THE VOYAGE HOME

THE VOYAGE HOME

THE VIKING SAGA, BOOK 5

GARY DOC NELSON

Waterside Productions

First Printing, 2025

ISBN-13: 978-1-968401-10-8 print edition
ISBN-13: 978-1-968401-11-5 e-book edition

Waterside Productions
2055 Oxford Ave
Cardiff, CA 92007
www.waterside.com

*Dedicated to Sir Ted Olsson, a true Swedish Knight,
and a fast friend.*

THE VOYAGE HOME

CHAPTER 1
DRY DRAYTON, ENGLAND

The lorry rolled to a stop in the alley. The young driver got out and moved to the back of the canvas-covered bed. It was dark at 5 AM, the full moon's light not penetrating the narrow space between the old stone buildings. There were only four keys on the keyring, which corresponded to the number of deliveries the driver had to make this evening. Eight cases to unload at this his first stop, thirty-five in total. If he didn't waste time, he could be finished and back at his college dormitory in less than two hours. He opened the back door to the pub and brought the first case in, removing the one with the empties and placing it back in the truck, repeating the process through six trips. On the seventh load, a light came on behind a curtained window on the ground floor of the building directly across from the pub's back door. He heard voices muffled by the heavy material and the closing of an inner door. As he placed the emptied case under the flap, one voice rose above the others.

"Royals ... dead!"

The words were accented but clear. Several more voices covered the speaker with what sounded like murmurs of assent. The young man moved from the lorry's side to the window, where the voices again quieted, letting the words of the speaker be clearly heard.

"The wedding might offer the perfect opportunity. They will all be in the same area."

The young man stood still, trying to process what he had just heard and determine what exactly to do. Before he could move, the curtain was pulled slightly aside, and part of a face showed as a shaft of light hit him. Momentarily stunned by the realization that he had been seen, the driver moved quickly to the cab as three men erupted from the door next to the window. One of the men ran at him with a pipe, hitting him across the forehead. The driver fell to his knees, dazed, unable to see for the blood pouring into his eyes, which was merciful, as he never saw the second man step behind him, drawing a knife across his throat.

CHAPTER 2
PARIS, FRANCE

"Mister Falconi, we have a problem."

The voice coming over the speaker of Mats Falconi's cell phone was obviously that of Cathal Magee, the Irish brogue identifying him as clearly as his name would have. The old man was the brew master at the Harp and Hawk Brewery in Donegal.

"And what would that be?"

Mats was in Paris, completing arrangements for a new wine label from Avignon to be added to his exporting license. Magee would not bother him needlessly. The Harp and Hawk was firmly established, providing an ever-increasing flow of non-alcoholic beer for Mats to import to the States. He had bought the brewery almost four years ago upon the death of the owner and his wife. He had deeded the entire operation to the previous owner's sixteen-year-old son, whom he and his wife had adopted.

"It's my pure fault. I should have told you about it before. About six months ago, an Englishman came through Donegal and struck up a conversation with my nephew. After a few pints, maybe more than a few, the lad gave him a tour through the works. I was having dinner at the Seascape with Charlie Tobin, going over production and delivery schedules, and didn't know about it until later that week."

"And what's wrong with that?" asked Mats. "We often provide tours. No one is hiding production figures, are they?"

"Good glory, no," said Magee. "The problem is the bloke owns a brewery, and I'm sitting in the office with one of his new non-alcoholic beers and I can't taste the difference between his and ours. He's stolen your process, and most likely the germs as well."

With the help of a Swedish biochemist, Mats had developed a process for brewing non-alcoholic beer, actually fermenting the final product without having to boil or filter off the alcohol. The key was keeping the process at a specific temperature and the addition of a manufactured bacteria, both of which Mats had numerous patents on. Magee didn't like the product, even though blindfolded he couldn't tell the difference between it and the 7% beer that was Harp and Hawk's main offering. He was fond of saying that the only advantage was that at the end of the evening, you were standing up when you took a piss.

"Okay. Email me all the information on the guy and his brewery. I'll fly to London tomorrow and check it out. What's the name of the beer and the man who took the tour?"

"Whistling Pig. Terrible name for a beer. The owner's name is Nickolas Rigsby. The place is located about an hour north of London."

Mats arrived in London and drove a rental car from Heathrow, taking the Ring Road east toward Cambridge. Magee's information had come just before he had boarded the plane. It was detailed enough that Mats knew Magee must have had help with the research, or perhaps had it already at his fingertips when he called the day before. The brewery was located just north of Cambridge in the small town of Dry Drayton–a curious name for a place with a brewery. The Whistling Pig had been established in 1918, just at the end of World War I, and had been in the same family until two years ago, when it was bought by Nickolas Rigsby, whom Cathal had mentioned on the phone. It was a small concern, almost a craft brewery, producing one tenth of what the Harp and Hawk did in a month. Until recently it had only had two offerings: an IPA and a dark lager. A non-alcoholic beer had been added less than two months ago and, from the previous month's sales figures, it was already equaling the other two beers in sales. Magee had included a phone number and postal code, which allowed Mats to set the GPS in the rental car. Magee said that he was doing more research on Rigsby and would send it as soon as it was complete.

It took Mats an hour to get to Dry Drayton, which was nothing more than a cluster of houses and a large stone barn-like building with a small loading dock adjacent to a door. A sign over the door in blue paint proclaimed, "The Whistling Pig." It was just after noon, and Mats had only had a breakfast roll on the plane. He drove around a green area that turned out to be a golf course next to the small town of Bar Hill, where he found a pub that served lunch.

"What can you tell me about the Whistling Pig Brewery?" asked Mats as the bartender brought him a meat pie.

"Not much to tell. We carry it. Only comes in bottles, though, not on draft."

"You have the non-alcoholic stuff?"

With a nod, the guy returned to the bar, welcoming a couple that had just entered. The beer was good, the label terrible. Mats didn't bother with the glass. He could see why Magee had been concerned. It was not quite as heavy as the Harp and Hawk's, but the similarity was unmistakable.

"Do you know the owner of the brewery?" he asked as he paid the bill.

"A little. Most of the time he delivers it himself locally. He's a newcomer–bought the place a couple of years ago. Quiet. I think he's from Yorkshire, at least he sounds like it. He treats the pubs fairly. Why do you ask?"

"No reason. I like the beer."

Mats drove back to Dry Dayton and parked. The door to the brewery was not locked, so after knocking and getting no response, Mats stepped inside and yelled "Hello!"

"In the back," came a reply from deep inside the building.

As he walked through the brewery, Mats noticed equipment that almost duplicated that of the Harp and Hawk plant in Donegal. There was even a specialized temperature stabilization tank that looked new, a piece of equipment that was specific to the brewing of non-alcoholic beer. He rounded the corner of a large fermentation tank and found a man on a platform that surrounded a large mixing vat, round in circumference and open at the top. Large fans lifted the air above the liquid mixture out through a venting system to the outside.

"Be with you in a moment," the man said, adjusting a mechanical arm that was slowly mixing the content of the vat beneath him. He climbed down to the main floor, wiping his hand on his apron before extending it toward Mats. "Nickolas Rigsby."

Mats looked at him, unsure exactly how to approach the subject of the stolen technology. Rigsby was shorter than Mats, probably shorter than the average Brit. He had a full head of hair, but it was thin, cut to an inch in length. His face was wider at the lower third than across the eyes. An image Stan Laurel flashed across Mats' memory, and he wondered if the man rumpled his hair when confused or accused. The man's eyes showed no sense of comedy, however. They were dark and quick, and flashed with the intelligence of the man behind them.

"What can I do for you?"

"Mr. Rigsby, I believe you are in big trouble."

"And how would that be?"

"My name is Falconi, Mats Falconi. I own the Harp and Hawk Brewery that you visited last year. I believe you stole my process for non-alcoholic brewing. That process is protected not only in Ireland but England as well."

"Your process is easily found on the web for anyone to see. I have modified it enough not to encroach on any patent," said Rigsby, not denying his contact with the Harp and Hawk.

"The process does not work without the bacteria."

"You can pick up bacteria anywhere. What the hell do you want?"

"Not that bacteria. It is engineered. It is not found in nature and it's not for sale. It is strongly protected not only for itself but as part of the process."

Rigsby went from belligerent to deflated in the space of a heartbeat. He was not a large man to begin with, but he shrank in front of Mats, sliding to a sitting position on a pump casing. "You'll not get anything if you sue. I'm just breaking even what with paying off the debt. The bank will get everything before you see a penny."

"Why don't you tell me the whole of it," said Mats, sensing that the man was perhaps an unwilling thief.

"I bought the Whistle two years ago. Took a loan and all of my savings. The beer had a good reputation locally and I thought I could expand it. Then they passed the zero-tolerance law and people stopped driving to pubs for a drink. If you haven't noticed, there aren't a lot of houses around here, mostly small farms, and that's where the majority of my sales were from. I thought I could keep the place if I had an NA brew to sell."

"What made you go after my process? You must have known it was protected."

"One of my sisters is married to an Irishman. He mentioned the Harp and Hawk. I'm a good brew master, Mr. Falconi. I give full value and quality. I was amazed at the flavor and body you were able to keep in an NA. I never thought anyone would notice the small amount I was producing, even though it was enough to keep up payments and keep me afloat. I guess I was wrong and I'm dead."

"I've tasted your offerings. They're good–no, better than good. What stopped you from expanding?"

"Same thing that caused me to turn to brewing NA– lack of money. I'm the whole thing, though I used to hire a lad when I bottled. He would make the evening deliveries when I was busy brewing. He cut out and left me without a driver a week ago. Found the missing lorry at the

Little Chef on the carriage way minus twenty-eight cases. The kid was gone. Now I drive all the deliveries, buy the grain and hops, everything. I work fourteen-hour days. How can I expand?"

"How much money do you owe the bank?"

"190,00 pounds. Down a little with the payments I made the last two months."

Mats took out a card and handed it to Rigsby. "You can keep up the brewing cycle for now. I want you to send your loan and debt information to that email. I'll be back to see you in a week. Send me all your contact information as well. Perhaps there's a way to work this out."

CHAPTER 3
THE MEDITERRANEAN
SEA–955 AD

Jarl felt the dragon ship flex beneath his feet. They were fortunate, as the wind had been at their backs since they had left Ajaccio on Corsica. They'd been sailing for eight days, only stopping once to replenish their water, with the added advantage of killing a few goats on an island to the east of the land of the Spaniards. Jarl stayed on the beach for a full day, wanting to rest his men for the passage through the Pillars of Hercules. This also had given him a chance to haul the boat ashore on the rocky beach and inspect the hull and calking. It had been Leif's first ship, and it had surpassed Jarl's expectations, both in function and sailing ability. Stored in the hull were each man's treasures, gained when they'd served as Varangian guards for the Eastern emperor. They would all be rich men when they arrived back at Falkhand Sted, Jarl more than the others, as he had served as captain of the force that protected the emperor. Still, he would have given up all the vast wealth carried in the hold if he could have had by his side his wife, Gun. Her death at the hands of the emperor's vizier was the reason they had left the great city after he had exacted his revenge. Bringing news of her death to her father, Red Hand, was a duty he could not avoid.

As they sailed further east, Jarl could feel a subtle wind shift. The wind that had been at their backs slowly veered toward the north, blowing hot and dry from the sands of Africa. Two more days and it swung further, coming more from the west. Not only had the direction changed, but the temperature had dropped; even the smell of the air changed, now seeming full of the tang of salt. It forced them to drop their sail and row. Jarl left the mast stepped and posted one of his men up it to act as lookout. He wanted to split the difference between the coast of al Andalus and the African coast, mostly for safety reasons should any leave those shores to try to intercept them, but also because despite his map and the oral directions he had received from those in Miklagard and Rome, Jarl suspected that they were filled with inconsistencies at best, overly imaginative and badly inaccurate at worst.

The morning of the third day after their stop and nine days of sailing since they had left Ajaccio, they could see the coasts converging from both north and south. The mainland was visible on both sides of the longboat. Only the water directly in front of them and the expanse behind them remained clear and unobstructed. As they rowed toward the opening, the current beat against them. Even the shallow draft of Leif's creation felt the tug of the water resisting their effort. Outside the opening between the converging land masses, Jarl could see clouds billowing high into the sky.

The decision to sail equidistant between the two continents proved wise. Jarl, then the crew, saw two galleys come out from the southern shore, and a single cog that tried to overtake them using sail from the north. The galleys came the closest to intercepting them. From the number of men crammed into the closest ship, Jarl thought they must be rowed by slaves. They came close enough to hear a drum beating out a cadence that the oars matched. His Vikings matched the beat, then after the two vessels remained at their distance from one another for a league, the crew of the longboat responding to a nod from Jarl standing at the steer board. The longboat shot ahead, the blades of the oars biting deeper into the choppiness of the waves without increasing their cadence. The galleys increased their beat to try to stay with the escaping longboat but lost distance and eventually gave up the chase.

After two days of constant rowing, as the shore to the steer board retreated to the north, Jarl and the men experienced the power of the ocean. The waves became larger, the winds milder and more consistent than they had been at the Pillars, where the water had been funneled between the two land masses. The color of the water turned grey, without a hint of the blue that had dominated the inland sea. Jarl turned their course to the north, keeping the land just in sight over the horizon. The westerly wind kept trying to force the boat back toward the shore. Jarl constantly provided pressure on the steering oar to maintain the seaway necessary for safety, both from grounding and from unfriendly vessels.

Vikings were the only seafarers who were comfortable spending nights at sea, but even they were hesitant in unfamiliar waters with winds and waves that could push them onto a lee shore. Jarl knew there were two possibilities: to row into the wind easting as much as north, keeping at least part of the crew at the oars throughout the night, or to head toward shore and find a secure inlet or a beach to pull up at for the evening. His crew was relatively fresh, despite the effort that had taken them through the Pillars. The constant turmoil on the mainland helped make up Jarl's mind to stay at sea. At first light, out of sight of land, he raised the sail and made as much of a northern course as the square rig would allow. He let all but two of his men sleep until noon, when the first hint of land to the steer board showed below the low clouds. He stayed under sail for another two hours, running at forty-five degrees north to the approaching coast; then he lowered the sail and again had the men row north-east, as he had the previous day.

Jarl repeated this pattern for six days. Soon he knew that he would need to seek the shore, as the replenishment of their water and fresh meat became, if not a necessity, at least prudent. On the eighth night, after rowing north-west for the better part of it, they again raised the sail and made as much of a northing as the west wind would allow. On this day, however, no land came to view as the sun climbed to its zenith. Jarl unrolled the map he had taken from Miklagard and saw a great break in the headland, with days of open sailing approaching. The coast eventually curved to the west as it went north, giving shape to a great bay. His map was filled with drawings of the heads of children blowing wind, their cheeks puffed out with the effort and force of their breath. The wind also changed with the absence of the shore, veering more to the north. Jarl quickly calculated that they could sail for three more days before it became necessary to ration their water, more if it rained and they were able to capture enough to fill a cask or two. The sail was adjusted to the new course, and the men slept after their night at the oars.

On the dawn of the third day, the lookout at the mast-head shouted that there was land both to the east and north. Still a couple of hours away, Jarl steered the ship toward the eastern shore, instructing the lookout to look for an inlet where they might find fresh water. At first landfall there was nothing promising, so Jarl dropped the sail and had the men row west along the shore. An hour under oars and the lookout saw a cleft in the cliff that would in all probability contain a stream that had cut it, and Jarl steered for the break in the land. There was a small spit of sand on the eastern shore of the inlet, large enough to beach the ship, and a stream flowing from a small waterfall scarcely taller than a man.

When the ship was secured, Jarl sent a man to the top of the cliff to act as sentry. The rest he watched with laughter as they walked with dizzy steps, trying to gain their land legs after almost two weeks at sea. They had left Corsica with twenty-six men–eighteen of them Norsemen, six slaves, and two Guibega. After passing through the Pillars, he had told the slaves that they were now free men. Only the Guibega had shown signs of seasickness, and they had become used to the roll of the ship by the third day.

"We need our water casks filled," Jarl said to Lars, who had shown himself to be a leader during the voyage and was trusted by the men. "I'll take Svante and one of the Guibega and look for game. It would be good for the men to taste red meat after so much fish. We will shelter here tonight and row west in the morning."

The three hunters, armed with bows, climbed the cliff to the grassy plain. In the distance there were trees where the inlet narrowed to a shallow creek. Drinking from the stream was a small group of sheep. As they spread out and made their way toward the animals, they failed to see a young boy on the opposite side of the narrow crevice, slipping through the grass. Once he was out of sight, the boy headed north at a run. Jarl took the lead, circling around the sheep, blocking them from the woods. At his signal the three stood as one, each killing an animal with their first arrow. The Guibega, after his shot, threw aside his bow and ran directly at a ram that had started to flee. He jumped on the animal's back and drew his dagger across the throat. The ram took six more steps before going to the ground. Svante had also taken down two sheep, but more conventionally–both with arrows. Jarl was content with one; his shield, which hung on his back, had interfered with the drawing of his arrow for the second shot. The sheep scattered.

"These will provide a fine feast, as well as meat for the next few weeks," said Jarl. "Let's get them to the ship."

Each man picked up an animal, placing it on their shoulders, and carried them back to the edge of the cliff. Jarl yelled down to the crew to come and pick up the carcasses as the three hunters went back for the other two kills. The ram was twice the size of the other they had left, large enough to require two men to carry it. The Guibega quickly tied its hoofs together and ran Svante's spear below the knots. They hoisted the load between them as Jarl went to the remaining animal. He had just hoisted the sheep onto his shoulders when the first horseman appeared, galloping full speed toward him with a dozen or more following in the dust that his passage kicked up. Running alongside him, trying to keep up, was the shepherd boy. The trailing riders moved right toward the cliff, attempting to cut off Svante and the Guibega, but the two had enough of a lead that they arrived at the cliff first, throwing the ram over the edge and yelling at the crew that they were under attack. Without orders needing to be given, the crew still on the ship threw weapons out of the hull to the men on the beach, then dragged the ship back into the surf. The rest of the men, now armed, started climbing the cliff to join Svante.

Jarl still had over a hundred yards to the safety of the cliff. It was evident that the rider who had singled him out would easily overtake him before he went a fourth of that distance. He thought for a minute that he might reason with the horseman, give him money for the sheep they had taken, but as the man neared and the head of his spear came down, he spurred his mount to even greater effort. Jarl had only moments to react.

With the slain sheep still across his shoulders, he couldn't draw his sword in time. He threw the animal off his shoulders directly in front of the charging horse just as the spear came down to impale him. The animal stumbled, moving the tip of the spear slightly to the side. At the same time, the boy, who was running hard and spinning a sling around his head, let go with a rock. The rider went over his horse's head, landing awkwardly, lying still as the horse trod over his inert body. The rider's spear went directly toward Jarl, deviating slightly as the rider was thrown. It carried between Jarl's side and his arm, its point sticking in the wood of the shield slung across his back. As he started to go down under the impact of the spear, the rock from the boy's sling hit him squarely on his temple, just at the junction of his forehead and his helmet. His knees buckled, and he fell unconscious on his back, the spear imbedded in his shield sticking straight up to the sky.

The men from the ship arrived at the cliff top just before the horsemen who were after Svante and the Guibega. Weapons clashed. The horsemen, surprised at the sudden appearance of the warriors and finding themselves outnumbered, were still intent on the two they had chased. The horsemen lost two of their number, one to a thrown axe, one to a spear that had taken his horse. The man who threw it landed on top of the thrown rider with his knife.

The Guibega saw Jarl lying on his back with the spear sticking up above him and ran back across the meadow to his aid. Two of the horsemen overtook him from the side. He slid under the first horse, his knife out, gutting the animal and spilling his rider. The second horseman ran over the Guibega before he could regain his feet, then turned and speared him fatally through the neck, a fountain of blood spraying high from the man's carotid artery.

More men on foot were now arriving at the north of the meadow, running to support the nine horsemen facing the warriors at the cliff.

"Jarl and Luca Guibega are dead. Get to the ship," shouted Svante.

The men responded by spilling down the steep trail and across the small beach to the ship, which had been pulled into the surf. Those on board already had oars out. As more men gained the boat, they took oars. When the last man was onboard, the men powered the ship through the small breakers toward the open sea. Along the edge of the cliff, spears were being thrown, and several of the men on foot had crossbows sending bolts at them from above. In the ship, those not rowing protected those at the oars by raising round shields above them, and soon they were out of range.

They rowed against the wind, directly to the west, and when they passed the headland to starboard, they turned north, again catching the wind and allowing the oars to be shipped. As they passed the point, they saw their mistake. Nestled along the shore, just a few miles from where they had landed, was a fair-sized village with a castle protecting it. They watched the men who had attacked them file back down the cliff and into the dwellings, noting that there was no vessel tied up at the jetty that fronted the water. The men looked at Svante for reassurance now that Jarl was gone. He had none to give.

CHAPTER 4
LONDON, ENGLAND

Mats met Suzanne at the airport shortly after 10 am. He'd called as soon as he had met with Rigsby. Something the man had said had caused him to worry, and it was something that his wife could help him with. After the violence of the events in France, it would also be good to spend time in England, where there was less chance of them finding themselves in the spotlight. As they drove to the hotel, Mats explained what Cahill Magee had termed a problem.

"This guy, Nickolas Rigsby, visited the Harp and Hawk last year. Four months later he's producing a non-alcoholic beer at his own brewery. I talked to him yesterday."

"And what was his story?"

"He admitted he stole the bacteria. He needed a non-alcoholic label to keep afloat. He seemed like a decent guy–has a good reputation in the pubs he supplies. He's just in financial difficulty. Doesn't have the money to expand. He has a beer, an IPA, and the non-alcoholic–all very good. He's in debt to the bank for 190,000 pounds, and he's working twelve hours a day to keep things going. That's not why I asked you to come over, though."

"I was thinking of coming anyway. The work on the Bougainville library is down to just administration, which

I can do by computer. The Constantinople library is out of my hands. It was never really our discovery anyway, and the Turkish government is impossible to work with as a woman. It's enough that the mystery was solved and the books announced to the outside world, so the volumes that conflict with the Koran can't be conveniently lost again. But why did you want me in England, not that I'm complaining?"

"Rigsby said something before admitting what he'd done. He said that our process was available online—that he didn't have to steal it. It made me realize our security is lacking. We have more to do to protect than the Harp and Hawk's brewing process. Ever since the drug deal and the death of Colletti in France four years ago, we've been trying to keep our names out of the media. You're much better than I am with computers. I'd like you to find a security expert. I would also like you to find a full history on Rigsby. Cathal is supposed to be researching him, but I would trust you to find out more about the man."

"That should be easy enough."

They spent the night reaffirming their love. No alarm was set, and no wake-up call was placed. They awoke, and even though the morning was half gone, mutually agreed to resume their late-night activities before showering and going downstairs for brunch.

"Did you pack a jacket or a suit?" asked Suzanne. "While we're here, I'd like to see a play."

"Nope, I have the sport coat I came over in. That should be all right."

"Mats, that thing has seen its day. Why don't you ask the concierge for a recommendation and buy a good suit, jacket, and slacks? You haven't dressed since Monte Carlo, when you were still trying to impress me, and that was black tie. While you shop, I'll work on the security question and look for information about Rigsby. And I'll try to find some tickets to a good play."

What Suzanne said was true, but underlying her words was the goal of getting Mats out of the hotel. She had a strong feeling that if he were in the room while she was working, there would be more interruptions like the one that had already made them late for breakfast.

It was after five-thirty when Mats arrived back at the room, followed by a bellhop with three garment bags and three shopping bags. Suzanne opened the door and giggled.

"This is how I'm supposed to come back from shopping. Did you have fun?"

"Not really," said Mats. "I really don't like shopping, but the tailor the concierge called for me was amazing. He altered every piece in less than three hours–two jackets, a blue three-piece suit, and two pairs of slacks. He insisted that I couldn't possibly wear his stuff without new shoes, so I got two new pairs from a store he recommended while he worked on my purchases. It kind of reminded me of the service at Gene Hiller's store across the street from our Sea Hawk restaurant in Sausalito."

"Well, don't just stand there," said Suzanne after Mats had tipped the bellhop and he had left the room. "Let's have a fashion show."

Mats grumbled, but he dutifully put on every one of the new garments, each of which fit perfectly. He even put on the new shoes, although without socks. As he put on the last outfit, the blue suit, Suzanne whistled. Not only did each item fit perfectly, but they accentuated Mats' broad shoulders and narrow waist, which she had noted was getting smaller by the notches taken in on his belts.

"British style is so different from French, but I have to admit that you might look better in it."

"Enough ogling my body. Did you find a security expert?"

"I did, and I have a full dossier on Nickolas Rigsby as well, but next time I get to go shopping with you. I hope you kept the name of the haberdasher."

"I have his card, and he has all my contact information, though I don't think his place is the type that will be announcing a sale anytime soon. How did you find the expert?"

"I called the U.S. consulate, and the French one as well, and asked who they would recommend. The same name was given by both, an English firm, although the French suggested a French outfit as their first choice. After Googling them, I think the English group is the best for us. It's a small firm run by a woman named Katherine Radcliff Stoner. I talked with her on the phone. She seems really sharp, so I hired her to do the check on Rigsby as a test. It came back in less than three hours. It even included four personal interviews. I didn't print it out, but it's on my computer. It's very thorough. We have an appointment with her at her office tomorrow at eleven to see if you like her. If she's as good at security as she was at getting the Rigsby information, she should solve your problem. Now get the suit back on. You're taking me to dinner. We have seven-thirty tickets to *The Mousetrap* at the St. Martin's theatre."

The play was good. Agatha Christie provided twists and turns to keep them thinking, and the actors as well as the audience seemed to be having a good time. They were in a cab by 10:00 and back in their room by 10:30.

The next morning after breakfast, at a more normal time, they took a cab to the security firm's office. As they neared it, they passed Baker Street, the residence of Sherlock Holmes, which the cabbie pointed out with practiced enthusiasm. The security firm was housed in a two-story converted residence, painted pale yellow with white trim. All it was missing was flowerpots in the windows. It looked anything but secure.

Inside, they got a different impression. There, in a narrow entry room just large enough for a small couch and a high-backed chair, they were met by a young woman who looked like she was in her late twenties. As she was strikingly good-looking with blond hair and blue eyes, Mats and Suzanne assumed that she was a greeter, a secretary whose job it was to offer them coffee and a place to wait while her bosses took whatever time they needed before seeing them. They were surprised when the young woman stuck out her hand and said, "Good morning. I'm Katherine Radcliff Stoner. You must be Suzanne."

"I am, and this is my husband, Mats Falconi."

"Pleased to meet you both," Katherine said, giving Mats a firm but delicate handshake. "Before we go inside, could I have you both remove any cell phones or recording devices? It's company policy inside the building. You could take your cell phones inside, but they wouldn't work." She handed them a yellow plastic container. When it was loaded with three cell phones—one from Mats, two from Suzanne—Katherine took the container back and placed her hand on a small device next to the door leading to the interior. Just inside the door there was a scanner, similar to the kind found at airports but much thinner, almost acting as a door jamb. It might have been missed for what it really was except for a red light blinking above the entry as their guide passed through with the phones, and the chiming of a soft alarm. Through it Mats could see a larger reception area that at one time must have been joined with the area at the front. Several people could be seen at desks behind computer screens, smiling at their guide as she passed them. She dropped the yellow container on one of their desks.

"We like to test various security procedures that we offer our clients," said Katherine, turning back to them. "Let's go to the conference room and we can discuss your particular needs."

She led them to a room with an oval table, its surface marked by electrical outlets and computer hookups, and lined notebooks and pens in front of every seat. When they were comfortable, Katherine took a seat across from them. "Can I offer you coffee, tea, or water?" she asked. Receiving an affirmative for the coffee, she pressed a button. "Donald, would you bring two coffees, a tea for me, and whatever you would like as well to the conference room?"

Katherine turned to Mats and Suzanne. "Rather than explain to you all of what we do here, I'd like to hear exactly what your concerns are."

Mats looked at Suzanne before taking the lead. "What precipitated our call is that the process we developed for a brewery we own was found and copied from the internet even though it was protected by patents. That started me thinking about our business emails and correspondence as well as our personal information."

The door opened, and a man entered with a tray of cups, spoons, cream, and sugar. He was youngish, or at least trying to look youngish with a ponytail, tee shirt, and Levi's.

"This is Donald Leitch. He's in charge of our internet and computer division," said Katherine. "Donald, would you please join us? There are some questions that you would know best how to answer."

Leitch sat down with his own cup while Katherine explained the problems Mats had outlined.

"It should be possible to scrub the process information off the internet. I would first like to find out how it got posted in the first place," said Leitch. "I assume that you or the brewery didn't do it. As to your personal communications, we provide a service that allows all your devices, cell phone, tablets, and computers to be encrypted to a level that no one with the exception of the United States government, and possibly the British or the Russians, would be able to breach. We can even protect a land line if you still use one."

"Sounds expensive," said Mats with a grin, giving the impression that price would not be a factor.

"That's Katherine's area. Is there anything else?"

"Yes. I assume that anything I tell you will be held in the strictest confidence," said Mats.

Katherine looked at him, her eyes hard and penetrating. "I know that you received your referral from the U.S. and French embassies. Your request raised some questions as to why you would want to know what security firm they used. They called me to ask if you were legitimate, so I have already done a background check on you. Some of what you are probably going to tell me I already know. The main point is that once you are our clients, your secrets are our secrets. It is the reason for the precautions you've seen that we take, and for many that you have not noticed, such as this room being completely secure from all known listening devices."

"If my file is as thorough as the file you sent Suzanne on John Rigsby, I would like to see it," said Mats.

"Oh, it is much more detailed than that. But as much as I learned, there was a lot left unsaid. There was almost nothing until four years ago. Just normal stuff until your father died. Then a flurry of activity in four different countries, with very professional cover-ups. It made me curious. I couldn't wait to meet you two."

"I hope we have met with your approval," said Mats with a hint of cynicism in his voice.

"Please don't take what I said the wrong way," said Katherine. "Any time I can't find the whole story, or I sense a cover-up, it makes me look deeper until I find answers."

"Okay. You're right. In the last four years, things have happened that we don't wish to be associated with, at least not in the press. The first was the death of a drug dealer named Colletti in France. The second was when we bought the Harp and Hawk Brewery in Ireland. The owners had been murdered. I didn't know that before we decided to buy the brewery. Then there were some deaths associated with a fringe religious group, which had nothing to do with us or the brewery, but there's a chance that some of my employees were involved."

"Yes. Then there were references to you in the discoveries of some stolen Impressionist paintings in Ukraine. First indications were that you were involved, then not, then Suzanne was given credit for the find. Russia's response was cryptic as well. Just a month ago, there were the terrorist attacks in Turkey, France, and Belgium. Again, it was a mention of an unnamed person here, an unidentified man there–information given to the authorities by an anonymous source. Do you want Donald to scrub these things as well? I can tell you that I am most curious about how this all started. I assume there is a common link between each of the events, but my research has not uncovered it. In all cases, it seems you've worked with the police and committed no crimes."

"It is true that we've committed no crimes," said Mats. "And yes, I would like all references to us deleted, except for the credit given to Suzanne academically. You can see how, if my name were linked to those events, it could be a problem for me personally."

"It can be done," interjected Donald Leitch. "But it would be useful to know the whole story of each of the events and your full involvement in them. It would be of great use to be preemptive in our scrub. Do you plan on any more heroics for me to worry about?"

Mats gave the computer expert a soft laugh. "I hope I'm done for a while." Turning to Katherine, he said, "I'm guessing you will take us on as a client."

"Yes. I'll ask you both to come in and give the details of the events you want us to scrub and monitor. I'll have Angus MacKee write up the contract. Most of this can be done in house, which will save you money. It would help if you could bring all your devices that need encrypting here and buy new ones for your associates, if they can't come in themselves."

Mats looked at Suzanne. "We should get them for your parents, and Audrey too."

"The paperwork should be done by tomorrow, if you would like to come back then. We can buy the hardware for you as well if you text me the names and numbers of the phones and other devices. We buy with a discount. I do have one more question. Do you have any hard items that need protecting? So far all that we have discussed is cyber work."

"We have warehouses in Corsica and Paris for our wine-exporting concern as well as one in California, but we have our own security that is more than adequate. We also have bank accounts in France, Ireland, and the US. We would want to know about any unusual activity in those accounts." Mats hesitated, trying to decide whether to say more. This interview had gone far beyond a discussion of how to remove the non-alcoholic brewing process from the internet. That was due to the feeling of trust that both he and Suzanne were developing for Katherine Radcliff Stoner.

"I take it we have an agreement that we are your clients. Could we speak privately?"

"Of course. Donald, I will get you all the information and the list of devices as soon as the Falconis get it to me. Thanks for your input." As the door closed behind Leitch, Katherine turned back to Mats and Suzanne.

"This is something only five or six people know, and only three of them know the true significance," said Mats. "I would like to keep it that way, even within your organization. If a single person could help me, it would be preferable."

"As long as what you tell me is not illegal, I can probably take care of it personally. If I can't, I will let you know now."

Mats turned to Suzanne and had a short-whispered conversation that ended in Suzanne nodding her assent.

"It has to do with the events you mentioned previously. You were looking for some common link drawing me into violent situations."

"You have to admit, it is curious. I was even confused as to the number of murders, so much had been covered up," said Katherine, wondering what was coming next from this man.

"When my father died, he left me a journal," said Mats. "Parts of it were hundreds of years old. In Turkey, we recovered another of my family's journals, even more ancient. It was these journals that led me to the events you found over the last four years, providing me with information that protected me and Suzanne once we were involved. So far, I've been able to safeguard them, but I can't keep taking them with me. Suzanne can photocopy and digitize them in her lab, but we are afraid that somehow they will end up on the web, like the brewing process. If it were possible to put them on a protected flash drive so that only I could read them, then Suzanne could properly preserve them."

Katherine looked at them across the table, her mouth open, her eyes wide with shock. She seemed unable to move, a pen in her right hand poised above a notepad. Minutes before she had seemed like a supremely confident young professional, secure in an environment of her own making; now she was clearly shaken to her core.

"Are you all right?" asked Mats after a long silence in which Katherine did not respond to his question.

Katherine shook herself. "Oh, oh yes. The best way would be to encrypt the information and link it to a single device. That way even the U.S. computers couldn't break it unless they had your device. You say you have two journals, both written by ancestors?"

"Yes, but the one my father gave me had sections written by two individuals. I suspect there are more journals that we haven't found yet. There is also a larger one, more a manuscript than a journal, that was specifically about my family. It was discovered with the Bougainville find. Keeping it secret is the only illegal thing we have done. It was not listed in the volumes we submitted to the French Minister of Antiquities."

"If you trust me with the journals, I will personally perform the digital transcription and the encryption for you. I can do it without actually looking at the text, and I would insist on doing it alone. There is something else, though. I would like you to meet my husband. He is an American and will be back from Washington D.C. the day after tomorrow."

CHAPTER 5
DNIEPER RIVER–945 AD

Svante let the men rest, the adrenaline of their narrow escape burning off. Two Rus had been struck with arrows from the cliff. One had a nicked shoulder, the other a more serious arrow wound in his thigh. But when the shaft was broken and drawn out, there was little blood, revealing that the major artery had not been hit. With no ship visible at the piers of the settlement, they only had to make sure that no one would attack them from the sea. Svante sent a man to the mast head as a lookout. Then, with the ship rocking in the gentle waves, he reviewed the situation with the crew.

"I saw Jarl and Luca, the Guibega, struck down. Jarl was first with a spear to his chest. The Guibega went to aid him and was run down by several horsemen," said Svante, seeking confirmation of what he had seen.

"I did not see Jarl fall, but I saw him on his back with a spear in his chest. The Guibega was brave but foolish," said Bjorn Ragnarson, a seasoned warrior who had served eight years in the Varangian guards.

"What are we to do now?" asked Neil, the Viking at the second oar, who had been with Jarl from the beginning.

"We will continue north to Jarl's sted," said Svante, surprised at the question. He thought it clear what they should do.

"But is that the best course?" asked Lars, the Viking across from Neil.

"It is what Jarl planned. Why would we change?"

"Because Jarl is dead," said Neil. "I for one came on this voyage because Jarl was our leader."

"We should stay true to his wishes," said Svante. "But this is a Viking ship, and each man gets a vote. Jarl freed the six slaves as we started the voyage, so they can vote as well."

"Red Hand might not take the death of his daughter well, and Jarl was killed while under our protection," said Lars. "He might blame the messenger. At the least, he would take the treasure."

Svante stood on the steering platform, looking at the crew, which now numbered twenty-five: eighteen Vikings, six men who had been slaves, and after the death of Luca, a single Guibega. What Lars, Bjorn, and Neil had said was true. "We should consider these points, but I think it would be wise to wait before we discuss our future. First, how much water did we bring on board before the attack?"

"All casks are filled, but we left one on the beach. Three sheep are also on board," answered Bjorn.

"Let's butcher them and eat. After we are full and have had a portion of wine, we can discuss the journey."

In the meadow that they had fled, the boy with his sling was straddling Jarl, who was still unmoving, lying on his back with blood trickling from his temple. The spear of the fallen rider was stuck fast in Jarl's shield, which was on his back between him and the ground. The shaft was between his arm and his chest, rising toward the sky. The boy bent down, his hand moving under Jarl's kirtle, looking for his purse. He barely had stuffed it into his own, tucked tightly under his left arm, when a soldier, accompanied by a priest, came up from behind.

"Is he dead? Did the spear take his heart?"

"The spear is like a child's trick. It struck between his torso and his arm. He is bleeding a bit," replied the boy. "I brought him down with my sling. He hasn't moved, but I think he is alive."

"Where is the master?"

"Over there in the tall grass," said the boy, still straddling Jarl. "He was thrown when this man threw the sheep in front of his horse."

The soldier and the priest moved to where the boy pointed and found the rider who had tried to impale Jarl. His head was bent at an impossible angle, his neck broken by the fall. The horse stood nearby, his head lowered to the grass of the meadow, his saddle empty. The soldier grabbed the reins and led it back to where the boy stood over Jarl.

"I asked if he was alive," said the soldier gruffly as he moved toward the fallen Viking.

"I think so," said the youth.

"I can remedy that," said the soldier, unsheathing his sword and moving toward Jarl's head. He raised the sword, about to drive the tip into Jarl's throat, when the priest stopped him with a hand placed firmly under the guard.

"Hold! This man is a Christian." The priest knelt down and lifted the Greek crucifix from Jarl's chest. "This insignia on his armor is that of the Varangian Guard of the eastern Pope." He placed his fingers on the man's throat and felt a pulse.

"That matters not. He killed the master," replied the warrior, trying to break his sword loose of the priest's grip.

"It is everything," said the priest, standing and putting a hand on the other man's chest. "He did not kill your master. The fall from the horse did. This man is a warrior of the church."

The boy with the sling felt his chance of riches from the man he had felled slip away at the priest's words. Then, as if sensing danger, Jarl moaned.

He opened his eyes, unfocused and seeing double. He tried to remember what had happened. He saw a head bend down toward him, blocking out the sun and blue of the sky. He remembered killing a sheep, but that was all. Slowly the two angles of the face above him merged into one, still spinning but at least forming a single image.

"What happened?" Jarl asked in his native language of the north.

The priest, guessing what the Viking had asked, answered in Latin. "You were hit by a rock from a sling. It appears that your helmet took most the blow. You are lucky to be alive."

Jarl tried to sit up, but the soldier put his weight on the spear that was firmly embedded in the shield strapped to Jarl's back. "Take his sword and knife," he instructed the boy.

Once Jarl was disarmed, the man put his foot on Jarl's shield and pulled hard on the spear, releasing it from the back of the shield.

Jarl tried to stand but fell to his hands and knees as dizziness overcame his sense of balance. The man put the tip of the spear under his throat.

"Do not harm this man," said the priest, holding his hand up at the man with the sword.

"He killed the lord. He should die."

"Your lord died of a fall. This man has not unsheathed his weapon," said the priest. "He is a Christian in the service of the eastern Pope. He is under the church's protection."

Several more men at arms came up to the group, surrounding Jarl.

"Help this man to his feet," the priest said to the newcomers. "We will bring him to the village. You!" He pointed at the man with the spear. "Bring your lord and his horse back as well. Is there anyone else who is injured?"

"One of the Vikings was killed," said one of the newcomers.

"Take his body as well. We will bring this to the burghers, as the lord is no longer with us."

There were four burghers, the priest, and a nephew of the dead lord crowded into the small guild hall along with Jarl and the soldier who, still holding the spear, acted as his guard.

"You attempted to raid our town," said the burgher who sat at the head of the small table. He was dressed so as to hide his paunch, but his double chin made this an unnecessary exercise.

"We did not. I was unaware that your town even existed."

"You landed secretly on the other side of the peninsula and would have come down on us at night if we hadn't been warned."

"We are traders, not raiders. We have been at sea for a fortnight. We stopped for water and to hunt meat. We were unaware of your village, or we would have docked there and traded for what we needed."

"And you expect us to believe that?" asked the obese burgher with a throaty laugh. "Our village with the castle watch tower is hard to miss."

"We came from the south, from the inland sea. Your village is hidden by the headland. We beached where we did in order to refill our water casks in the stream."

"Harrumph," snorted the burgher. "Peaceful Vikings? Ha!"

"What he says has the ring of truth," said the priest. "He wears the armor and insignia of the Varangian Guard, the protectors of the eastern Pope. That alone should tell you he comes from the south, from the inland sea."

"Priest, you have only been with us for two weeks. Our village is not for you to protect," said the burgher.

"Yes, and you know that I was sent by our Holy Father in Rome to bring the word of Jesus to the heathen tribes of the north. I would not be here except that I was told I could arrange passage on a trading vessel from here. I take the arrival of this Norseman as a message from God."

"If you were here to trade, why didn't you offer to buy the sheep from the shepherd boy? You would have had a purse for that, ech?"

"I saw no one tending the sheep. Upon landing, we thought to get a deer. The sheep were unexpected." Jarl reached for his purse under his kirtle. "My purse is

missing. It must have been lost when I was struck down."
Knowing what he did of fighting and battles, he suspected
that the soldier with the spear or the priest had already
claimed it. Jarl was a veteran of the streets of Miklagard–a
city known for its pickpockets. He had long ago learned
to keep a readily accessible purse with a few coins tucked
under his kirtle, while keeping another concealed deep
in his clothing at his back, but he thought it would be
unwise to offer this information to the burgher.

"The church will pay for the sheep," said the priest
quickly, trying to answer the dark looks being exchanged
by the burghers.

"Your men must have seen things," said Jarl, his voice
raised like one accustomed to holding authority. "There
were only three of my party in the meadow. All the rest
were on the beach bringing water to the boat. They must
also have seen my ship. All the shields faced inboard, and
the bow was empty. It did not have the figurehead that all
Viking ships attach when raiding. I will pay for the sheep,
and even for the loss of your lord, though his death was
caused by his own poor horsemanship as he tried to kill
me without reason." He nodded toward the young noble,
who had remained quiet.

"And how will you do that?" sneered the fat burgher.
"It is unlikely that your ship will return. As I see it, we
have three choices." He turned to the other burghers.
"We can execute him as an example to those who would
attack us, putting his head on the jetty facing the sea. We
can sell him to the priest for whatever that would bring.
Or we can ransom him."

The priest began to respond, but Jarl put a hand on
his arm and said in a low tone that implied a threat, "If

I am murdered for butchering four sheep, you and your town will suffer. You may already be in danger if my men believe me dead. We were to meet my father's fleet in two days' sailing. Within a week, ten longships with Vikings intent on revenge will be on your shores. You've neither the numbers nor the courage to want that to happen. I have said that I will pay for the sheep and for the loss of your lord. If I do, I will go north with the priest. If you attempt to ransom me, my men will free me and destroy your village. You will gain nothing but misery if I am not set free."

The burgher looked shaken for the first time. He glanced at the other town leaders for confirmation. "Take him away. We will decide his fate."

The guard motioned with the tip of his spear to the doorway. Jarl started to leave but stopped and turned toward the burghers. "Do not take long with your deliberations. It will take me time to contact my men. They could be planning revenge for your foolishness already."

Darkness had not yet fallen when the priest came to the room where Jarl was being held. "You have made them afraid," he said. "But they are greedy men and want to know how you will pay what you have offered."

"They have my sword, my bow, and my knife. The jewel in the knife's pommel is by itself worth the whole flock of sheep, but I should not wish to lose that knife or the rest of my weapons. I know where my purse is, and there is enough that the church will not be liable."

"If you can pay, then I will negotiate a price. The earlier we leave this place the better. The lord who was killed will not be missed, at least not by the burghers or his nephew.

It would still be best that they think the money comes from the church. If they think you still have a purse, their greed could overcome their cowardice."

"Tell them that when I have my arms back, you will give them the money. If not, I'll not agree to accompany you north."

The next morning, the priest, with his belongings packed on a donkey and with Jarl in possession of his weapons, paid the burghers the amount they had demanded. Jarl thought it was inflated about three times what he would have paid in trade.

Turning toward the nephew, he said, "I am a lord in my own land. If I am going north, I would ride. Give me a price for your uncle's horse, or another as good."

The young noble smiled, a sly look in his eyes as he quoted the price, which was inflated as much as the sheep.

"That includes the tack and saddle, of course. Pay the man, priest," said Jarl, glad that he had thought to give the churchman sufficient funds to cover the transaction. If the young noble had said no, he would have taken the horse anyway. As it was, he felt unfulfilled in not killing the guard, who he was sure had his first purse. The priest was gaining his trust.

"I thought you might kill the soldier," said the priest.

They had ridden almost two hours in silence. The priest had tried twice to start a conversation but was answered only by Jarl spurring his horse ahead, causing the priest's donkey to try to follow with a very uncomfortable gait.

"The man stole my purse," said Jarl in a tone that brooked no dissent.

"I was with him from the time we came to your body. He didn't touch you until you had awoken."

"You are my second suspect," said Jarl in the same dark tone.

"I? I did not touch you either. If I had, the man would have said so. The shepherd boy was standing over you as if you were his possession when we arrived. You awoke shortly after."

"The shepherd boy!" said Jarl loudly, laughing with joy. "You are absolved of all blame, priest. I'll ride with you with pleasure, and I thank you for saving me, although I will tell you now, I am no Christian. The other things you have surmised are true, however. I was captain of the Varangian Guard."

CHAPTER 6
LONDON, ENGLAND–THE
PRESENT

On Saturday, two days after their meeting with Radcliff Stoner, Mats and Suzanne were invited to dinner to meet Rodney, Katherine's husband. They anticipated joining their new acquaintances at one of the more fashionable London restaurants or at a private club, but they were invited to the Radcliff home instead.

Since Katherine had seen fit to do a background check on them, Suzanne felt compelled to reciprocate. After leaving her office on Thursday, they went back to the hotel, and Suzanne immediately phoned the security firm recommended by the French embassy and had them do a background check on both Katherine and her husband Rodney. It took less than four hours for a courier to knock on their hotel door, Mats having given the front desk permission to give out his room number. If the speed with which the file had been compiled stunned Mats, the information inside was even more surprising.

The file on Katherine was much like the information that had been given to them by the embassy before they had hired her, but there were some astounding additions. She was also known as Lady Katherine, heir to large estates west of York. She was older that she looked–thirty-one rather than the mid-twenties both Suzanne and Mats had estimated. She had taken over the leadership of the security firm seven years ago and turned it into a major firm in the field while earning for herself an impressive fortune, which she invested conservatively.

Her husband, Rodney Hamerton Stoner, was an American. He was from California, actually from the same area as Mats, although fifteen miles north of Sausalito in San Rafael. After graduating from college, he had worked as a speech writer, first for Senator Naomi Shapiro and then for Kent Beck during his presidential campaign. He now was President Beck's press secretary, a position he shared with Adam Kappe, who was the one most often seen on TV. That would have been enough, but a series of newspaper clippings brought back into their memory events that had been on the news over the past few years. There had been a car bombing during an economic con-ference in London, which Scotland Yard had felt was con-nected to Beck. Then, in America, Katherine had been abducted and held until Rodney saved her and killed the man, who turned out to be a member of Senator Shapiro's campaign staff. All of this had been headline news during the campaign, then rehashed in the papers when Senator Shapiro was murdered. It seemed as if Katherine and her husband had been involved in their own share of vio-lence. If Katherine had been anxious to meet Mats and Suzanne in person, the feeling was certainly reciprocated now in their desire to meet her husband.

The cab dropped them off in front of a modest three-story residence surrounded by much larger houses in the

Kensington neighborhood of London. They were met at the door by Katherine. Her husband was at her shoulder. The men shook hands, looking at each other with more than the usual interest. They looked to be of an age. Both were just over six feet and similarly built, strong through the shoulders, and ruggedly handsome. After introductions, Katherine led them to the sitting room, where an elderly woman stood to meet them.

"This is my grandmother, Margaret Radcliff–Lady Radcliff," said Katherine.

"Posh," said the woman with a twinkle in her eye. "Surely by now these young people know there is a sir and a lady behind every door in this country. It's nice to meet you both."

They sat, and while Katherine excused herself to go to the kitchen, a woman Mats had seen behind a computer in the security office came out with sautéed brie and small crackers. Setting the food down on the table in front of them, she took drink orders, which were easy, as all took her suggestion of wine.

"I understand we're both from Marin," said Mats when the drinks arrived. "What high school did you go to?"

"Redwood. And you?"

"Tam. Play sports?" asked Mats.

"Not really. Freshman basketball. I did a little Bok Fu at a dojo in San Rafael."

"How often do you get back home, Mr. Falconi?" asked Margaret, handing him the brie.

"I try to get back once a month for a week, but it's been hard these last few months. I have a restaurant and a liquor-distributing company back there, but I have great managers for both. How about you, Rod?"

"Not as often as you. I work for President Beck in Washington. Fortunately, he allows me to do a lot of work by email and take a lot of time with Katherine here in England. He even allows her to travel with me sometimes when I'm with him on the road."

"That must really be exciting, being that close to the president," said Suzanne. "I understand you have had a lot of excitement in your personal life as well."

"We can talk about that after dinner," said Margaret quickly stopping Rodney's response.

Katherine and the other woman, whose name was Jane, came back into the dining room to serve the meal. Katherine sat, and Jane went back to the kitchen and returned with her plate. The meal was fantastic. The main dish was two filets of salmon with bay shrimp in a light buttery sauce between them, baked in puff pastry. Small sliced finger-length potatoes, roasted and seasoned, and fresh peas were the perfect complement to the salmon.

"You've outdone yourself with this one," said Rodney to his wife.

"Katherine, did you cook this?" asked Suzanne. "It is simply superb."

"It really takes no time to prepare. The salmon only takes twenty minutes, and I like to cook. I just don't get the chance very often. If you want a real treat, let Margaret cook."

Dessert was Zabaione with a curious hint of lemon, which also got rave reviews, with much scraping of spoons inside the large wine goblets in which it was served. Jane came in and cleared the table after both courses, then returned with a tray of glasses, and bottles of port and Carlos Primero brandy.

"All the dishes are in the dishwasher, Katherine. Is there anything else you would like me to help with?"

"No, that's all we need. Thank you very much for the help tonight. I couldn't have managed without you."

Katherine got up and walked with Jane to the front door, again thanking her for her assistance. When she returned, Margaret had moved everyone back to the sitting room along with the tray of liquor.

"The dinner was wonderful, dear," said Margaret. "But now that Jane is gone, it's time that we discuss the purpose of this evening. Mr. Falconi, you mentioned to Katherine a family journal, one that was instrumental in placing you in some dangerous situations."

"Yes, I did, and she was sworn to secrecy concerning them." Mats gave Katherine a withering glance, but she seemed unfazed by the look.

"Katherine has told me and her husband about the journal, and if you give me a minute to explain, I think you will understand why." During the meal, Margaret had been the picture of the perfect grandmother; now she leaned forward in her chair, her eyes burning with authority and intelligence. "I ... we have been the guardians of journals written in our family for eight hundred years. They warn the men of our line of danger. You have had your journals these last four years, and Rodney and Katherine have had theirs as well. It is too much of a coincidence that you just happened to employ Katherine's firm."

"But it is a coincidence. I did not know of her or her firm a week ago," said Suzanne.

"I did not mean that you knew of our secret. I meant that our journals tend to lead us or advise our men in courses of action. It sounds like yours do as well. I suspect that we are somehow connected."

"When you first mentioned your journals," said Katherine, "I wanted to tell you immediately of the coincidence, but I needed to talk to Rod, because our journals are his legacy. I needed his permission before Margaret or I could tell you of ours. I have one question for Suzanne, though. Do you read them?"

"I read the beginning of the original journal when we were first trying to translate it, but I have not read them since. Why do you ask?"

"The women in our line don't read the journals. In the past, when they have, things turned out badly for them," said Margaret, again taking over the direction of the conversation.

"I was in danger, for a while," Suzanne said. "But Mats kept me away from the possibility of harm by placing himself in danger."

"I'm warned of threats that dictate my actions," said Rod. "Sometimes I find that I have skills that were previously unknown to me. Do you have the same experiences?"

"Exactly," answered Mats. "Often after reading part of the journal, I will have dreams that add to or elaborate on the written text."

"I take it that neither of you has ever heard of anyone else with journals like these, or premonitions?" asked Margaret.

"I always thought that I was unique," said Rod, under his breath.

"The journal my father left me tells of an ancestor with similar abilities," volunteered Mats. "The Guibega tell me that it was passed down over the centuries, some having greater abilities than others."

"The Guibega?" asked Margaret.

"A family, a very close-knit family on Corsica, that has been friends of the Falconi for centuries," said Mats.

"So, they know about the journals. Do they know about the dreams?" Again, Margaret took the lead.

"I don't think they know about either, although they might have guessed. Mainly they talk about the Falconi knowing exactly what to do before events unfold. They say that early on, the Falconi seemed to read each other's minds, but that ability has been lost over the centuries."

"It seems that we have much in common," said Katherine in a soft voice. "I suspect that these common-alities brought us into contact–not luck or coincidence. If we could, I would like to go back to the issue of secu-rity. Most of what you asked for has been done. All your phones and computers have been safeguarded, as we discussed. Donald has removed information as to your involvement in the events you mentioned, but he told me there was remarkably little left to scrub. He will continue to monitor the web for any re-entries."

"I have a friend in the French police, who limited the press access to much of the information," said Mats.

"The White House staff, specifically the Secret Service, did the same for me," admitted Rod.

"As to the security of your journals," said Katherine, bringing the focus back to what she considered the most important aspect of the conversation. "Ours are held in a safe location that is tightly controlled for both tempera-ture and humidity. It is known only to those in this room.

I suggest that you construct your own, or place the journals in a bank vault, probably in Switzerland. How many are there in total?"

"The original journal, two texts that are more like books, and the journal that we recently found in Turkey," said Mats. "How many do you have?"

"We have what we believe is a journal for every male in our line since sometime after the Magna Carta was signed in 1215," answered Margaret.

"I still haven't gone through all of ours," said Rodney. "But every now and then, I'm drawn to one of the volumes, seemingly at random. But it's not random. Whichever one I choose is almost always relevant to whatever is happening to me in the present."

"I haven't translated the one we just found in Turkey," said Mats. "Like the first, it's written in a number of languages. Different ones than were used in the first one. It makes reading it difficult, but mostly I haven't gone through it because it did not seem to be the right time. Suzanne is still concerned that someone will accuse us of smuggling it out of Turkey. One of the other discoverers knows about it. In fact, it was how he got Suzanne to help him with the announcement of the lost library in Turkey."

The conversation turned to how the journals had predicted or helped with the adventures that both Rodney and Mats had faced over the previous years, and how the two women were involved and protected. It was remarkable how similar their experiences were. The bottles slowly diminished in content as the evening moved on, with Margaret doing her fair share of damage to the bottle of port.

"We must not forget what brought us together," said Katherine. She and Suzanne had drunk the least. "The process for the non-alcoholic beer has been removed from the web, I'm told, although someone could still theoretically be able to get it from the patent filing. What do you plan to do about the brewery?"

"Yes, what to do about the Whistling Pig and Mr. Nickolas Rigsby?" said Mats in a low voice, as he reached for the bottle of Carlos Primero.

CHAPTER 7
GAUL–945 AD

Jarl and the priest rode north, passing small farms and staying at the castles of local lords when they could, and in the rough if they couldn't. The priest had a letter, signed by the Pope, which even the surliest of the nobles honored, giving them food and a place to rest.

The mule determined their rate of travel, which Jarl figured was only about fifteen miles a day, far less than the 25 to thirty he would have made on his own, even if he had been on foot. The priest had saved his life, though, and he was reluctant to leave him alone. He had no expectation of rejoining his ship. The bluff he'd made to the burghers about his men returning had frightened them, but it was truly a bluff; there would be no attack if his crew thought him dead.

On the sixth day, they were on a road wide enough for a wagon. The sun beat down on the grain growing on either side of the road, turning it to deep gold. The smell was intoxicating. It brought to mind the bread they had been given as part of their fare as they traveled north, so different from the heavy dark loaves of his homeland and the flat bread of Miklagard. Its crust was crisp, the inside white as the winter snow at his sted. Smelling the grain that surrounded him, he could understand where the bread gained its flavor.

Shortly after stopping for their mid-day meal, which the priest never neglected to obtain from the kitchens of the manors where they rested, a band of armed horsemen came around the bend in the road ahead of them. With no evasion possible, they dismounted and moved the horse and donkey off the road to allow the horsemen to pass. These men, numbering twelve, rode two abreast with a single rider at their front. The leader was richly attired, and his mount had silver fastenings on its bridle and tack. The man rode past them, giving the priest a nod and casting a critical gaze at Jarl. As the rest of the troop rode past, dust kicked up from the horses' hoofs, causing both Jarl and the priest to turn away from the road. The last pair had passed when Jarl heard a horse galloping back toward them. He looked through the dust that hung close to the ground and saw the leader returning. Jarl reached for his sword as he saw the whole column turn behind their leader. To resist would only result in death. Slowly, he slid his sword back into its sheath and stood shoulder to shoulder with the priest.

"Jan! I almost didn't recognize you in that uniform. What are you doing so far south?" said the leader as he dismounted and moved toward Jarl, clasping him by the shoulders.

Jarl didn't understand the words spoken in French, catching only the word Jan.

"He thinks you are a man named Jan," said the priest, seeing the confusion on Jarl's face.

"Tell him Jan is my brother, and ask him if Jan is near."

Jarl listened to the priest talk with the man for far longer than was necessary to ask the question he had posed. The man had not let go of his shoulders but was looking curiously at Jarl's face as he and the priest spoke. Jarl was irritated that he did not know the language of the Franks. He was good at languages and promised himself that he would learn it.

"Tell him Jan Falkhand is my twin brother," said Jarl, extending his hand to the leader. It was taken, hand to forearm, and Jarl could tell by the grip that this was a warrior not to be underestimated.

Several of the riders dismounted and clapped Jarl on the back. Then their leader said something to them, and they looked at Jarl in confusion. They stood at the side of the road, the priest acting as interpreter for almost a quarter of an hour. It was determined that Jan, Jarl's brother, had occupied the land and was the protector of two villages that adjoined the land of the noble who led the column. They had become allies when Jan had offered to help the lord with a band of Britons that threated his borders. His manor was located a day's ride away on the same road, then a half day's ride to the east. They parted with the noble, who offered an escort that was politely declined by the priest.

When they had ridden off, Jarl said, "Priest, I would like to use the time we are together to learn this Frank language. I know you speak Latin. Do you know other languages as well?"

"I know the language of the Angles and I will be glad to teach you both if you return the favor by teaching me your Nordic tongue."

"That I will do. I didn't know where my brother had settled. I knew when we parted that he was going to raid the lands of the Franks, but I didn't know that he had settled here. It's a good omen."

They followed the directions the noble had given them, but it soon became evident that the distances had been given in horse miles, not donkey miles. Jarl used the time to learn words in the Frankish language. He found the language similar in some ways to Latin, and the pronunciation came easily to him. The priest, on the other hand, had trouble with the Norse words Jarl gave him in exchange.

It took them a day and a half to reach the village where they had been told to head east. There was no church, but they were offered a room with a bed to share in a farmer's house. Not knowing how long it would take to reach Jan's holdings, they decided to avail themselves of the farmer's hospitality. The next morning–after the priest had blessed the farm, the animals, and the farmer's children, in that order, and had procured the inevitable sack of lunch–they were on the road two hours after sunrise.

Again, the half-day ride was optimistic, and it was nearing supper time when the road, which was little more than a wagon rut, opened to a large, fortified manor house located at a bend of the river. The river had come from the northwest, after bending almost completely around the mound on which the small castle was raised. As it passed the castle, it skirted a small village of huts made of wood, with a raised path that led to the front gate. To Jarl's delight, on the bank of the river, suspended on racks, was a dragon boat turned keel up.

Jarl had not seen his brother Jan for almost five years. Part of his desire to travel north was to tell Red Hand that his daughter, Gun, who had become Jarl's wife, had been killed by the head of the palace guards of Miklagard. It was Red Hand who had insisted that the triplet Falkhand brothers–Jarl, Jan, and Kjell–split up. There were rumors that they used black magic. The rumors were true in that they could read each other's thoughts and had had the ability from birth. It gave them a tremendous advantage in war, but the difficult birth of three had killed their mother.

It was this ability that had allowed Kjell to warn Jarl that Red Hand's young daughter was about to strike him from behind. Jarl had pivoted and taken the sword hand of the young girl. When a truce was made, Jarl became responsible for the girl, taking her back to his sted and later marrying her. Jan joined the Danes, and Kjell became Red Hand's second in command. Three years later, Gun had taken charge of one of the two boats that had gone down the inland rivers to Miklagard, where Jarl had become the head of the Varangian Guards, protecting the emperor.

Jan had said at their parting that he planned to go south to raid the Franks, but it appeared that he had liked the land and had found a stronghold that suited him. This was the first that Jarl had heard of either brother, but with their birth-bond abilities, he felt he would have sensed it had either brother met with death.

Usually, the priest was the first to seek an audience at any place they were to spend the night. This time it was Jarl who rode to the closed gate in the wall that surrounded the manor house and hit the stout frame with the pommel of his sword, shouting, "I seek Jan Falkhand!"

A helmeted head appeared at the top of the wall looking down on Jarl and the priest. Seeing no threat, a signal was given, and the gate swung open.

Once inside the courtyard, Jarl dismounted and gave his reins to a boy who looked at him with wonder. From the main door of the house, the door opened, and Jan, dressed in a loose-fitting knee-length tunic of bright blue and yellow, stepped out, still in the process of buckling his sword to his waist.

Brother, is it really you, came into Jarl's mind.

It is. I am happy beyond words to see you, my brother.

Jan and Jarl walked quickly toward one another, grasping each other's forearms and moving in a circle.

"How is it that I find you at my door with no warning?" asked Jan.

"It is a long story and one that I am sure will leave us both thirsty," replied Jarl. "But first I think that both the priest and I are due for a wash in the river. We have two weeks of dirt to remove before we will be presentable."

Dinner was served, followed by wine, and the priest was welcomed along with the retainers and men-at-arms. Jarl told Jan that he would describe his journey to him in private. Jan had no such reservations.

"The first year, I joined a fleet of Danes, as Red Hand suggested. Our raid was successful, but I didn't like the company. They accepted me, but I was always assigned the least profitable duty or the one with the highest risk. We had an argument." Jan looked away, as if there was more to say. "I saw this tributary and followed it." Jan stopped and took a large swallow of wine.

"The second year, I came alone. Many Northmen had conquered the lowlands near the sea and settled there. This is further inland, but as you can see, it is easily defendable, and the river is always available should I be attacked. The castle did not have the wall that you see now. It was easy to capture. The lord was not a warrior, and better yet, he treated his serfs badly. It did not take long to win them over. The nearby nobles did not have much use for him either. The one who told you of me is Sir Laurent. I helped him with a small skirmish, and he came to trust me, as have the other local lords. There is plenty of empty land, which I give to my warriors, and every year I send my longboat for others and their women who would like to settle. Things are good, sometimes too good."

"Why is that, brother?"

"Most of my men want to farm. They still owe allegiance to me and fight when I call them. I provide them protection as they raise families, and they provide a fighting force when I am threatened or want to expand my lands. However, many no longer want to go a-viking."

"I fail to see the problem, brother. Is it not what you are doing?"

"Yes. The problem is not with those men, but with many of the younger single men. Their blood still runs hot. Without women, they don't want to be tied to the land. If they don't raid, then I must provide for them. That means the others must send me more of their laborers to feed those in the village. It is good to have a ready band of warriors. It was they who built the wall and deepened the moat, but I weary of keeping them busy and sending them on raids."

"How many are in your band?"

"Fifty, all told, but in truth, never more than thirty-five are here in the village at one time."

"It seems like a good problem to have, my brother," said Jarl with a short grunt that could have been the start of a laugh. "My story is more complicated, and much of it for your ears alone."

It will have to be in my chamber. Many of the men sleep in this hall.

Jarl found it strange to hear this voice in his head after being away from his brothers for five years. They had even invented their own spoken language by the time they were ten. No one knew of their ability; not even Gun had known, or Red Hand.

"Could you show me my room?" asked Jarl. "The priest can sleep in the hall with your men."

Jan grabbed the jug of wine and motioned to Jarl to bring his goblet. They went through an opening at the rear of the hall. A stone stairway carried them to the upper floor. There, a short hall brought them to a room overlooking the wall that spanned the isthmus, leading to the hill on which the manor had been built. The room was huge for a bedroom. It had a large bed that was lifted above the floor by posts, and a table with two chairs was placed by one of the windows. On the left side of the bed was a table with evidence that a woman slept there. A hairbrush and comb sat beside several colored bottles with liquid in them.

"You have done well," said Jarl as he looked around the room, placing his glass on the table.

Jan noticed that Jarl's eyes had lingered on the woman's things laid out next to the bed.

"I am content. I miss going a-viking, but this is a good place. I have married Laurent's daughter as well, so I am doubly content. Elinore is visiting her younger sister, who is due to give birth. She will not be back for a week. Now, what have you been doing? I have heard nothing of you or Kjell in four years."

"First, you should know that I married Gun."

"Gun! She is a child," laughed Jan.

"You know that Red Hand sent her with me for training. She was just turning fourteen then. Two-and-a-half years passed. Then Red Hand came to our sted and told me to go south, following the rivers to Miklagard where they needed replacements for the Varangian Guard. He said that Gun would be taking a second ship full of trade goods with me. She was no longer a child; she was a woman, and she was voted to command her father's ship."

"A woman in charge of a Viking ship. That must have been interesting," laughed Jan, slapping his brother on his back.

"It was. We were not halfway down the Dnieper when she killed two Rus warriors–though they did not deserve the name of warriors. The Rus are a displaced clan of Norsemen. They control the river."

"You must have taught her well."

"When we arrived in Miklagard, the men were welcomed into the Varangian Guard, but Gun ran afoul of the vizier, who controlled the trade of the city as well as the palace guards. After two years, she was forced to leave, going back up through the Black Sea and the Dnieper.

The vizier sent men after her and killed her. Only one man escaped to bring me the message. When the vizier found out that I knew of her death, he presented me with her shriveled, handless arm."

"You killed him, of course!" said Jan, no longer finding any mirth in Jarl's tale.

"The emperor forbade me from killing him. After six months, I resigned my position and outfitted my ship to sail the inland sea through the Pillars of Hercules and north to our home. I knew I had to tell Red Hand of our marriage and her death."

"I know you, brother. You would not have left her unavenged."

"I did not. My ship was loaded with treasure we had accumulated while in Miklagard and ready to sail. It was almost a week before the opportunity was given to me. I killed the vizier and immediately went to the ship. We were away before the news reached the emperor."

"And how is it that I find you walking with a priest in my land?" asked Jan.

"Before I left, the emperor gave me a scroll to give to the emperor of Rome. Just before arriving at that city, we surprised a pirate fleet that was attacking a Roman galley. We were able to capture one of the pirate ships and drive off the others. Afterward, we were well received in Rome, and I was given a gift of land in one of the great islands in the inland sea–Corsica. It is good land, and like you, I think I will return and settle. I built a second dragon ship. As soon as it was finished, I took men who wanted to return home. Some had women there. Some slaves and three of the local Corsicans who had become my allies craved adventure and filled out the crew."

"And where is this ship and the men now?"

"Ah. Almost a moon ago, we landed to take fresh water and find meat. We didn't know that just around a narrow headland was a village with a foolish lord. We found his sheep unattended, and three of us killed some of them while the others took on water from a small creek that flowed to the beach. The three of us on the plateau were attacked by horsemen, and I was felled by a rock from a sling. One of my men was killed. I was left for dead, and my crew took to the sea. I have not seen them since."

"Your men left you? What kind of crew does that?"

"I believe they had no other choice. They were greatly outnumbered, and on the beach with the villagers above them. I was down on the ground, and it looked like I had a spear in my chest."

"How is it that you were not killed?"

"It was the priest who saved me. He recognized the insignia of the Varangian Guard on my tunic and armor and thought me a Christian. I was taken before a council of the town's burghers, where the priest defended me. I paid for the sheep and for the lord's death, bought a horse, and we have been traveling north to get to Le Havre ever since. Two days' ride south, we came across the noble you called Laurent. He thought I was you at first and ended up giving us directions to your manor."

"What will you do now, with no ship or crew?"

"I would spend a fortnight with you. It has been too long, brother. Then I would crew on a ship going north. I still have to tell Red Hand of his daughter's death and the revenge I took on her killer."

"Won't your crew continue the journey?"

"I suspect they will, but with me presumed dead, they will elect a new leader and decide what to do. There were some who had reason to go north. The rest were going because of me. They will have little reason to continue."

"Brother, you are more than welcome to stay with me as long as you wish. When you tire of the food and the wine, I myself will take you to Le Havre and find you a ship going north."

The morning broke on the long ship. The skies were clear, the wind gentle from the southwest. The lookouts had seen no sign of other vessels during the night. While the scene was peaceful, the situation on the ship was not. Svante still retained command as Jarl's chosen second. Neil and Viktor stood beside him while Lars, Bjorn Ragnarson, Nils, and three other Norsemen huddled mid-ships.

Svante had convinced the crew to rest until morning and then make a resolution about their voyage. It was obvious that there were deeply divided opinions as to the future of the journey.

"We should not go north," shouted Lars in Norse. "Also, the slaves had no part in accumulating the treasure we have on board. They should not receive any share. In fact, it would be better if we sold them at the nearest port. We cannot expect their loyalty."

"What of the two Guibega? Would you sell them as well?" answered Svante. "And me if I do not agree with your scheme?"

The three men at mid-ships were joined by three others–Akel, Isak, and Emil–all with their hands on the hilts of their swords. The two standing with Olaf in the stern did the same. Violence on a ship the size of the Dancing Horse would be fatal not only to the participants but to those around them. There would be no place to escape the carnage should the eight Norsemen draw their weapons. One of the free slaves had been chained in a galley for almost a year with a Dane. He had learned enough of his tongue that he understood what Lars had said about the status of the slaves on board. He had quickly translated it into the two languages spoken by the rest of the slaves. Now they also gripped their weapons but faced the dissident band, rather than Svante. Seeing this, Lars told his men to stand down.

"I call a Thing," shouted Svante above the voices of the crew. The rules of a Thing were rigid, and to violate them made one an outcast, never to be trusted by any Norseman. No weapons were allowed, and every man was given the right to speak, with disagreements settled by the leader. The leader was chosen by a vote. These were the rules that governed a Thing. The freed slaves and the two Guibega were confused, but the majority of the crew, including the two injured men, grunted their acceptance.

"I call for a vote for leader," said Lars from the waist of the boat. "I propose Bjorn Ragnarson."

"I propose Svante," said Viktor quickly.

"What of the slaves? They should not have a vote in the Thing," said Lars.

Svante answered quickly. "I am still the leader until another is voted such. These men are free men of our crew now. They have a full say."

The vote was explained to the non-Norsemen members of the crew and the vote was taken. It was close. Most of the Norsemen except the two wounded men sided with

Bjorn Ragnarson, and all the others sided with Svante and the two at the stern. Svante retained the role of leader by a single vote, but he could see great dissatisfaction in those who had voted against him. He didn't know whether it was because the former slaves' vote had been given same value as their own, or whether it was true dissatisfaction with him as their leader. Whatever the reason, it would be well to prepare for violence after the Thing was concluded.

"Most of us have treasure on board that belongs to us individually," started Svante, taking on the simplest issue first. "There is no change in that. But we must decide what to do with Jarl's treasure. He has no wife, although he and the Guibega woman on Corsica lived as one for almost a year. He has no children. I propose we divide his into equal shares for the entire crew, with one share for the Corsican woman."

Discussions followed, with several crew members stating their opinions of Svante's proposal.

"I say again that the slaves had no part in obtaining the treasure and should not receive a share," said Lars.

"Lars," responded Svante in a low, firm voice. "I am not speaking of our own individual shares of treasure. I am speaking of Jarl's treasure. You did not have any part in Jarl's obtaining riches. None of us did. Why should we be different from those who Jarl freed at the start of this voyage?"

General agreement was given to Svante's logic and a vote took place. All would be given a share.

Svante knew that he would not have the power to force the opposing crew members to continue the journey north. "I propose that we sail to the next large Frankish port. Those of us who wish to continue north can leave with our shares and find another ship. The former slaves can continue with the ship or leave, as they desire. If the ship needs additional crew, you others can either buy slaves or bring on new men. You can also buy women, or if you should not want to spend part of your wealth, you can raid the lands you find as you go a'viking."

The vote was taken with only two dissenters, and the men relaxed. Svante wondered if there would be a resumption of bad feelings when the treasure was divided and the former slaves left the ship. It would be best if they arrived at a port quickly. He ordered the sail set, taking advantage of the prevailing winds, and the oars to be used to supplement their speed.

The long ship slid easily to the jetty. Svante moved the steering oar expertly as the gunwale stopped inches from the stone wall. Two of the crew beside Svante were still insistent on going north. Svante, Viktor, and Nils all had wives and family awaiting their return. For Svante, it had been only four years, but Viktor had served the Varangian Guard for nearly eight. They had spent a day sailing, dividing Jarl's share of the treasure into equal shares for all the remaining members. Some of the items were hard to divide, but eventually all were satisfied with the disposition. Those remaining with the Dancing Horse had voted to buy female slaves to bring with them back to Ajaccio. The two remaining Guibega had had enough of sailing the seas, and with Jarl dead they, as well as four freed slaves, had decided to stay ashore. The Guibega would travel overland and take a short sail back to Ajaccio. The two other freed slaves went along with the majority of

Vikings who wanted to return to the island. Olaf wondered if they would be treated well once they were back at sea. Both were from the northern mainland, and as such had been more accepted by the Norsemen than the other slaves.

There were over two dozen ships in the harbor, and little attention was given to the crew members as they left the ship loaded with their heavy sea chests. All were on their way within two days.

CHAPTER 8
DRY DRATON, ENGLAND–THE PRESENT

Mats wanted to talk to Nickolas Rigsby in person. He had not yet decided what he would do to the man for stealing the Harp and Hawk's brewing process. His choices ranged from filing suit and shutting the brewery down completely, demanding a license fee for the use of the process, sending Rigsby to jail for the theft of the bacteria, or buying him out. He knew from Katherine's report that Rigsby was up against it economically. He had put in everything he had and borrowed to the max to buy the brewery and equip it for the production of the non-alcoholic beer that was keeping him afloat.

Mats parked in front of the building and found the door open, as before. Again he yelled out a greeting and was answered by a call from the back.

"Mr. Falconi, you have great timing. Would you do me a favor and turn that valve open when I tell you?"

Rigsby was standing on the platform above the mixing tank, wearing rubber gloves and a mask. He pointed to a large valve wheel at the base of the platform, about a dozen steps from where he was standing.

"I could do it, but I would lose several cases worth of brew. Okay—now."

Mats turned the valve open and then closed it a quarter turn, a habit he had learned from his father on the fishing boats that always let you know the valve was open, not closed. As soon as he had finished, Rigsby climbed down the short ladder to the main floor and took off his gloves and mask.

"Thank you. Since my employee left me, I've had to do everything myself, like opening that valve at the same time I'm closing the one on the tank. Bad design for a one-man operation."

"Are you free to talk now?" asked Mats.

"Sure. Just let me adjust the temperature on the batch and we can talk in the office."

The office was bigger and better furnished than the production of the brewery would suggest, showing that the original owners had expected a higher return on their investment. Still, Mats noticed that several pieces of furniture had recently been removed, if the subtle outline of their former presence was any indication.

"I want to thank you for allowing me to continue brewing, Mr. Falconi. But to tell you the truth, I don't see how I can go on much longer. I haven't found another delivery man yet, not that I have much to pay him. I'm barely covering the loan payments, and the fourteen-hour days are wearing me down."

"Let's see if we can find a solution," said Mats, opening the file he had brought with him. "You actually owe more than the one hundred and ninety thousand pounds you mentioned the other day. Your house is also mortgaged, and you owe on both the delivery van and your car."

"I was planning on selling the car," said Rigsby, his voice barely above a whisper.

"You wouldn't get much from it after you paid off the loan," said Mats, leaning back in his chair. "Let me make you a proposition. Everything I've learned about you tells me that despite your theft of my process and bacteria, you are an honest, hardworking man. You must realize that if I stop you from brewing the non-alcoholic product, you will go under, and maybe that'll happen even if I let you continue."

"Why do you think I'm working like I am? Of course I know it."

"What would you say if I proposed to buy and pay off all of your debt, even the debt on your house and car, as well as put two hundred thousand pounds into the business itself?"

"What would you expect in return?" asked Rigsby, his eyes flashing.

"I would become fifty-one percent owner of the Whistling Pig Brewery. You would retain forty-nine percent and would own your home and car outright."

"I would lose control of the brewery," said Rigsby. "I didn't buy it and go into debt because I wanted to work for someone else."

"I understand your feelings, but forty-nine percent of something is worth a lot more than a hundred percent of nothing, which is what you will have if the banks foreclose. Which will probably happen even if I don't sue," said Mats. "Besides, if you agree, I would leave you in complete charge of the business. I don't want the brewery if you don't run it. The money I put into it will allow you to hire help and expand your distribution, as you had planned. I will require that my export company be given exclusive rights to distribute the brand in the States. That alone will increase production and profits, as well as brand recognition."

Rigsby's Stan Laurel face spread into a grin that widened the lower half of his face, showing disbelief. "And after the place becomes profitable, you can sell it out from under me!"

"That is not my intent, but I understand your suspicions. We have reason not to trust each other. On my part, I might doubt your character because you stole my process, and on yours, you might think my requiring fifty-one percent ownership is not a good way to begin a partnership. I want the majority ownership in the beginning because I want to make sure that several things are done to produce a better-quality beer, as well as to establish a distribution network and greater sales. Also, you need to change the label on all your offerings. They're terrible. But after those things are in place, and a profit is being made, I guarantee that you would have the option to buy back two percent of the shares at a price we would agree upon beforehand."

"Why would you do that?" asked Rigsby.

"Still suspicious," said Mats, with a chuckle. "I don't have time to run a brewery. I have deeded the brewery in Ireland to the previous owner's son. He's young and has managers run it for him at a good profit. I really don't want yours. I am primarily interested in controlling the exportation of your premium offerings. Your IPA is excellent, but your dark lager and the NA, while very good, could be improved. After that is done, I just want a profit on my forty-nine percent holding. I think that is only fair."

"More than fair. Would you draw up the agreement and let me look at it? If it is as you say …"

A loud knock in the entryway caused both Rigsby and Mats to turn around.

"Come in. It's open," yelled Rigsby.

"And put in a remote door lock and intercom," said Mats, laughing at the silly grin on Rigsby's face as he went to the office door and opened it onto the brewing floor.

Two men entered, one in a police officer's uniform and one in slacks and a sports jacket.

"Inspector David Small," said the man in the sport coat as he showed his badge. "Which of you is Nickolas Rigsby?"

"I am," offered Rigsby, extending a hand to the inspector.

"You filed a report on a missing delivery lorry on the fifteenth of September."

"Yes, you found it abandoned four days later with my beer gone. I picked it up from your impound lot. It's parked out front."

"Have you used it since you picked it up?"

"Yes, certainly. I've used it for deliveries at least three times since."

"You drove it personally, not your employee?"

"I haven't seen Mason since that night. He's a student at Cambridge, just down the road."

"Have you tried to contact him?"

"Yes, several times. I've left messages on his mobile and at Cambridge. He's a post-doctoral student, so his hours are irregular. Have you found him? Did he take my beer for a party? That's what the officer I reported the incident to thought."

"Where were you the night of the disappearance?" asked the inspector, looking at the gloves that Rigsby had taken off and placed on his desk.

"At home sleeping after a twelve-hour bottling run," said Rigsby. "What is this about?"

"Can anyone verify that you were at home?" The inspector did not bother answering Rigsby's question.

"No, I live alone. Why?"

"We found Mason Crawley in a shallow grave earlier today. Actually, a dog–an Airedale–found him on a walk with his master. His body was in good enough condition that we were able to make a positive identification. He was murdered."

"How?" asked Rigsby, shaking his head in disbelief.

"That is still under investigation. So you have no one who can corroborate your whereabouts that evening?"

"No. I didn't know anything was wrong until about ten in the morning, when one of the pubs called to tell me that they hadn't gotten their delivery the previous evening. I had noticed the delivery lorry wasn't out front, but sometimes Mason used it to get to school and brought it back after his class."

"What was the name of the pub that called you?"

"The Regent, but I got another call from the Bar Hill Arms later in the morning with the same story. I was about to call Mason when I got a call from the Swan. They had gotten their delivery, but it was incomplete, and Mason had left the back door open, which really upset them. That was when I called in the missing lorry to the police."

"But you did not file a missing person's report. We are impounding the lorry," said Inspector Small. "I will require you to come to the station for fingerprinting and further questioning."

"Am I a suspect? I hardly knew the lad. He had worked for me less than three months."

"At present you are a person of interest. We need your prints to be able to eliminate them from others inside the lorry."

"I can take you to the station," said Mats. He had a strong instinct about Nickolas Rigsby's honesty. It was a big part of why he had decided to go into partnership with him rather than close him down. The situation was not parallel to the murders that had eventually resulted in his buying the Harp and Hawk, but it was close enough for Mats to strike a pose in Rigsby's defense.

"And who are you?" asked Small, seeming to notice Mats for the first time.

"My name is Mats Falconi," said Mats, rising and taking the inspector's hand. "Mr. Rigsby and I were just concluding a business transaction."

"You're welcome to come with him, but I warn you that it might take some time."

"Thank you for the offer, Mr. Falconi," said Rigsby, visibly appreciative. "I can take my own car."

"Here is my card," said Mats, quickly writing on the back with a pen he took from the desk. "It has my cell phone. Let me know when you are free, or if you require any legal assistance. I'll give you a call later. I already have your cell."

"To save time, Mr. Falconi, where were you on the evening of September 15?" asked Inspector Small.

"In Paris. I'm sure plenty of people can vouch for me, but I would have to look at my calendar and ask my wife for precise details."

The officer with Inspector Small opened the door. Outside they could hear the sound of wind and distant thunder. Mats remembered too late that in England, you should never be too far from an umbrella.

CHAPTER 9
LONDON–THE PRESENT

"They must blame the Irish."

The four men sitting around the table listened intently to the man who was standing in front of them. All were dark complexioned, two with beards, and two with mustaches. The man who was speaking was clean shaven and tall. He was also dark, but on him it could have been a tan.

"It is essential if we kill a royal. The British love their monarchs. No one will believe that they weren't the primary target. We will leave enough evidence to make them think so, even if someone suspects otherwise."

"Can we be sure that they will be together?" asked one of the men at the table.

"If they are not, then we abort, and I find another opportunity. Two things must happen. A royal must die along with the Prime Minister, and not one of us must be caught. No possible blame must ever be traced to the brotherhood. That means that you cannot even be found dead. This must be clean. You men have been chosen because you are our best. It is my job to put you in the right position with the right tools; yours is to follow my plan precisely."

The tall man gave a phone to each of the men at the table. "Use this only to call me. My number is saved under 'Florist.' From now on you will refer to any royal by calling them 'Flower'– the PM is 'Greenery.' I am the Florist. Word recognition has gotten too good for us to use names or titles that will flag our calls. You are not to use the phones except to call me or receive orders from me. Does everyone understand?"

All at the table nodded and examined their new burner phones. Each one came with a charger.

"Abdul, you and Hasan find a room south of the Thames. Bashar, you and Habib rent a room between Heathrow and London—the closer to the airport, the better. Use your English names and identifications to rent the rooms. Use cash. You are not to talk to each other, only to me. We cannot afford another mishap like the one in Bar Hill. If you must tell the other group something, call me and I will relay the message. Also, shave–no facial hair. Do that before you look for your rooms. When you find them, call me with the locations."

There was a flash of light at the window, and the bulbs inside the small apartment flickered. Thunder followed quickly and was close enough to rattle the windows.

"Better wait until this storm passes. Not even Englishmen would look for a room in this weather."

CHAPTER 10
GAUL–945 AD

The fortnight Jarl had asked to stay with his brother, Jan, eased into two. A full moon passed before Jarl finally said that he must continue his journey north.

Jan's Frank wife took after her father, whom they had met on the road north. She was tall, coming up to Jan's nose, and beautiful, with red hair so dark that in certain lights it could be taken for black. She was some five years younger than his brother, and Jarl could see that he loved her. Jarl suspected it would not be many months before her cousin would reciprocate by coming to Jan's manor to assist in a birth.

In the end it was not the company or any imposition that caused Jarl to announce his departure but the turn of the season, which brought with it shorter days and winds that increasingly veered from the north. Jarl worried that it would become difficult to find a ship in which he could sail north.

On the chosen day, Jan had his longboat up-righted and moved to the grassy riverbank, where his men quickly readied the craft for the short journey down the river to Le Havre. They didn't bother stepping the mast, as the Seine twisted north and south far more often than it went west toward the coast. Le Havre occupied the north bank of the estuary as the river met the ocean. If the wind was favorable, they would raise the mast then, but until they reached that point, they would row. The current would be with them going down river, and the trip would take a day. The way back for the crew would take a day and a half.

Jan had given his brother several sets of clothes to replace those still on the Dancing Horse, as well as several more gold coins that Jarl put into his purse. He also added to the hold some gifts that Jarl would give to Red Hand on Jan's behalf. The priest had accepted nothing and was dressed as before, in a simple robe, although it was made from fine wool. The two had kept acquainting each other with languages they wished to know. Jarl was becoming much more familiar with the Frank tongue than the priest was with Norse.

They spent the first night on the banks of the Seine, roasting a haunch of boar they had brought with them over an open fire. The mood was jovial, with Jan telling stories of his first-year raid with the Danes. Jarl thought he was leaving parts of the story untold, which was unlike his brother. Jan persuaded Jarl to tell of his voyage down the inland river. Gun's killing of the two Rus who attacked her was told and retold. Everyone laughed, but the telling made Jarl morose, and he soon took his robe to the edge of the gathering and tried to go to sleep.

The previous evening did nothing to dampen the men's spirits; they were on the boat, rowing toward Le Havre, by daybreak. The river widened and as it did, the current lessened and the crew took to singing a chant to give power to their stroke. Jarl could smell salt in the air when

Jan ordered the mast stepped and the sail set. The wind was not very favorable, coming mostly from the west, but it helped as they entered the wide mouth of the river and turned north.

Le Havre's waterfront was a hive of activity. As they approached an empty pier, Jan's longboat was recognized. A number of men ashore, dressed in the Norse tradition, waved in greeting. As they tied up, Jan jumped ashore and clasped one of the men by the shoulders before embracing him in a bear hug. Jarl followed his brother, recognizing the man as one who had sailed with Jan before they were separated by Red Hand. It took a moment for him to remember his name. Was it Axel? No—Arne; the name came to him.

"Arne. It has been too long," said Jarl, taking the man's hand as Jan released him.

"Kjell, it is good to see you as well."

"It seems it is my fate in this land to be taken for my brother–first Jan, then Kjell! I am Jarl."

Arn stepped back, his mouth open, his eyes wide. "But I have heard that you died, a spear thrust from a Frankish horseman."

"Where did you hear this?" asked Jarl, knowing it could only have come from one source.

"Almost a moon ago. A longboat came here. The crew split up, and at least nine left the ship. Three went north on a Danish ship. Some former slaves and two others bought horses and pack animals and rode east. They were a rough-looking lot. I don't suspect they will be bothered on the road. The rest stayed with the ship, which spent eight days here before it sailed."

"How did you hear of my death?"

"Arne left me to run an inn here," said Jan, slapping the man on the back. "Although he sells more ale and mead than beds. If there is a tale to be told or a secret to be known, he will hear it."

"As I said, they were a close-mouthed group," said Arne. "The ones I helped find berths on the Danish ship said nothing, nor did the former slaves. The crew that stayed on the Dancing Horse, for that was what they called their ship, were at my tavern every night. They spent freely and drank much. In their drunkenness, they told me of your death and the disagreement among the crew about whether to continue north. They bought ten women slaves, spending small fortunes for the young, best-looking ones. They also took on two men and bought two male slaves to round out their crew, but I still think they were undermanned. They certainly didn't have enough on board to go a-viking. It is probably why they bought the women rather than raiding for them. I am sorry to mistake you for Kjell."

"That is all right. We are used to being taken for each other, although Jan looks to be getting soft in the middle with the life he leads now."

"This is what I get for offering you my hospitality this past month?" laughed Jan. "We don't know where our Kjell is. Neither of us has seen him in over five years. In fact, it is only fortune–good or bad, depending on your view–that brings Jarl here."

"Did they say where they were going in the Dancing Horse?" asked Jarl.

"No. I don't think they were even sure themselves, but they left the day after buying the slaves, and they looked to head south. At least, they were rowing against the wind and didn't have the sails up. That was three weeks ago."

"I'll be asking for your services as well," said Jarl. "I need passage north for myself and another passenger."

"Can the passenger row?" asked Arne.

"Not well. He is a priest."

Arn took a deep intake of breath. "That might be hard. Most Danes and Norsemen think a priest on board brings bad luck."

"He will pay well for his passage."

"There are several possibilities. First, though, come to my tavern and drink with me, and we will tell lies about the old days." Arne linked arms with the two brothers and led them toward a large building that sat close to the center of the wharfs.

Three nights, two barroom brawls, and five gold coins later, Arne announced that he had found Jarl a berth on a Danish ship that was going all the way north to the land of the Swedes.

CHAPTER 11
DRY DRAYTON, ENGLAND–THE PRESENT

"I would like Nickolas Rigsby, the owner of the Whistling Pig Brewery, to have proper representation with a lawyer." Mats was sitting with Suzanne in Katherine Radcliff Stoner's office. It was still storming outside. The lightning was even more spectacular as the light was fading in the early evening. "He was taken to the police station over six hours ago. I've called him three times on his cell and he has not picked up."

"Which station?" asked Katherine.

"I'm not sure. He was picked up at the brewery outside of Dry Drayton, just north of Cambridge. The officer was Inspector Small. I don't recall his first name."

"Was he arrested or charged?" asked Katherine, reaching for the phone on her desk.

"Not before they left. The police had found the student who used to work for him. He went missing a couple of weeks ago on a delivery run. Evidently he was murdered."

"In this country we have a different system than you do in the States," explained Katherine as she punched in a number on her desk phone. "If he hasn't been charged, he probably needs a solicitor. If he has been charged, then he needs a barrister for any court proceedings. Regardless, he will need a solicitor first, because it is he who retains the barrister."

She turned away and spoke into the phone. "Harry, it's Katherine Radcliff. Yes, nice to talk to you as well. I have a favor to ask. A man named Nickolas Rigsby has been picked up by an Inspector Small in Dry Drayton for questioning about a murder. That was six hours ago, and we haven't been able to get in touch with him since. Could you check into it, please? It's for a client of mine. Yes, thank you." She hung up. "We should get word within the hour. Harry Lapidas is very good. May I ask why you are interested in helping this man?"

"A couple reasons," said Mats. "First, I've met with him a couple of times and he doesn't seem the type to murder anyone. He's a hard-working guy who's under it financially. Losing his worker just put him under more stress. The police brought him in because he is their only suspect. I've mentioned that we bought a brewery in Ireland a few years ago and learned that the previous owners had been murdered. My going into business with Rigsby is just too eerily similar."

"We should know more in a few hours," said Katherine, opening a file on her desk. "In the meantime, let's review the security measures we have put in place for you on your mobile devices and computers. They take advantage of fingerprints as well as facial recognition. Once Suzanne has supplied us with the images of the journals, we will place them on your computer. The journals will only be able to be seen on your device, and they will be read-only. No one will be able to copy them."

The phone rang, and Katherine looked at the number before picking up. "Yes, Harry." She listened for a minute without comment, then said, "That's great. Thank you for doing that so quickly. Yes, please stay on the case until further notice. Send your statement here."

She turned to Mats. "That was the solicitor. They were holding Mr. Rigsby as a suspect, but they found a neighbor who saw him park his car at his house the evening of the murder and parked in back of him. The neighbor swears that Rigsby couldn't have used his car without asking her to move hers, so they let him go for now, at the insistence of Harry, who is now his lawyer."

"Thank you for your help," said Mats. "Would you please give the lawyer my name and number? I'll pay his fee, and I would also like him to write up some documents for the purchase of part of the brewery, and an exclusive export arrangement."

"We would like to invite you to dinner," said Suzanne, as they finished the business matters.

Rodney came into the meeting room from somewhere in the back of the building before Katherine could answer. "Sorry I'm late. I had to finish two speeches and write two press releases. Katherine has an isolation booth of an office in the back where I can work undisturbed, but sometimes I lose track of time."

"You're not late at all," said Katherine, rising and kissing her husband. "And even if you were, I don't think there will be many people out in this storm. We should take one car, though, in case we have to park away from the restaurant. That way only one of us will get wet."

Katherine had been correct about most people not braving the storm to go to dinner. Rodney dropped the others off and walked back under a large golf umbrella. The restaurant was less than a third full. He was led to a table where the others already had drinks and three plates of appetizers in front of them.

Over a dessert of gulab jamun and his second beer, Mats asked, "How did you two meet?"

"Margaret watches over a thatched house and church in a village called Hamerton a couple of days a month. It's not far from Cambridge," said Katherine. "I was visiting her when Rodney came to see the church on a promise he had made his grandmother. When Margaret found out that his mother was a Hamerton, she sent me up to see if he had any questions."

"It was my first time in England. I was with Senator Kent just as he started his presidential campaign. Katherine helped me with a speech, and the rest is history," explained Rodney, giving his wife a squeeze of the hand. "How about you guys?"

"Kind of similar, actually," said Mats, pushing his beer to the side. "I couldn't read the journal my father left me. I went to Corsica to see where my father had been born. I thought the ancient manuscript section of the Bibliothèque would have scholars who could help me. First guy I met I wanted to punch in the mouth. Fortunately, he had a great assistant in Suzanne. She read it like it was a comic strip."

"The translation of the journal led to the discovery of the Bougainville library," said Suzanne. "Things just came naturally after that."

"I guess you have to meet the one you love somewhere, but it's probably more than a coincidence that we both met our wives seeking information about our family heritage," said Rodney.

"And we were both involved in violence shortly after discovering what was in the journals," added Mats. "Clues from our ancestors helped us protect our loved ones. My father left a note saying I would know when to open the journal. Events had already gotten violent when Suzanne helped me translate it."

"Same with me, now that you mention it," said Rodney. "A guy tried to kill me with a hammer. I didn't even know about the journals until after I met Katherine and Margaret. Then they kind of gave me guidance."

"Do you think the purchase of this brewery–what is its name, the Whistling Pig?–has put you into another dangerous situation?" asked Katherine.

"That's its name, all right," said Mats. "It's a terrible name. Catchy, but not inviting. I'll probably change it if I buy in, or at least change the label we export to the States. There has been violence–the murder of the delivery boy–but it doesn't feel personal like the Harp an Hawk did. This is just a business deal that became necessary because of Rigsby stealing our brewing process for non-alcoholic beer."

"It might have been the vehicle for bringing our two families together," said Katherine. "I mean, both of us thought we were unique. Without Rigsby filching your process, you wouldn't have come to England and hired me to help you with security. We are both richer because of it."

"Speaking of richer, what's in this gulab jamun dessert you ordered for us?" asked Mats, spooning a second full load out of the round ball that had been placed in front of him.

CHAPTER 12
LE HAVRE, GAUL–945 AD

T he ship Arne had found for Jarl and the priest was, like most Danish vessels, wider of beam than the dragon ships of Jarl's homeland. Likewise, the Danes themselves were thicker, and as a group not as tall as Jarl or his brothers. While their language was the same, Jarl thought they spoke it like they had pebbles in their mouths.

Their first evening at sea, a third of the crew kept at the oars, only enough to give the ship headway against the waves that moved down the channel from the north. As dawn broke, the winds picked up and the clouds took on a fiery blood-red hue that told of the weather to come. The waves increased both in size and fury, and within an hour the ship was being tossed about like a leaf in a windstorm. The steersman struggled to keep his oar in the water as the boat ran up and over the oncoming sea. Every fifth wave came from a different angle from those before. Jarl was on the steer board side at the last oar. The stern-most rowers were usually the ones who gave the ship the most power, with the front oars providing the stroke. The priest had proved a disaster at the oars, alternating hitting the oar in front of him or pulling himself off the thwart. He was settled next to the stern platform, just aft of Jarl, trying to keep warm, his eyes wide with fear.

Jarl thought it was good that the priest still had not been able to master the Norse language. An hour after what must have been sunrise, the dark storm clouds blotting out all light from the sun's position above the horizon, the Danes rowing in front of them started to blame the storm on the presence of the priest. They all agreed that the waves would calm as soon as the priest was thrown overboard.

"Reach under the platform and place my sword between my legs, priest," said Jarl in Latin, hoping the leader at the steering oar did not know the language.

The priest looked at him as if he didn't understand the words.

"Now," said Jarl, sharply. The priest pushed the hilt of the sword between Jarl's knees in response to his urgent tone.

Almost immediately, Jarl heard a rattle as the two pairs of rowers behind him shipped their oars. Jarl bent, pulling his sword from its scabbard in one motion while turning to face the crew. He held the tip of the sword to the throat of the man who had seconds before been rowing at his right shoulder.

"Priest, take my knife and face the steersman. Tell me if he leaves his position or takes a weapon." Jarl's action had stopped the four men just out of the sword's reach. All had daggers. If they charged, they would take Jarl, but they would lose three, maybe four, counting the man threatened by his blade.

"The priest will not be harmed," shouted Jarl. "If you don't return to your oars, the ship will surely broach, and we all will die. I am Jarl Falkhand, and if you have heard my name, you know I have weather luck. I say the storm will slacken soon. Then you can turn with the wind and drop us at the nearest coast. If you attack, I will take the steersman and enough of you that you will not be able to work the ship."

"Do as he says. To your oars!" shouted the man on the steering platform. He had heard of the Falkhand brothers and knew that the man in front of him, if he truly was a Falkhand, would be true to his word.

Whether it was as Jarl had said—he had good weather luck–or that Jarl could read weather patterns better than other men, the storm started to subside an hour after the Danes tried to rush him. First, the wind abated in intensity and began to maintain a constant direction. Then the waves became less violent, so the ship was not in danger of broaching. By the third hour, Jarl turned to the leader of the Danes and told him that he could turn, raise the sail, and take him and the priest to the shore that was visible on their port side.

The storm had blown them to the southwest, toward the shore of the Angles' Isle and almost into the estuary of the great river leading to the city of Londinium. Jarl had not been there, as his only time on the island had been spent raiding the northeast coast with his brothers. The crew dropped the sail and took up the oars again, bringing the ship to a swampish north bank that was barely inside the river mouth. Still holding the crew at bay with his sword, Jarl had the priest retrieve their packs.

Jarl looked at the muddy bank toward which the Danes rowed. If he and the priest were left there and the crew decided to avenge his earlier actions, there would be no doubt of the outcome. The confines of the boat and his weapon at the ready to strike the steersman had kept the Danes at bay until now. There would be no such restrictions once he and the priest were ashore.

"The priest has already paid for his passage," said Jarl to the steersman. "I was to crew for mine. This should give you luck and pay for the time I spent with a sword rather than at the oars." He flipped a coin to the leader and pushed the priest off the boat onto the soggy shore, throwing their belongings onto the muddy bank before following him with his own leap. If the crew had followed them, it would have been over quickly.

"We will not kill you or the priest," yelled the leader as they moved away from the boat. "For that, Jarl Falkhand, do not use your black magic on us for the remainder of our journey. We will not speak ill of you, and I will never spend your lucky coin."

The coin Jarl had given to them had made a difference–that and his name. It was one thing to kill a man. It was another when the man had two brothers, known for their success in battle, who would surely take revenge.

The priest hiked up his robes and slogged toward a slight rise visible in the distance. Jarl followed, glancing back repeatedly at the longboat, which was backing oars and moving into the muddy stream of the river.

"Where do we go now?" asked Jarl as he caught up with the priest.

"Thank you for saving my life," said the priest, ignoring Jarl's question. "I lived in this land as a young acolyte. If we follow this bank, we will arrive at a great city, but it is not a place that a Viking, even one who served the eastern emperor, would be welcomed. It is best that we find you a robe so you can act as my disciple. We should go west until we get to solid ground, then head north. In the far north the Norse rule. If we get there, you will be safe."

"You said when we first started traveling together that you spoke the tongue of this land," said Jarl as he followed the priest across the bog. "I will continue to teach you Norse, and you can now instruct me in this language."

Three days later, having not eaten and having slept rough, they came to a small village that carved its existence through fishing on a tributary of the main river. There was a small church, and luck was with them, as the monk who divided his time between four flocks was present. Jarl hid while the priest entered the village.

"A woman is making you a hooded robe," said the priest as he sat down next to Jarl, opening a cloth containing bread and fish. "It's not much of a task. It will be ready this evening before dark."

"How did you explain the need for the robe?"

"I told them you were naked. You had been robbed by Vikings and I found you three days ago near the banks of the river. You had best hide your clothes, your sword, and your axe, in case one of the women gets curious. Give me one of the smaller silver coins. I will need to pay for the cassock as well as the food we eat. They would find your weapons more useful than coin. I doubt that they have much need for coin in this village."

CHAPTER 13

DRY DRAYTON, ENGLAND–THE PRESENT

"Inspector David Small?"

Small was caught as he was parking outside the station in Northstowe, five miles from the town of Dry Drayton. "Yes."

"This is Gerald Bawkin from the home office. I called earlier about an individual you had detained, a man called Rigsby, but you were out."

"Yes, my assistant told me of your interest. Do you want Rigsby on a warrant? I could find no record of one or of any previous criminal record."

"I was actually calling at the request of Lady Bridget, Katherine Radcliff. She has a client who is providing legal assistance to Mr. Rigsby should you file charges."

"Is the client's name Mats Falconi?" asked Small.

"As a matter of fact, it is. I have no intention of interfering in your investigation, but I do have an interest and would greatly appreciate your keeping me informed."

"There's really not much to tell. I just got the case this morning," said Small. "Would you mind if I called you back in a minute or so? I would like to move to my office."

Bawkin was familiar with the technique. Small would go to his room and call the Home Office's exchange to confirm the identity of the man who had called him. Bawkin's estimation of Small went up a notch.

His office phone rang only once before Bawkin picked up. "Hello, Bawkin here."

"David Small. Sorry for the interruption. You were saying that you wanted to be kept informed?"

"Yes, well first I wanted to give you a heads up that a solicitor, a very good one in fact, would be representing Mr. Rigsby if he were charged. Lady Bridget asked me for a referral in the name of her client, Mr. Mats Falconi."

"Yes, I've met Mr. Falconi. He was at the brewery where we picked up Rigsby. He said he was there for a business meeting."

"Lady Bridget mentioned that the American was in talks to buy half of the Whistling Pig. I hope the beer is better than the name implies."

"Ah. That would explain his interest. The officer who came with me says that the beer is excellent but hard to find outside the Dry Drayton area. It's brewed in limited quantities. But what is your interest, if I may ask?"

"Perhaps you remember the bombing of a taxi a few years ago during a meeting confirming the monetary situation between Britain and the United States. We were debating if we should leave the European Union. As it turned out, it was meant for a member of the American senator's staff, Rodney Stoner. The bomber turned out to be on the staff of another American–Senator Shapiro–but before I could solve the case, he tried again and was killed by Stoner in self-defense.

Actually, it was in defense of Lady Bridget, whom the man had tied up."

"I do remember that. Stoner killed the assassin in Washington, did he not?" asked Small. "But what is your interest in this case?"

"Stoner and Lady Bridget are now married. She seems to have more than a casual business interest in Mr. Falconi and his French wife. If Katherine Radcliff is interested in your murder investigation, then I am interested."

"Well, as to the murder investigation. We're only holding Nickolas Rigsby for questioning at this point. He has an alibi of sorts. A neighbor parked behind him and would have made it impossible to move his car until seven in the morning. That doesn't preclude him from leaving in another vehicle, but for now we are looking at other possibilities. For one, the victim had three deliveries that evening. Two pubs got nothing, and one an incomplete order with the door to the pub left open. We are going with the possibility that that is where the lorry was taken, and perhaps where the driver was killed. Officers did a door-to-door in the neighborhood. It seems that the renter of the rooms directly across from the pub's delivery entrance has gone missing. We are looking for him, of course. Right now, he is either a suspect or another murder victim."

"Do you have a name?"

"We do, but I'm almost certain it is false. None of the neighbors saw much of him after the rental was taken, but they say that he had visitors staying with him."

"I'll thank you for keeping me informed, and if I can help at the Home Office, please let me know." Gerald Bawkin hung up his land line. Truth be told, he was still bothered that he had not caught the bomber of the cab while he was still in England. He'd identified Rodney Stoner as the most probable intended victim, but the lad was far down the ladder of importance on Senator Beck's team, to be sure. He'd put extra security on Beck while he was still in the country, but as far as he could tell, there had been no further attempts. Those came after Stoner had returned to the States and almost cost Katherine Radcliff her life. Violence was in the recent past of Stoner and Lady Bridget, and from the initial reports he had seen on Mats Falconi, in his as well. Yes, If Katherine Radcliff and Mats Falconi were interested in the murder and in helping Nickolas Rigsby, then he was as well. Very interested.

Inspector Small looked at the phone on his desk. Home Office, he thought, a tight grin on his face. Gerald Bawkin had the scent of MI6 all over him. The number of clicks it had taken after the call to the Home Office was the first indication. Lady Bridget, Katherine Radcliff, was another indicator that this murder of a delivery lad might have some other significance as well. The Radcliffs were well known to have played important parts in both WW II and in domestic politics, if only from behind the scenes. Katherine's marriage to the American, Stoner, was big news in the tabloids, which paid particular attention to Britain's nobles. If she was important enough to ask favors of MI6, then he would have to be very careful with the handling of this case or he might find himself walking a beat.

CHAPTER 14
ENGLAND–945 AD

"Priest, I should know your name," said Jarl. The cassock that had been made for him had needed to be brought back to the woman to be lengthened by six inches. Her original offering reached to only above his ankles. Jarl refused to give up his traditional Norse leg wrappings, and if they were visible beneath the robe, it would defeat the purpose of the disguise.

"I have saved your life and you have saved mine," said the priest in Latin. "We've traveled together for over two moons, and now you would know my name?"

"If I am to act as your acolyte, it would be odd if I kept calling you 'priest.'"

"I am Father Giacomo. My full name is Giacomo Hambley."

"Your Frankish sounded different from the language of those we met at my brother's castle. My Latin sounds different from yours, even though the words are the same. Will the same be true of this Angle language you are teaching me?"

"No," said the priest. "I was born on this island, but I was sent away to Rome at the age of six to become a priest. All languages sound different when spoken by people from different areas. It is the same with the Norse that the Danes used and that which you have taught me, true?"

"The Danes speak like there's mush in their mouths," agreed Jarl. "Is it the same in this land?"

"Yes, there are at least three languages used on this island, depending on who holds the area. Saxon is the most common, especially this far south. It is a tongue that sounds a little like your Norse, but with different words and accents. We will hear others as we travel north toward the lands that the Danes hold, and in the highlands where the Scots hold sway."

A call for the priest from outside their camp interrupted their conversation. Jarl quickly pulled a blanket over his head as a woman hobbled into the clearing with the finished robe.

The priest took the garment, quickly inspecting the addition, and blessed the old woman. Jarl peeked out from beneath the blanket as the woman took his blessing with a sneer and spat several words at the ground. The priest looked shocked that his blessing was not enough compensation. He removed a copper coin from his purse, giving it to the woman as she moved away. She mumbled a few more words over her shoulder and hobbled down the path.

The priest tossed the robe to Jarl, who caught it in flight, slipping it over his undershirt, mail, and leggings.

"We should be on our way," said the priest, picking up his pack and heading upriver.

Three days later, after following footpaths that skirted the banks of the river, they stopped on a slight rise. They had only an hour or two of daylight left to them. Jarl saw a yellow smudge on the horizon to the west.

"Do you see that?" he asked the priest.

"I do. It is our sign to turn north, away from the river."

"What is it? I have never seen the like."

"It is the settlement that I told you about, Londinium. That cloud hangs over it most days. It is not a place that will do us any good. There are fine roads, left over from when Rome ruled here, but we should not use them, as there are many soldiers and other roaming bands that are friends to no one." Without further explanation, the priest turned north, following a path that was only wide enough for one.

The walking was easier once they left the river. They no longer had to cross bogs or move inland to traverse tributaries of the great river. The terrain changed to rolling hills and grassland interspersed with forests of oak. They passed small villages but only stopped for food on days when they had not found game, which Jarl killed with his bow.

After seven days of walking north, Jarl wished they had brought the horse and donkey. The priest walked at a pace that Jarl had trouble matching. The man never seemed to need to stop and rest. If it were not for the mid-day meal, which Jarl insisted upon, and the encroaching darkness, he thought that the man would not stop at all.

As they made their way north, the land became somewhat hillier, and forests dotted the landscape in patches. They were traveling through such a grove near mid-day when they heard a scream. Jarl had his weapons inside his robe. His sword was strapped to his back in its scabbard, his axe and knife in his belt, all covered by the robe.

His re-curved bow was unstrung and acted as a walking stick, there being no place to hide it.

The priest was first to react, running forward toward the scream with Jarl right behind. They came to a small clearing with a brook running through it. There were three men keeping two servants at sword point, and a fourth holding a struggling woman.

"Stop in the name of God," shouted the priest, still running toward the group.

The men did not stop, and Jarl thought it would be unusual if they did, as he suspected they did not care about the priest's God. They were Danes. They had leggings like Jarl's and tunics made of spun cloth rather than the furs preferred by his own people. They glanced at the priest and Jarl in his robe, seeing no threat.

"Go, priest, before you anger us," said the Dane holding the woman.

"I will not. You will release the woman," said the priest, moving closer and reaching for her.

"Now you irritate us," said the Dane holding the woman, using a Danish word for a man who is less than a man. The leader nodded to two of the others, who left the third to guard the servants. One pointed his sword at the priest, although he was still some steps away.

"I am a man of God," said the priest, slowly backing out of the sword's reach.

"I am not," shouted Jarl, dropping his backpack and drawing his robe over his head. "Do as the priest says."

"Teach this non-priest a lesson," said the Dane holding the girl.

The two who had left the servants moved apart and came at Jarl, the priest for the moment forgotten.

Jarl stood his ground. As the two approached, he swung his sword from over his head and slashed one Dane across the throat before he could raise his sword. Ducking low, he swung his blade back against the rear of the second man's knee. Where the first couldn't scream, the second bellowed in pain as his left leg could no longer hold him upright. The leader thrust the woman away, but as he released her, she raked her nails over his eyes. The man's hand went to his face, giving Jarl time to reach him and bring his sword down, first through the man's wrist and then deep into the angle of the neck and the shoulder. The fourth man was no coward, but seeing three of his friends taken so easily by the monk, he turned and ran. Jarl reached to his side and brought his axe back to his ear before releasing it. Slowly revolving, it struck the man in the back, just below his neck. The man collapsed face down on the trail. He tried to push back to his feet, but only his arms worked. His effort to roll over onto his back was stopped by the handle of the axe. He was still chest down when Jarl reached him and pulled the axe from where it had crushed his spine. Without hesitation, he brought the axe down hard on the back of the man's skull, the conical helmet he was wearing having fallen a pace up the trail.

The Dane Jarl had hamstrung had pushed himself to his feet, standing on his left leg, his right hanging flaccid below his knee. He had his sword point down in the ground, supporting his weight and helping to keep his balance. Jarl moved to him, his sword in one hand and the axe with bits of his comrade's brains still clinging to its edge. The Dane lifted his sword, balancing on his left leg. Jarl looked at him with distain and flicked the man's sword aside, sweeping his own back and severing the tendon just above the man's left ankle. The man dropped like a stone, his sword falling just out of reach.

The woman, who had been silent except for a short scream when Jarl took the life of the man holding her, moved to the other side of the downed Dane. Her two servants still stood where they were, shaking in fear. Jarl could now see that she was more a girl than a woman. Her body was mature and full, but her face, framed with white-blond braids, was clear and unblemished, except for the drops of blood that had splattered from her assailant's neck.

"I thank you, priest, for saving me from these men." Her voice was high, a small tremor showing that she was shaken by what had occurred. "I would know why they are on our land and whom they serve."

Jarl looked at her, not understanding a word of what she had said but impressed that she was composed, when she might be expected to be hysterical. Jarl had been with strong women before. His murdered wife, Gun, had been the equal of any man, and Lesia Guibega on Corsica was also without fear. This woman seemed to be of the same ilk, not in terms of physical strength–she was thin and appeared delicate–but where it mattered most, in character and intelligence.

Father Giacomo moved to Jarl's side and put a hand on Jarl's sword pommel. "She says not to kill him. She wants to know where the Danes came from and who they follow," he told Jarl in his halting, half-learned Norse.

Jarl saw the look on the priest's face. His companion had never seen him use his weapons. In fact, since he had found him unconscious and unable to defend himself,

Giacomo probably thought he was a poor warrior. His insistence on keeping his weapons when buying his freedom from the burghers should have told the priest that he was a fighter, but he had only drawn his sword once, and that was on the Danish ship, where he hadn't used it except to threaten the crew. Jarl could not decide if the priest showed surprise, respect, fear, or a mixture of all three.

"Who is your leader and what are you doing here?" Jarl asked the man in Norse.

The man kept silent, as if he had not heard Jarl's words. Jarl stepped on his right wrist and pulled a knife from the man's waistband. He held it to his throat. "Answer my questions. If you don't, I will cut out your tongue and leave you here to die. Your wounds will bleed slowly. You will be without a weapon to hand and will not enter Valhalla. Or perhaps you prefer the blood angel that your tribe favors."

"What do you want?" answered the Dane, stifling a sob.

"Where do you come from and who is your leader? Answer my questions, and I will give you a weapon and a quick death."

"We are part of the crew of three longships come to summer with Soren the White. We were separated from the rest of our crew and sought to find his encampment on our own. It should not be far from here."

"Do you know of Soren the White?" Jarl asked the woman, with the priest quickly translating from his Norse tongue.

"Soren is a Dane. He has held lands to the east for the last three years. His hold is near the river, some two or three hours' walk distant. I have never been there, but he has visited my father. They are allies of a sort."

"And who leads the three crews?" demanded Jarl of the man at his feet.

"Blood Axe. He has four other ships that he uses to raid the coast. He uses Soren's sted as a base when ashore."

Blood Axe. The name hit Jarl like a physical blow. It was Blood Axe who had caused his separation from his brothers by Gun's father. Blood Axe had been humiliated by Jarl during a raid on the island's north coast, the Dane's actions causing loss of life among his crew and yielding very little plunder. Jarl had broken away from Blood Axe and raided a community up the coast with opposite results. In retaliation, Blood Axe had claimed that Jarl's success was the result of dark magic and had commissioned a demeaning saga to be written and performed throughout the north lands. It was this saga that had caused other Viking leaders to refuse to join the brothers. Now he had killed three of Blood Axe's crew after he and his brothers had given their word to Gun's father not to seek revenge on the Dane.

"When will Blood Axe be back with Soren?"

"I know not. We had just separated. If it is like last year, he will return some three moons from now."

Jarl kicked the man's sword close to the man, who grasped it with both hands. "You were the best of your band, not running or hiding behind a woman. Know who will take your life so you can brag of it in Valhalla. I am Jarl Falkhand."

The Dane's eyes widened in recognition. "I was with Blood Axe six years ago when we raided this coast with you. Blood Axe was wrong, and many men died that day. You were right and did not deserve the saga that he caused to be written. I told you only half the truth. We were lost but we were not going to Soren. We were on our way to another lord near here on Blood Axe's orders."

"What is this lord's name?"

"You have killed the only man who knew. He was holding the girl. I have told you all. Please, if you do have black magic like the saga says, don't use it to send me between. I will sing your praises in Valhalla."

Jarl pressed the point of his sword into the man's throat, severing both carotid arteries as well as his vocal cords. The Dane died holding his sword to his chest.

CHAPTER 15
ENGLAND–THE PRESENT

"Suzanne, this is Katherine."
It was just after breakfast. Mats was brushing his teeth when the phone rang.

"Harry Lapidas, the solicitor, dropped off the papers Mats needed for the purchase of the brewery here," said Katherine. "He was uncomfortable leaving them at the hotel desk if you were not there."

"Mats will be thrilled," said Suzanne. "Wait a second. Here he is." Mats took the phone as Suzanne mouthed, "Katherine."

"Hello! I was just telling Suzanne that the brewery purchase papers are here at my office. There are a couple sections you might like to have explained, as they are unique to British law."

"Super," said Mats. "I'd like to get them signed and recorded as fast as possible. How long will you be at your office?"

"All morning. I have to go up to Hamerton later. I mentioned that Margaret takes care of a cottage and the church there. The church was damaged in the storm. I must inspect the damage for Margaret. It crossed my mind that we might drive up together. I could meet Nickolas Rigsby, and you could see the church where Rodney and I met."

"We could be at your office in forty-five minutes. Will Rod be going with us?"

"Rodney is at the airport. He has to go back to Washington for a week. His plane leaves at noon."

They drove north in Katherine's Volvo, arriving at the brewery just after one. Rigsby was waiting. It took him five minutes to express his gratitude to them for hiring Harry Lapidas to represent him and get him released. It took another hour to go over the sales documents, Mats asking Katherine to explain a few points before he signed.

Business concluded, Rigsby got four glass mugs from a refrigerator and poured four Whistling Pigs in celebration. Then he gave the women a tour of the brewery. Suzanne could see how excited Mats was about the signing of the brewery. It didn't have the same emotional impact as the purchase of the Harp and Hawk, but then there was Brian so closely connected with that agreement.

When Rigsby finished the tour, Mats made an appointment for a meeting in two days. He told Rigsby that funds would be available before the end of the week and advised him to hire two employees, one for inside and one to replace the delivery lad.

The drive to Hamerton took twenty minutes. Katherine directed them down a road that was paved but only wide enough for a single car, with turnouts to accommodate oncoming traffic every quarter mile. Mats wasn't sure why Katherine was so determined for them to see Hamerton. She'd said it was where she and Rodney had met, but it seemed like more than that. Mats didn't know what to expect of the town but was surprised when Katherine directed him to pull over and park.

"Is this it?" he asked as Katherine began to climb out of the car. She studied him closely, looking for a sign of an emotional connection to the small village. There was none.

Mats saw a short row of small cottages. All were painted white over stucco. All had thatched roofs, and the one at the end had a garden with neatly tended rows of herbs and vegetables. A thick clutch of red roses spanned the entire length of the white picket fence that protected the garden from the road. The color of the flowers contrasted perfectly with the white of the house and fence, and the fragrance from the blooms permeated the air around them.

"This is Margaret's cottage," said Katherine. "I'll get the keys to the church."

She was back in less than a minute, holding a large brass ring with two improbably long keys on it and another ring with a more modern key attached. "We might as well walk," she said, starting across the road toward a stone bridge spanning a small watercourse that was rushing with water from the recent storm. "About two miles down, this joins a small river that empties into the North Sea at King's Lynn."

Once over the bridge, a path led them to a small hill. Mats could see a church's bell tower rising above the horizon.

"About ten years ago, Margaret's cottage needed a new roof," said Katherine as she guided Mats and Suzanne up the incline toward the church. "She wanted to keep it in thatch, but she couldn't find anyone locally who knew how to replace it. Thatching was becoming a lost art. So, she started the Thatched Roof Society– funded scholarships for young apprentices, and salaries for a few master thatchers."

"She seems like a remarkable woman," said Suzanne.

"She is. This church is her main charity. It was first built by William the Conqueror, although it has been added to over the years. Margaret heard that it had been damaged in the storm and wanted me to take a look for her."

They came to the top of the hill and saw the full extent of the church. It was made completely of undressed stone, and the roof was covered by slate. To the side was a graveyard, which looked like it was only occasionally tended, and below it an expansive view of the surrounding countryside. Mats was surprised by the view, as the hill on which the church was perched did not seem that high. Again, Katherine watched Mats for any sign of recognition. Again, he showed nothing but simple curiosity.

Katherine began keying the three locks in the large door, which appeared to be the only entrance to the structure.

"Look at this," said Mats, interrupting her progress. He pointed to the right side of the building. Katherine left the key in the third lock and moved to where Mats stood, looking at the stone wall of the church. A jagged line wended its way down from the top, from just under the eaves to the ground. It was black, as if someone had tried to burn the rocks. The stones themselves had moved from their neighbors as the crack extended to the foundation.

"My goodness," exclaimed Katherine, placing the tip of her index finger in the crack. Looking up, she could see the roof sagging at the top of the crack and the roof missing a number of slate shingles. She quickly backed up, as if afraid the building might collapse. They walked around the whole exterior but could see no further damage. At the door, Katherine turned the last key and pulled, but the door didn't open.

"Are you sure all three locks are open?" asked Mats, watching Katherine repeat the procedure with each key.

"Yes. The door should open."

Mats pulled harder on the door, feeling a slight movement. He put both hands on the large handle and gave an even more forceful tug. The door opened with a squeal; a cloud of dust came down on him. As the door fully opened, the frame settled.

"I don't think we're going to be able to close the door. It looks like the jamb has settled," said Mats, stepping inside, followed by both women. Inside, the damage was more apparent. On the right wall leading to the altar, the crack on the outside had spread so that there was an inch of separation. As the crack neared the floor, it passed through a rose-colored marble marker reading in Old English block lettering:

KNIGHT OF HAMERTON
1268

"I don't think it's safe in here," said Mats, looking at the roofline, where the distortion of the ceiling was more dramatic than when viewed from outside. A fine stream of dust was drifting down from the ceiling over the entrance. "The crack goes all the way through the wall. Look, here you can see light from outside."

"Margaret will be devastated. I wonder what caused the crack," said Katherine, looking up at the shifted stones near the roof.

They moved outside at Mats' urging, closing the door only halfway before it wedged against the porch floor.

"I think this is the problem," said Suzanne, pointing at a severed cable just under the eaves. "It looks like your ground to the lightning rod either split or burned through. I bet the crack was caused by a lightning strike. We certainly saw enough of them in the last two days."

"I'll call Margaret," said Katherine. "She'll have to put up some danger signs and get a crew of stonemasons up here to repair the damage."

As they turned to leave, a rock above the head of the door shot out and landed ten feet in front of them. They turned to see a cloud of brown dust in the half-open entryway.

CHAPTER 16
LONDON–THE PRESENT

There were four people in line in front of the well-dressed man at the counter in the first-floor café.

His phone rang in his suit pocket. He did not recognize the number, which was not unusual. His main contact in England would only use a burner phone. He moved away from the crowd and entered an alcove selling woman's scarves before opening the line.

"Hello. This is the Florist."

"Would you be able to deliver a single red rose in London in two days' time?" asked a voice that he recognized, even having never met the man.

"Possibly. I have the event you assigned to me on my calendar. I have items to prepare for it."

"This is in preparation for that party. Can you deliver?"

"I'll need the particulars to make sure, but I will try."

"Good. I'll send the name and address to your shop."

The Florist shut his phone off, looking around for anyone who might have overheard the conversation. No one was nearby. He pocketed his phone and set off briskly for the entrance.

It took less than twenty-five minutes for the Florist to get to his apartment and pull up the message on his computer. On the surface, it looked like an easy assignment—hardly one that called for his level of skill. He was to rob an official of his briefcase. Making it look like a normal mugging would be the problem, especially as the case would be handcuffed to the man's wrist. He had two days before the job was to be done. The instructions were clear. Each day the target had the same routine. He left his townhouse at seven-thirty, walked two blocks to the underground station, and spent ten minutes on the train, then an additional three minutes getting to the office. The mark's evenings were less predictable, as he often took dinner out, stopped at a store, or went straight home. Morning seemed the best time to do what needed to be done, but two days gave him a chance to check out the route in person. The write-up was detailed, but knowing the route personally was essential for a professional.

The Florist clicked off his computer, took off his jacket, and pulled on a sweater and hat. He would walk to the target's house. No cab, no cameras in the underground that could catch a glimpse of him. He would take note of any cameras on the route used by the target.

The mark's neighborhood primarily contained expensive townhouses. Trees lined the narrow street, allowing only one car to pass those parked along the curb. The Florist retraced the man's route from his front steps toward the underground. Half a block down the sidewalk, there was a narrow alley, left over from centuries past, now just a thin passage to the street behind. He could see a single security camera on that first block. Still, he kept his head down, his face obscured by the hat. He would trash his sweater on the way home.

The next day, the Florist, dressed again in a suit and tie and carrying a backpack on his shoulder, arrived at the target's house. Attached to an extension rod he had a spray can, which he sprayed over the security camera. He waited in the shadows until the mark's door opened, then walked toward the house as the man emerged at precisely seven-thirty. They were five feet from each other, adjacent to the alley, when the Florist grabbed his chest, staggered, and gasped, "My heart." He stumbled into the alleyway.

The target saw him stumble and followed him. As the target reached the Florist, he straightened, and in a single motion slashed the man's neck, turning him so that the blood that spurted against the far wall did not hit him. As the man stopped twitching, the Florist moved him back down the alley, putting him into a sitting position. The man's briefcase was handcuffed to his wrist, as the instructions had said. The Florist reached into his own pocket and pulled out a set of keys. The first two didn't fit, which worried the Florist. If the third and last didn't open the cuffs, then he'd have to cut off the man's hand. He did not want to waste the time. On the third try, the cuffs sprang open. He reached into the man's jacket and took his wallet, then stripped the man's watch from his wrist and his ring from his finger. He stood, placed the briefcase into his backpack, and left the alley, striding like a man on his way to work.

"The flower has been delivered. I have the receipt. Do you want it?" asked the Florist, speaking into his phone.

"Yes, in one hour. Leave it under the bench in Hyde Park at the intersection of Serpentine Road and the Broad Walk. I will send my man to pick it up. Is the case open?"

"Yes. It opened when I uncuffed it."

"All right. You'll have the payment in your usual account by this afternoon."

The Florist would have to take a cab to get to the park in time. The case had a splatter of blood that needed to be wiped off, and he wanted to give himself time to look through the papers that had made the killing of a man necessary. He was only mildly surprised to find that the case contained a draft of the European settlement for moving ahead with Brexit, a document that had many people speculating–a document that held the key to immigration across Europe.

CHAPTER 17
NORTH OF LONDINIUM–945 AD

Four Danes lay on the ground dead. One's hand lay half in the water. Blood was flowing in the stream, feathering away in the small current.

Jarl looked first at the priest, then at the woman. It was the priest who was more shaken by the violence.

Jarl pulled the robe over his head after replacing his weapons. Underneath, he was exposed as a Viking: leggings, leather baldric, full shirt, and two long braids extending past his shoulder blades. As he let the garment fall, he saw a look of alarm on the woman's face. She stepped back a single pace.

"Tell her she has nothing to fear, priest," said Jarl. "Is her home near here?"

"It is," said the priest, after talking with the girl. "She asks you to take her there."

The two servants hovered behind her, still looking in fear at Jarl, who retrieved his pack. He removed the surcoat of the Varangian Guard, placing it over his head, and then replaced the monk's habit. The sight of the insignia of the cross calmed the two servants, who still put their mistress between themselves and Jarl.

The woman took a step forward and put her hand on Jarl's forearm, saying something Jarl only partly understood from what he had learned of the language during their trip from the river.

"She says that she thanks you for saving her," said Father Giacomo. "And that her father will reward you."

"You welcome," managed Jarl, looking first at the girl and then at the priest, who nodded that he had spoken understandably.

"Tell the servants to pick up the packs of the Danes," said Jarl. He went to the dead men one by one, removing their weapons, arm rings, and purses and putting them in his own pack. Then he dragged the man from the pond and cleaned his sword on the man's shirt.

The woman knelt just upstream of Jarl and cleaned the blood from her face. When she was finished, she raised her outer garment and dried her hands and face.

"These men should be buried, but we do not have time. Can the woman's father send men to do it?"

Another flurry of talk and the priest said, "Yes."

"Then let's go," said Jarl, lifting his pack, which now weighed well over a hundred pounds.

The servants struggled, carrying two packs each, but still led the way, keeping the woman behind them as a buffer from the priest and Jarl. They followed a creek that flowed from the pond for a mile before it emptied into a small river. They followed it downstream for another half mile before coming to a stone castle surrounded by a moat. As they approached, the girl took the lead. Workers in the field stood, giving her a slight bow, and followed her with their eyes. A drawbridge was lowered across the moat, but the gates to the enclosure were shut until she stepped onto the wooden bridge; then both sides flew open, and an elderly man stepped out–the young woman's grandfather, perhaps.

The woman ran to him, throwing her arms around him and unleashing a torrent of words, pointing first to the priest, then Jarl.

Still holding the woman, the old man turned toward the priest.

"I am William Hamerton," said the old man. "My daughter, Bridget, tells me that you and your companion saved her honor and her life. I thank you and offer you the hospitality of my house."

The priest nodded, almost a slight bow. Lord Hamerton had spoken in Latin, and the priest answered in the same language. "Thank you, sire, but it was Jarl Falkhand who saved your daughter."

"Kindly tell him that my thanks extend to him," said the old man.

"I appreciate your thanks and your offer," said Jarl, responding directly to the old man in Latin.

The lord turned toward Jarl, still holding his daughter in his right arm, surprise clearly showing on both their faces.

"You speak Latin!" she said, releasing herself from her father's grip and moving toward the Viking. "Then I must thank you personally. You were most brave in taking on those four Danish warriors."

Her Latin was good, better than the lord's. Jarl wondered what tongue she and her father had used, as he recognized not a word from the lessons of the island's speech he had learned from the priest since they had turned north.

"They were taken by surprise, believing I was a monk," said Jarl. "It would have been harder if they were prepared."

"I doubt it, Father," said the girl, turning to the lord. "He gave them no chance. I have never heard of such a feat, although I admit that I was frightened when he took the life of the Dane who was holding me. It is his blood that I have on me."

The lord looked at her, noticing for the first time the stains that covered the front of her dress and the splatters of red on her face.

"You did not appear afraid. You looked brave," said Jarl.

The girl smiled, her eyes downcast, which made her appear younger; a moment before, she had looked like a mature woman. "I pray you will accept my father's offer of hospitality."

The priest stepped forward. "We have been on the trail north for near a fortnight. Both Jarl and I would relish a wash and a chance to rest."

"You will have it," said the lord, "and a feast tonight after you are refreshed." He turned and motioned to two servants who stood inside the gates to show the visitors to their rooms. The two who had returned with them were speaking excitedly to others inside the wall, pointing at Jarl as the gates closed behind them.

Jarl looked around the enclosure. It was of a size with his brother Jan's castle on the mainland. It was situated on the bank of the river, which fed the moat at high water, but the riverbank was straight and only protected the fortress on one side, relying on the moat on the other three. The moat was less than half as wide as the riverbed. His brother Jan would have raised the height of the wall by a man's height and strengthened its supports, but that was not the main weakness that caught Jarl's eye. There were boys near the livestock enclosure and servants in the yard and at the door to the castle, but Jarl could only see three men-at-arms, and of those, only one stood atop the gate as a lookout.

"It would be wise to send men to bury the ones I have killed. They were part of a larger band," said Jarl. "Your servants can show the others where they lie."

The lord said a few words to his daughter, who motioned to the two who had accompanied her. Jarl and the priest were led to a room on the second floor, the lower floor being occupied almost entirely by the great hall. Two servants carried a copper bowl, large enough for a man to sit in, to the center of the space. The boys Jarl had noticed inside the fort began filling it with water from buckets. As the bowl filled, a woman brought two sets of garments and placed them on the bed. She stood, waiting, as the last bucket was poured into the bath. Both men looked at her until the priest cast his head toward the door. The woman departed, leaving the door open. The priest quickly closed it.

"You first, Father," said Jarl. "You are far less dirty than I, and you have no blood on your hands, as I do."

The priest moved to the bowl, lifting his robe over his head. In the bowl was a stick with an eel skin stretched over its length. A few tentative strokes showed that when used against the grain, it could remove dirt caked onto the legs, feet, and ankles. When Father Giacomo had finished, Jarl moved to the bowl, first removing the blood that remained on his face and arms, then moving to his feet. He remembered his bath in Miklagard and the one he had constructed at Ajaccio. The feeling of the hot water completely surrounding his body came back to him, but most of all the memory of the two women who had bathed with him.

CHAPTER 18
LONDON–THE PRESENT

Mats was about to drive north to Dry Drayton when Katherine called and asked him to drop by her office on his way to the brewery. Inspector Gerald Bawkin had given her new information on Rigsby's status, and she thought that security issues might be involved.

After quickly describing the repair work needed on the Hamerton church, Katherine passed out sandwiches and poured tea, remembering that Mats took his white.

"A friend in the government has been in contact with the local police inspector who detained your man," said Katherine, settling into her seat. "He's no longer considered a suspect. First, they found a woman who had blocked his parked car the evening his driver disappeared. Then they interviewed an elderly woman who has insomnia and reported that she had seen a light go on in his apartment at five AM. Her window looked out on the area where his car was still blocked. Right now, they are concentrating on a group of men who were occupying a small apartment directly opposite the pub's delivery entrance. Evidently, no one has seen any of these men since the night of the murder, and the leaser gave a false name on the rental agreement."

"Anything else?" asked Mats.

"Fingerprints. Rigsby's were all over the lorry, but they were smudged on the steering wheel and the door handles. Someone wearing gloves drove the car after Rigsby and the delivery lad. Your man is in the clear. Oh, that reminds me. All the sales documents have been filed. You now are legal majority owner of the Whistling Pig."

Mats thanked Katherine for lunch, picked up the file containing the legal copies, and went back to his car. An hour later, he pulled into the parking lot in front of the brewery. As before, the door was unlocked, and Rigsby was tending to a batch of fermenting beer. "I'll just be a few minutes," he called down from the railing.

When Rigsby finished, he came down and offered Mats his hand. "Good to see you Mr. Falconi," he said. "The money has been deposited in my account already, but the buggers won't release it until tomorrow–that is, if the check is good."

"It's good," said Mats with a chuckle. "And it's not a check. It's a money transfer between banks. It should be ready to draw on immediately. I suspect your bank, being a small local branch, is just being cautious."

"Couldn't come at a better time," said Rigsby. "From here through Christmas, demand usually goes up. I have already started looking for a new part-time employee. Have three possibles."

"You'll need more than a part-time employee after we discuss some changes I would like to make. Let's go to the office and I can get your take on them."

Nickolas Rigsby sat behind his desk with a worried expression on his face. Mats knew why he was worried. He had sold controlling interest in the brewery and now it seemed he was about to pay the piper.

"First," said Mats, "I would like my brew master from the Harp and Hawk to come over and take a look at your set-up and process."

"I've spent time with him," said Rigsby, looking even more worried.

"You spent time with his nephew. Cathal Magee is the brew master. Cathal has been saying for a while that the Hawks Brew NA could be improved, but it has become so popular in Northern California that I don't want to risk changing the product. Yours is an exact copy. Not a surprise, since you used our process and our bacteria. I see no need to import two items that taste exactly the same. I thought we could try the improvements to yours before I start importing it."

"I wouldn't want to lose any of my customers here if it were changed too much."

"Tell you what," said Mats. "It just doesn't make sense to make three NAs. The Whistling Pig's production is by far the lowest. Changing it carries the least risk, but if all three of us don't agree that the final product is an improvement, we will go back to the original. I'll have Cathal come over in a day or two and talk with you."

"Inspector Small said they might want me back at the station in the next couple of days, though."

"I think that you are cleared of that worry," said Mats. He told Rigsby about the smudged fingerprints and the bathroom light coming on. "Right now, they are looking for some men who rented the apartment across from the pub. They've disappeared and have not been seen since that night. I don't know how successful they will be, as they don't even have descriptions."

"Mr. Falconi, I ..."

"We're partners. I think you should call me Mats, and I will call you Nickolas," said Mats.

"Nick would do just fine. Men, you say?"

"Yes, three or four, maybe even five. I don't think the landlord knows how many for sure. Right now, they think your driver might have seen or overheard something."

Rigsby opened his desk drawer. "I was about to call you when you called and said you would be coming up this afternoon. I found this stuck deep in a crack in the passenger's seat." He passed Mats a small object with an open chain attached to it.

"What is it?" asked Mats, turning the object over in his hand. It was about a third of the size of a matchbook.

"I think it is a miniature Quran. When I lived in Leeds, I saw some of the Muslim shop owners with them."

"Have you reported this to the police yet?"

"No. I just found it last night while I was interviewing a prospect for the delivery job. I thought it would be wise to know if he could drive a stick shift. It was poking me in the bum the whole ride."

"Call Inspector Small now," said Mats.

Rigsby pulled a card from under the corner of the desk blotter and called a number on his cell. On the third ring, it was picked up by the detective. "Hello Inspector, this is Nick Rigsby over at the Whistling Pig. I found something in the van that your men might have overlooked. A miniature Quran, the kind worn on a key chain or around one's neck."

Mats listened but could only hear Rigsby's side of the conversation.

"Sorry, Mr. Falconi and I have both handled it. Yah, I didn't think, but I can give you a description of the men in the apartment. I was at the pub two days before the murder, having lunch. I left the back way. As I stepped out, there were three men outside the door to the apartment. One was trying to get the key to fit. When I came out, I startled him. He dropped the key at my feet. I can give you a good description."

Mats looked at Rigsby, trying to digest his side of the conversation. It was obvious that the brewer didn't yet realize the meaning of what he had just told the detective. Three men committing murder was a lot more significant than a random homicide. Mats got up and left the office. He walked to the front of the brewery. Taking out his cell phone, he punched a number on his favorites list and waited three rings before it was picked up.

"Yes, Mr. Falconi." The voice was crisp, the English only slightly accented.

"Ramondo, where are you now?"

"I'm in Switzerland, spending time with Brian. We just finished today's workout. He's getting good, very good. Is everything all right?"

"Yes, but I have a job for you. I'd like you to come to England. I just bought a brewery called the Whistling Pig. It's just north of London in a small town called Dry Drayton. I want you to take a job helping with brewing and delivering the product."

"I'll be there this evening," said Ramondo, without hesitation or questions.

"Good. My partner, Mr. Nickolas Rigsby, is working alone. His delivery lad was murdered last week. Nickolas doesn't realize how much danger he is in because he is the only one who can identify the likely killers. I'd like you to provide security for him."

"Brian gets a two-week school break the day after tomorrow," said Ramondo. "We were going to take a trip to Ireland. Suzanne knows about it. Would you rather I tell him to go to England?"

"That would be great. Tell him we're at the Mayfair. I'll call Suzanne and get him a room. I don't want him anywhere near the brewery or Nickolas Rigsby."

CHAPTER 19
LONDON–THE PRESENT

"You've done what?" the Florist asked, louder than he intended, into the cell phone.

"I can't find my Quran, the miniature one I carry on my keychain," said Bashar. "I missed it shortly after we moved here from the country. It's not in our rental car. It could be anywhere, but I might have lost it in the lorry when we were moving the garbage."

"Are there any identifying marks on it?"

"Not my name. My initials were on it, but they were almost worn off. It was a present from my uncle." The Florist could hear the fear in Bashar's voice. It was good that he was afraid of what might be done to him. A little mistake could cause the plan to fail.

"This is not good. Everything depends on casting blame on the Irish Protestants. At least the only person who could give a description of us is dead."

"Sir," Bashar said, with a hesitation brought on by fear that was plainly evident in his voice. "There is more. The lorry driver was not the same person who saw you when you dropped the key. That man was much older. You probably didn't notice since you left immediately after we silenced the driver. I thought you knew."

"You're sure of this? They're not the same man?" asked the Florist, his tone cold and threatening.

"I'm sure. It was a man in his thirties or forties who saw you, me, and Habib that day."

"And he was not the one who overheard our plans?"

"No, sir."

Everything is a worry at this point, thought the Florist. *Who was the man who saw us? It might not be important. He might never connect us with the driver's disappearance, but then again, he might.*

"Keep to my instructions. Speak with no one except me. I will be taking Abdul and Hasan with me for a few days. You stay put and let me know immediately if you find your Quran."

The Florist clicked off and called another number. It was picked up on the second ring.

"Meet me at the restaurant in two hours. Bring clothes for two days."

The Florist went to his laptop and typed in the name of the brewery that had been displayed on the side of the lorry. It was an odd name–the Whistling Pig. His search for an English brewery with that name brought up the name and photograph of the owner, Nickolas Rigsby. He recognized Rigsby as the man outside the pub–the man who might identify him. The site had very little else to tell him except the brewery's offerings and its address. He shut down his computer and went to the bedroom to pack an overnight case. He opened the bottom of the case, revealing a hidden compartment formed into a recess, holding a Glock subcompact pistol. He took the weapon out, checking its clip before replacing it in the case and folding his clothes over the hidden compartment. Satisfied, he removed his knife from his pocket, flicking its six-inch blade open with a snap of his wrist. He knew the edge was razor sharp, but he tested it with his thumb anyway. Resisting the urge to let the blade cut him, he snapped the steel back into the thin handle and returned it to his front pocket.

The Florist looked through the window of the restaurant. It was almost empty as it was 3 pm, midway between lunch and dinner. Seeing the lack of patrons, he decided not to enter but to wait outside for Abdul and Hasan. He didn't have to wait long, as they arrived less than two minutes after him. He didn't greet them, merely giving a soft wave of his hand to indicate that they should follow him to where he had parked the car. Leaving now, they'd be in the beginning of the rush traffic leaving the city center. It took until they were halfway to Cambridge for the roads to clear, enabling them to drive at speed.

It was just after five when they drove past the entrance to the Whistling Pig. There were no windows in the front of the building, but those on the side were dark, the doors closed. The lorry was parked off the street in a space on the right side of the building. If the brewery had been occupied, the Florist could have taken care of the problem that night. With the van parked and the lights out, he had missed his chance. He pulled over a few blocks away and tried to find Rigsby's home address on his phone. He was unsuccessful.

"We'll have to wait until morning," he said to his two passengers. "We'll stay in Dry Drayton. Tomorrow we'll take care of this loose end."

Twenty minutes after the Florist had left, a car drove past the parked lorry, pulled up behind the brewery, and parked. The car lights went out, but no doors opened. Inside, a man lowered the driver's seat and turned to his side. Setting a vibrating alarm on his watch for six, he went to sleep.

CHAPTER 20
HAMERTON, ENGLAND–945 AD

Jarl would have liked to wash his hair, but the water in the bowl had so much dirt and blood in it now that he would not have been able to get it clean. The priest was clearly uncomfortable in the hose and tunic that had been provided for him while his robe was being boiled, not only to clean it but to remove the lice that had taken up residence. Jarl's offered tunic was small on his frame, stretching tightly across his chest. He put on his leather tunic and spare leggings from his pack, but those came only to the middle of his calves.

They went down to the main hall together and found the lord waiting. The servants had brought a large table into the room and were setting chairs around it in preparation for the feast.

"It is good that we all speak Latin as a common language, but what manner of speech do Hamerton and his daughter use between themselves? I do not understand a word," said Jarl as they entered the room.

"They are Saxon. Their people originally came to this land from Jutland," answered the priest.

"We have an excellent nut-brown ale," said Lord Hamerton as they neared the table. "Or would you prefer wine or mead?" He motioned to the servant who was attending them.

"I would relish a cup of wine above all else," said the priest. "Although my companion usually selects mead. It has been a fortnight since we have had a cup of either."

The servant left, quickly returning with two large flagons. Another servant accompanied him with a tray of bread and cheese.

"I thank you again for your hospitality," said Jarl, taking a seat near Hamerton. He took a long draught of the honeyed liquid the servant had placed in front of him. "May I ask if you were expecting a group of Danes here?"

"Danes? Here? No, why do you ask?"

"Your daughter had me ask the last wounded Dane why they were in the woods. At first, he said they were lost and were trying to find Soren the White. When I threatened to end his life without a weapon to hand, he said that he and his companions were indeed lost but they were on their way to a nearby lord, not Soren. They were part of a larger group when they became separated."

Lord Hamerton thought for a second, shaking his head as he discarded one thought after another. "There are only two lords within a day's ride from here. Both are Saxons. Neither of them would entertain Danes."

"Who would not entertain Danes?" asked the lord's daughter as she entered the room. She was dressed in a gown of light blue with a matching ribbon braided into her hair, fastened with pins and combs high on her head. There was little trace of the young girl who had been in the woods; it was as if the dress had transformed her into a mature young woman.

"Lord Falkhand was asking if any of our neighbors might have summoned the Danes who attacked you," said Lord Hamerton. "I told him neither would have done so."

"Yet they were on their way somewhere, and it was certainly not here," responded Lady Bridget.

"Sir Roger Longtree is our closest neighbor, but we have a pact to aid each other in case of a Danish attack on either of our lands," said Lord Hamerton. "And there are not many who hate the Danish more than Sir Hubert Watley, north of Sir Roger's lands. The Dane must have told you false."

Jarl noticed that the names Longtree and Watley caused the young woman to turn away as if in disgust.

"I think not," said Jarl. "He was relieved to know who would send him to Valhalla. He would not have died with a falsehood on his tongue. I believe him, and it sounded like his group was not the only one expected."

"I'll send a runner and request that Longtree and Watley meet me here tomorrow. This is troubling news. But now I would hear the full story of my daughter's rescue."

The four were served while the tale was told, primarily by the priest and Lady Bridget. Jarl was shocked as to how their stories differed in perspective. Much of what he had done was instinctive, requiring training rather than thought. He had moved smoothly through the Danes, aided by their lack of alarm, as they had believed him a monk. But both the priest and the woman ascribed forethought and bravery to each of his moves, lending fear and excitement to the story, rather than the detachment that Jarl had felt.

"Was the life of my daughter not in danger when you took the man who held her?" asked the lord.

"He held his sword to her throat," Jarl said in Latin. "If it was a knife, he could have acted more quickly. I took little risk with her safety. I know the leader of these Danes who threatened your daughter. He has many men at his disposal, perhaps as many as three hundred. If his men are coming here, it would be wise to prepare for an attack. I suspect more than your daughter is at risk."

"Lord Falkhand was charged with the safety of the eastern Pope. He was the captain of the Varangian Guard. He could help you with your defenses," volunteered Father Giacomo.

This offer received a swift glance from Jarl, which the priest chose to ignore.

"I thought we were in a hurry to get to my homeland," retorted Jarl.

"There is always time to help those in need. It is the Lord's way," responded the priest, not at all cowed by Jarl.

"What would you do to improve our defenses?" asked Lady Bridget, earning a look of disapproval from her father.

"You must excuse my daughter, Lord," said Hamerton. "Her mother died when she was young, and she has grown up thinking that she must take care of me as well as the household."

"It is a reasonable question," said the priest, looking at Jarl.

Jarl took a deep breath, exhaling noisily through his nose. "The castle is positioned well enough, but the walls around it should be higher. Right now, two men holding another on a shield could reach the top. It would take time to raise it, and with the Danes already in the area, you probably don't have that time. I only saw the moat as we passed over your bridge, but it looks fouled with bracken and mud. It should be cleaned, deepened, and widened to come directly under the wall. How many men-at-arms do you have?"

"Sixteen, but there are four hundred who live in our lands, over a hundred and fifty of them men. I've always thought that men were better used for raising food than for standing on walls," said Hamerton. "We are well stocked for a siege."

"Sixteen are not near enough. You should have three times that number just to protect your castle. Unless the moat is cleared and dug, any siege would be a short one."

"Anything else?" asked Hamerton briskly, obviously offended that Jarl had found his defenses so lacking.

"Drawn up, your bridge acts as a gate, but the inner gate is wood and could easily be shattered. If you have a smithy, I would place a third gate of iron bars behind the inner gate, with a murder hole between them."

Hamerton's face colored. He was about to retort when his daughter put a hand on his forearm, whispering, "Father, I asked for his view, and it was given freely. If you had seen with my eyes how he dispatched four warriors, saving me from dishonor and perhaps death, you would trust his views on war."

The lord looked hard at Jarl and then at his daughter, his face softening. "You are right, daughter. Thank you for your advice, Jarl Falkhand."

The final dish was a sweet pudding, something Jarl had never experienced. The taste was pleasant but the slimy texture not to his liking. He stood and moved to the hearth at the side of the great hall. The fire was roaring, but its warmth was felt only a body's length into the room. After years in Miklagard's heat, the cold of this land affected him more than it should have. He held his hands against the heat of the flames.

"My father knows that you are right," said Lady Bridget, moving to his side. "He actually likes to build and design things. It is just that he tends to build more for comfort, for himself and his serfs, than for defense. You will understand when you go to your room. The flue from this fire separates and goes under the stones of the floors in the three rooms above, heating them before leaving the chimney. It is my father's design. You will find your room pleasant when you retire. He will consider your skill, and after some thought, he will heed your advice."

"It is well that he would. I know this Blood Axe. He is more than a threat, he is destruction–a blunt blade."

"So you will help us?" She placed the palm of her hand on his chest, an intimate gesture that stirred a feeling in Jarl's groin.

"I'll talk with Father Giacomo. His purpose seems to have changed. For almost a moon he has been all about charging on to my home, the northland. Now he seems content to tarry here and help you. About this alliance with your neighbors, when your father mentioned that he would call them here on the morrow, you seemed disturbed."

"Not disturbed, rather concerned that he would rely on them. One is as old as Father and the other is not welcome in this house, at least not by me."

"And why is that?" asked Jarl with an amused grin at the rancor in her voice.

"He seeks an alliance in more than protection. He has asked Father for my hand."

CHAPTER 21
DRY DRAYTON, ENGLAND–THE PRESENT

A soft vibration of his watch woke the man in the car. The morning sun was just infusing the clouds with a hint of red, but no light entered the parking lot behind the brewery. He got out and went to the back door. Removing a ring of picks, he quickly opened the bottom lock and went to work on the second deadbolt, which was slightly more resistant. When he heard a click, he turned the knob and entered, closing the door behind him and resetting the locks. Using the light on his phone, he went around the whole building before returning to the small office in the back. He took a seat facing the door, his elbow resting on the scarred wooden desk to his right.

Less than thirty minutes later, at exactly seven AM, he heard the door open, and the lights on the brewery floor turned on. He did not move, except to turn his chair to face the door of entry from the brewery floor. Ten minutes passed, and he listened to the sounds of electric motors starting around the building. He heard footsteps climbing the metal steps to the top of the vats, then coming back down toward the office.

The door opened and a man flipped on the light switch before turning toward the desk. He was a step in before he registered that there was someone sitting in front of him.

"Agh," he cried, stepping backward.

"I'm sorry. I didn't mean to scare you. I got cold waiting outside and let myself in."

"Who the hell are you?" asked Nickolas Rigsby, recovering quickly from his fright.

"I'm Ramondo." The man stood and extended his hand. "I believe Mr. Falconi told you about me? I'm your new helper."

Rigsby relaxed at the mention of Falconi's name and took the man's hand. "That was quick! We just spoke yesterday. How did you get in?"

"The back door was open. I've locked it behind me, though."

"What did Mr. Falconi tell you about the job? Did he explain that it was only part-time?"

Ramondo sat back down. "He said I would work for you full time but that he would take care of my wage. You do not have to worry about it. He said I would be helping you in the brewery and that you had someone in mind for delivering the beer."

"I'm not sure I have enough work to keep you busy full time. Have you ever worked in a brewery before?"

"Not as such, but I've been to Mr. Falconi's other brewery in Ireland. Recently I've been helping him with his wine and vodka selection. I think you'll find I'm a fast learner."

"Yes. Well, you might as well fill out these forms." Rigsby opened the third drawer in his desk and pulled out two pages held together with a paperclip. He handed them to Ramondo along with a pen. "Then I'll show you around."

Ramondo finished the forms, leaving many of the sections blank. He left the office and moved toward the front of the building, where he could hear Rigsby working. Rigsby was at a scale near the front door, measuring hops, when the front door opened and three men stepped in, closing the door behind them. Ramondo moved to the side of the room, concealing himself behind a stack of burlap sacks.

"Can I help you, gentlemen?" called Rigsby over his shoulder as he adjusted the flow of hops onto the cradle of the scale.

The man on the right was trying to get a look at Rigsby's face. The other two stayed still, five paces inside the building, their hands in their jacket pockets.

Not receiving an answer, Rigsby turned to face the nearest man. "You!" he said.

"Yes, you," said the man, pulling a gun from his jacket. The two men behind him did the same.

Ramondo moved up silently behind the man nearest to him, placing a hand over the man's mouth. The man shot wildly at Rigsby as Ramondo snapped his neck. The man slumped to the ground, releasing his gun, which Ramondo caught in mid-air. The man to the left saw the movement and turned. Ramondo's foot flew upwards and kicked the gun from his hand as it went off. The gunman's head followed the flight of the weapon, as Ramondo stepped in with a hard strike to the man's throat with the edge of his palm. The man's hands went to his neck as he dropped to his knees and then fell on his side, gasping.

The leader was focused on Rigsby but was just distracted enough by the gasping of the second man for the brewer to leap behind the scale as the leader's gun spit out three quick pops. Ramondo couldn't see if Rigsby had been hit. The assassin was moving around the cradle of hops to get a clear shot. Ramondo took a knife from a sheath at his belt and threw it underhand at the gunman, knowing that it would strike the man's shoulder. The knife was still spinning as he moved, watching the blade turn in front of him. The point of the knife stuck deep into the leader's left triceps. The grip struck the scale, causing a sound like a gong as the man turned his gun on Ramondo, who dove to the ground as the rounds went over him.

Rigsby grabbed the crucible holding the hops and swung it back, then forward. It struck the gunman in the back, knocking him forward. The man saw his two followers on the floor and decided to cut his losses. He ran to the door, opened it, and fled outside. Ramondo was following when three bullets hit the door. Seconds later, he heard a car pull away, tires protesting.

"Are you all right?" asked Ramondo as Rigsby came out from behind the scale.

"Yes, thanks to you," he said. There was blood all over the front of his shirt.

"Are you sure? You're bleeding."

Rigsby looked down and felt his torso with both hands. "I don't think it's mine. I must have picked it up from the hops carrier. It's covered with blood. It must be from the one who ran away. You're hired, by the way."

"Call the police." Ramondo went to the man who was holding his ruined throat, turned him over, and asked

Rigsby to bring some of the twine that was used to keep the hops sacks shut. With it he secured both the man's hands behind his back as well as his feet, which he bent backwards until he could tie them off to the bindings on his hands. That done, he reached into his pocket, took out his cell phone, and called Mats.

Rigsby went back to his office to find Inspector Small's card and returned to the front. "I'm not going to ask how you did that," he said, looking at the dead man and the other one gasping for breath. "Or why Mr. Falconi knew I would need your help. But thank you for saving my life."

"Mr. Falconi was worried when you told him you'd seen the man in the apartment. It will get busy when the police arrive. Why don't you tell me what my job here will involve, so I can sound like a real employee when the police come?"

Rigsby looked at the man trussed up, still gasping for air, and then at Ramondo. "All right, but who are you?"

CHAPTER 22
LONDON–THE PRESENT

The Florist drove through Dry Drayton and turned south, the knife still protruding from his arm, the grip rubbing against the backrest. After ten minutes, still on a two-lane road, he pulled to the side and went to the trunk, removing a first aid kit. He gritted his teeth against his current pain and the pain he was anticipating. He grasped the handle of the knife and yanked it from the back of his arm. Because of the angle he used, the blade opened half an inch of additional slash as it was withdrawn. Blood immediately started to flow from the cut and onto the seat of the car. He rolled up his blood-soaked shirt sleeve and wrapped adhesive tape over a piece of gauze he'd placed over the inch-long puncture. He wound the tape around his arm three times before the blood slowed, still seeping from the wound. He used the knife to cut the blood-saturated shirt sleeve off, throwing it deep into the weeds that lined the road, then took out his burner phone and placed it under the front tire.

He started the car and moved it forward a few inches, then got out and made sure the phone had been crushed and was still under the tire. Then he reentered the car and turned the wheel back and forth until he was certain the phone was not just crushed but pulverized. He moved the car again, then tossed the remains of the phone away where he had thrown his shirt sleeve.

Driving back to London, he stopped and bought two new burner phones, using one to call Bashar and Habib.

"Leave your room, now. Rent a new one, again use cash, and then text me the address. Take down this number, then destroy the phones I gave you and buy others. Do not take a call from Hasan or Abdul or try to call them. They have been taken."

He tried to look at his wound in the rearview mirror, but the angle was all wrong. It hurt and was still seeping. He'd been given the name of a doctor. A quick phone call arranged a meeting. His original plan had required four men–three gunmen and a driver. He was now down to two, three if he took one of the roles himself. He would have to modify the plot or devise a whole new scheme. It was possible but would be riskier.

By the time the doctor had met him in the back of a mosque on the outskirts of London, the Florist had conceived a new plan that would achieve his purpose. The original plan had been to kill three people, including two royals, making the real target's death look incidental. Now, with only two shooters, there would be a chance that the mark would look like the real target, rather than the royals. Fortunately, the disaster at the brewery could not be linked to the assassination, other than through his identification, and he would see that that would not happen. He would be out of England before any connection could be made. The Irish would take the blame. That was the whole point.

CHAPTER 23
HAMERTON, ENGLAND—945 AD

Jarl looked at the young woman and saw both disgust and determination in her face. The fire was burning brightly, providing warmth where they were standing, but not penetrating the main reaches of the hall. Her father and the priest were deep in conversation at the head table, far enough away that their words could not be heard.

"I take it Lord Longtree's attentions are not appreciated?"

"My father is getting old. He wants an heir, and since he does not have a son, that means a grandson. Roger Longtree's lands are adjacent to ours. Father feels it offers an opportunity to see me wed and consolidate the holdings."

"You obviously don't care for Longtree. Does your father not see this?"

"He does. I have told him so myself. I don't think he particularly cares for the man either. If Father should die without my being married or a male heir of his blood, the Crown would take over the Hamerton lands."

"I see," said Jarl. "But why would he want to force you on someone unsuitable?"

Lady Bridget stared into the fire, obviously thinking about her answer before speaking. "As you can see, we are a rural holding. We are Saxons living north of the Dane line. There are not a lot of possibilities. He feels that I am of an age, and as I said, he feels his own mortality approaching."

"When will the two lords arrive?" asked Jarl.

"Father has already sent a runner. They will be here on the morrow. May I ask you, Lord Falkhand– as a warrior, could you capture this place?"

"I could do it with ten men in less than a day. You have no defense if Blood Axe should attack. For one, I would not allow any Dane inside these walls to see your lack of men-at-arms. I suspect that is why Soren the White visited. It will be interesting to see what Lord Longtree has in mind with this defensive pact he has made with your father."

Jarl found his bed much more comfortable than sleeping on the ground, as he and the priest had done for the previous moon. The morning meal was also more fulfilling than the rations and gruel that had been provided for them as traveling clerics. Lady Bridget's comment that her father had provided more for comfort than for defense returned to his mind.

After breaking fast, Jarl donned his monk's robe and walked around the castle defenses and the surrounding countryside. Upon returning, he was surprised to find ten men in the moat, removing bracken and broken branches. More surprising was that Lady Bridget was outside the walls, directing the men's efforts as well as the women carrying the debris to a spot downstream on the banks of the river.

"It seems you have been busy, m'lady," he said as he came up behind her.

"Your comments last night were well taken. I have convinced my father to take your advice, though he does not truly see the need."

"It is good that he takes my words into consideration," said Jarl.

"There are more than a hundred and fifty men whom Father could release to work on the defenses you mentioned. And as you can see, the women can also labor. More will be here by mid-morning. I see you have put your robes on again. Is the air so cold?"

"My homeland is much colder, but in truth, spending years in Miklagard has made me feel the chill more than I did in my youth. It is not why I wear the robe, though."

"Then why?"

Jarl thought about the answer, looking at Lady Bridget as she faced him, her dress soiled at the hem with dirt. Her straightforward expression and the fact that she had taken his advice on the defense measures made up his mind.

"I know this Blood Axe, the Danish chief–the one the man in the wood named as his leader. We are enemies. If he knew I was here, it would go badly for you. He would give much to capture me. I would prefer to be known as a monk when these neighboring lords arrive. I will speak to your father and the priest. Tell your servants to refer to me only as a monk."

"There were only six who saw you in your Varangian tunic, but the two who were with me in the forest have told of your prowess. I am sure that the story will be circulated."

"That cannot be helped," said Jarl. "But my name should not be mentioned."

The lords arrived practically together, an hour past the sun's zenith. The bridge had just been raised for Lord Roger Longtree's arrival before Lord Hubert Watley's escort was seen coming through the wooded area to the north.

Even on horseback, the difference in stature between the two stood out. When Jarl had taken on his duties as captain of the Varangian Guard, he was considered a giant. Even Gun, a woman, towered over most of those in the city. Not only did Jarl's height contrast with those around him, but also his coloring. Norse men were generally fair-haired with blue eyes, with the occasional red-haired warrior. The people of Miklagard were dark-haired and dusky of skin. The first villages they had passed on this island were peopled by men who looked like Father Giacomo. They were dark-haired and slight of build, but unlike the people of Miklagard, they had white, almost translucent skin. As they moved north, they had seen more fair-haired, blue-eyed individuals, but unlike Jarl, they were stout, often broad-shouldered. The priest had called them Saxons. Their eyes were also blue, as were those of the Norsemen, but a deeper, darker blue, unlike the pale, nearly silver eyes of Jarl.

The two visiting lords were as different from each other as the Varangians were from the people of Miklagard. Lord Watley was of a kind with Lord

Hamerton, a Saxon, younger, but not by many years. He was strong shouldered and fair haired with blue eyes. As he dismounted from his horse, he stood at a level with Father Giacomo. Longtree was different. He was almost as tall as Jarl but with hair as brown as oak, hair that had not seen washing in many moons. He had a beard that a Viking would have shaved. It was scraggly, barely covering his jaw in most places. His hands were the most noticeable thing about him—small, almost like those of a woman.

"Welcome, my lords," said Lord Hamerton as he came down the small incline from his castle. "I am pleased that you came. It is past the mid-day meal, but I have left the table set, for I didn't know when you would arrive. Let us break bread together." He led them into the great hall while their men were brought to the kitchen against the fort's inner walls.

They sat at the table, with Lady Bridget to the right of her father at the head and the two lords seated along the side. Father Giacomo took the seat just down from Longtree, with Jarl, in his priest's robe, standing behind him to his right.

"I see you have men clearing your ditch," said Longtree. "Your messenger told of Danes in the forest who were killed. You need not fear. We have a pact. I will come to your aid if you are attacked."

"Your man gave me the same message," said Lord Watley in a voice that seemed to rumble from deep inside his chest. "Did they threaten you here?"

"No, but they threatened my daughter. With the help of Father Giacomo and his acolyte, my men were able to rescue her."

"Your man said they were killed. Four Danes," said Lord Watley. "Did any of them say where they were from? Were they Soren's men?"

"They spoke Danish, a language that I am only passing familiar with," said Father Giacomo. "One said that they knew of Soren the White but were not part of his group. But I may have misunderstood."

"Four Danes killed by two servants, two priests, and a woman," said Longtree with a sneer. "That seems highly unlikely."

"They were drunk, m'lord," said the priest, continuing the story that he and Jarl had agreed upon and shared with both Lord Hamerton and his daughter. "They were also giving all their attention to subduing Lady Bridget when we came upon her servants about to set upon them from the rear."

"And they spoke not, except for what you have already mentioned?" demanded Longtree, canting his head to the right from the center of the table while looking out of the side of his eyes at the priest.

"That is correct, m'lord."

"Did they carry any papers? A crest that would tell of their origins or purpose?" rumbled Lord Watley.

"None that we found," answered the priest, neglecting to mention the four packs still lying unopened in their sleeping quarters.

Jarl silently chided himself for not thinking of the possibility of papers and was grateful for the priest's quick mind. It would be something he would attend to as soon as the meal was finished.

"So, we are here at your bidding," continued Watley. "What plans have you made?"

"I have not made plans yet. I thought to seek your counsel," said Lord Hamerton, pushing himself upright at the end of the table. "Four Danes walking freely through my lands could be a harbinger of an attack. If I am a target, could you be far behind?"

"It's true that you are nearest the coast and closest to Soren," said Longtree. "What is unexplainable is how you could let your daughter go into the woods accompanied by only two servants. She would be much better off under my protection. My offer still stands to take responsibility for her."

Jarl watched Lord Hamerton's face as a series of emotions passed over it–first anger, then determination, followed by a quick glance at Bridget to his right. If Longtree had seen the reaction to his words, he did not show it.

"Sir Roger, we have discussed your offer of betrothal before. Bridget is still too young to wed. Have either of you had contact with Danes or seen them on your lands?"

Both lords said "No" in the same breath, shaking their heads to emphasize their answer.

Jarl could only study the face of Watley, who was sitting across from where he was standing behind the priest. Watley looked impatient and uneasy at Hamerton's question. Longtree was hidden from where Jarl was standing, but from his comment about Lord Hamerton's inattention to Bridget's safety, it was plain that the man had no respect for Hamerton's hospitality.

Jarl believed the Dane had told the truth. If so, one of the lords was lying, but he could not decide which one or guess at who would benefit more from an alliance with the Danes. One thing he knew for certain: no one would benefit if Blood Axe was involved.

CHAPTER 24
DRY DRAYTON, ENGLAND–THE PRESENT

When the police arrived at the Whistling Pig Brewery, it was like the reverse of a Le Mans start. Three cars and a van pulled to a stop simultaneously with an ambulance not far behind. Doors flew open and police, both uniformed and in street clothes, appeared. Rigsby had opened the overhead loading dock door as well as the entry the gunmen had used. The men spread out in front of the building while Inspector Small and another plainclothes man entered through the larger opening along with a uniformed officer.

Glancing at the gunman hog-tied just inside the entry and the other man lying near him with his head bent at an unnatural angle, the inspector strode over to Rigsby.

"Your establishment seems to be center of violence," said Small. "Would you care to tell me what happened here? Your account over the phone was not as clear as it might have been." Small sniffed the air. The smell of spent gunpowder was strong, mixed with the odor of wet grain.

"This one is dead," said the medic who had arrived with the ambulance. "The other one is alive but is having trouble breathing."

"Please explain," said Small, looking over his shoulder at the spot where the medic was cutting the twine holding the struggling assassin's legs to his hands.

"I was just starting today's brewing process," said Rigsby. "I'd added the grain and the water, and I was weighing the hops on the scale over there, when three gunmen came through that door and shot at me."

"With those guns?" asked the inspector, motioning at the two firearms that lay on the cement floor near the bodies.

"I'm not sure. Things happened very fast. There were three of them. The one who was shooting at me fired at least three times, but I ducked behind the scale. Those are his shell casings there near your foot. You can see where they hit the weighing crucible here and here. I don't know where the third one went."

"And what about these two?"

"I don't rightly know what happened to them, Inspector. I was busy trying not to get killed. The man shooting at me was the one from the apartment next to the pub. The one I told you had fumbled the keys."

"Perhaps I can help, Inspector," said Ramondo, stepping from the margins into the circle of police.

"Who are you?" asked Small, noticing the man for the first time since entering.

"My name is Ramondo Guibega. I work for Mr. Rigsby."

David Small observed Ramondo. Whereas Rigsby was visibly shaken and quick in his movements, as if he was on his sixth cup of coffee, Guibega was calm, looking directly at him without even glancing at the two men on the floor.

"Was it you who overcame these two?"

"Yes sir, I was lucky. I'd just come from the back and was about to raise the overhead door when they burst in. I ended up behind them. When they pointed their guns at Mr. Rigsby, I grabbed one from behind as he shot. I tried to twist him around, but he just fell at my feet. I swung at the other but missed his head and struck his neck. He was shooting too. I don't know what happened, but he dropped his gun and grabbed his throat."

"And the third man, the one who was firing at Rigsby?" Inspector Small's eyes narrowed skeptically at Ramondo.

"I had a knife, as I was going to cut open sacks of hops for Mr. Rigsby. I threw it at the gunman. I think it hit him somewhere. There is blood on the crucible. I thought that it was Mr. Rigsby's blood, but he wasn't hit. It is almost dry now, but you can still see it here and on the floor. The man turned and ran, but he fired more shots from outside. We were afraid to look out and see what kind of car he was driving."

"Go outside and preserve any tire tracks that might have been left," Small instructed the uniformed officer. "Don't let anyone touch the doorknob. Get the photographer in here but no one else until the techs arrive." Small looked at Ramondo, thinking, *Lucky, my mother's porridge! The man has military written all over him. Sounds French. There is more to this.* "Why don't we go back to your office while the men secure the scene here? I have more questions for you."

The three of them went to the back of the brewery, leaving the lieutenant in the suit to manage the murder scene. Halfway there, Rigsby stopped.

"Would you mind if I mixed in those hops? If I don't do it now, the whole batch will be ruined. It will just take a second."

"Go ahead, but don't touch the crucible that you pointed out."

"Thank you, Inspector. We run pretty close to the cuff here. Can't do with throwing out a whole batch. Ramondo, would you grab that gunnysack of hops there? I'll have to guess at the weight, but it shouldn't be far off."

Small watched as the Ramondo grabbed a piece of twine at the top of the sack. He handed it to Rigsby, who with a tug unthreaded the entire top of the bag. Rigsby tipped the bag over the vast vat and poured two-thirds of its contents into the large fermenting tank. Then he punched a button, which started a large blade slowly rotating the mixture. *Needed a knife to open a sack, did he,* he thought. *This should be jolly fun.*

In the office, the three took seats. Inspector Small reached into his pocket and pulled out a small recording device. "We will go over what you told me in a minute, but first I would like to find out more about you," he said, nodding toward Ramondo. He made a show of putting the recorder down without turning it on.

"I was hired by Mr. Rigsby earlier this morning. I had just finished filling out the forms on the desk there and had gone to the front to help him when the three men attacked with their guns."

"Let's dispense with the nonsense. Where have you worked before?"

"I've had many jobs, but I didn't want to speak until we were alone. There were too many ears on the brewery floor. I suspect the job that will interest you most is my five years' service in France in the National Police Intervention Force—the FIPN."

"So the disabling of two men and the wounding of a third was not a lucky accident."

"It was, only in that I was behind them when they entered and was unseen. It was unfortunate that there was not time to disable the dead gunman, as he was shooting at Mr. Rigsby. The second panicked. I was able to disarm him as he was firing at me."

"And the third man?" asked Small.

"He was the leader. He has a knife wound in his right arm. It was not enough to stop him, but it made him drop his gun. He turned and saw his two companions on the ground. That caused him to flee after picking up his gun."

Small was only slightly familiar with the French FIPN group and more with its reputation than its makeup. Its success in combating terrorism in Europe was legendary. The French operated under laws that were based on the Napoleonic Code–guilty until proven innocent. They allowed a much freer hand against subversion and terrorism than in Great Britain, and the FIPN was reputed to be ruthless in taking advantage of those differences.

"You realize that you could be held for murdering the man with the broken neck."

"I think you will find that both guns have been fired, and the only prints are from the two men on the floor," said Ramondo. "With Mr. Rigsby's testimony, I think any charges would be quickly dropped."

"Do you have someone who can vouch for who you are?"

"Certainly." Ramondo reached over and took the notepad and the pen he had used to fill out the employment forms. He wrote a name and a phone number on it. "Inspector Maurice Medau will confirm my identity. But I hope that your report will not mention my background, as it would hamper my ability to protect Mr. Rigsby."

"Protect me!" said Rigsby.

Ramondo turned to the policeman. "When Mr. Falconi heard that Mr. Rigsby had seen the men who might have been involved in the murder of the lorry driver, he thought he might need protection, and at the very least he needed help with the business. I don't think he knew my help would be necessary so soon."

"Are you still with the FIPN?" asked Small.

"No, not for three years now, but I would ask a favor. Could I be present when you question the prisoner? Although their dress did not identify them, they looked to be Persian, and the leader had an accent. I might be able to offer some insight into their motive for killing the driver and attempt to do the same to Mr. Rigsby."

"That might not be my call," said Small. "Meanwhile, I'd like to record what we've just gone over, for the record, keeping some things about your background unsaid." Small reached over and clicked on the recorder.

CHAPTER 25
MAIRFAIR HOTEL, LONDON–
THE PRESENT

Suzanne was overjoyed to see Brian, the boy they had adopted five years ago. It was hard to believe that he was seventeen years old. He had been just thirteen when Mats bought the Harp and Hawk Brewery, located in the town of Donegal in the northwest corner of Ireland. Mats did not know at the time he made the offer that the reason the brewery was for sale was that the Keohanes, Brian's parents, the owners of the Harp and Hawk, had been murdered, leaving their son an orphan. It had taken almost a full year for Mats and Suzanne, who had recently been married, to unravel Ireland's adoption regulations and receive custody of the boy.

Ramondo had picked Brian up at the airport and brought him to the hotel the previous afternoon. Mats couldn't believe how much Brian had grown—it looked like four inches in the last year. Ramondo and Wolfgang Schmidt, the German karate master, both worked with him in the martial arts. Schmidt often had him fly into Frankfurt on the weekends he had off from the American School in Leysin, Switzerland for instruction. The muscles in Brian's shoulders attested to the effectiveness of his training. Even though they kept up on Facebook, it was good to have Brian to themselves for his two-week break.

They were hardly seated when Suzanne asked, "*Comment vont tes études*–how are your studies coming?"

"*Est-ce que tu testes mon français?* Are you testing my French?" replied Brian in unaccented French, evoking a laugh from Mats.

"No more of that," said Mats. "We are interested in how you are doing, though. Do you like the school?"

"It's fine. I don't get to play much golf. The nearest course is forty-five kilometers away, and we only have a six-month playing season, but I'm learning to ski fairly well. I'd rather be with you, though."

"We'd like that as well," said Suzanne, "but with us moving constantly between Corsica, Paris, Donegal, the States, and now England, it would be impossible for you to get an education. Summer will be here before you know it."

"Ramondo tells me that you are ready to take a black belt test from Wolfgang," said Mats.

"Wolfgang is harder on me than Ramondo. It might be a while before I get that belt. He wants me to enter a tournament. If I do, would you come and watch?"

Ramondo grunted and shook his head, obviously surprised by Brian's comment. Knowing Ramondo, Brian's next workout would be a killer.

The meal was spent catching up. Brian was especially interested in Suzanne's expedition to Turkey and Mats' involvement in helping stop a street bombing in Belgium.

"I'll say goodbye now," said Ramondo. "I need to get to the brewery and be ready when it opens tomorrow." He stood and shook hands with Mats and Brian and kissed Suzanne's hand. "Thank you for the dinner. And Brian will have no problem earning the belt." He turned and walked quickly away from the table.

"I think you wounded him with the comment that Wolfgang was harder on you," said Mats.

"I didn't mean it that way. They teach different techniques. Both are equally brutal, but I think Wolfgang grades harder. It might be the German in him. At school, the hardest graders are the German teachers."

Mat had asked for the bill to be placed on their room tab, when his cell phone vibrated in his pocket. He took it out and snuck a look at it under the table.

"It's Katherine," he said in response to Suzanne's curious look. "I'll call her back when we get to the room."

Mats invited Brian to their room to continue to catch up. Brian's clock was an hour later than Mats and Suzanne's, and the meal had taken the edge off his excitement, but it had been almost two months since Mats had been with him and he didn't want to waste a minute.

In the room, Mats took out his cell phone and pressed Call Back.

"Hello, Mats," said Katherine, picking up the phone on the first ring. "I was hoping you'd get back tonight. Is there a way that you could meet Margaret and me tomorrow? Rodney is flying in from Washington in two hours on United and Margaret is driving down from Hamerton tonight. I thought we might meet first thing for breakfast."

"Is anything wrong?"

"No, but something very interesting has come up. Absolutely amazing, actually. Can you do it?"

Mats got a nod from Suzanne. "Sounds fine. Our son Brian has just arrived in London from school. Would it be all right to bring him?"

"Of course. It would be nice to meet him. I'll let you decide how much he should hear, though. I'll have breakfast set up at the office."

"Well, that was very mysterious," said Suzanne.

"That was Lady Katherine Radcliff, who helped us with a security matter and the purchase of the brewery that Ramondo mentioned," Mats explained to Brian. "She and her family have become our friends."

"Morning will come quickly," said Suzanne. "We should get to bed. Brian, we'll knock on your door at seven-thirty. Nice to have you here." She gave him a hug, noticing for the first time the beginning of stubble on his cheek.

Mats had wondered about the choice of Katherine's office as a meeting place for breakfast. He was even more intrigued when she immediately took them to the security room, which was set up with warmers containing eggs, thick bacon, potatoes, mushrooms, and tomatoes, plus carafes of milk and orange juice and insulated pitchers of coffee and tea. Rod and Margaret were already seated, waiting for the Falconis before serving themselves. Brian, unembarrassed, went back for thirds. After all had eaten, Jane, Katherine's assistant, came in and quickly removed all the dishes and the three warmers, leaving the beverages and closing the soundproof door behind her.

"Margaret has the most amazing news," said Katherine. "First, I must be sure that it is all right for Brian to hear about the journals we discussed before."

"Yes. Brian knows all about our journal and is undoubtedly related in some way to the original authors," said Mats, reaching over and squeezing the boy's shoulder.

"Very well," said Margaret, taking up the thread. "Nothing personal, Brian. It's just that this is something that pertains to both our families and should be kept to the very fewest members."

"I understand," said Brian, returning Margaret's smile.

Margaret took a quick breath, a mannerism Mats had noticed in their previous meetings. It was like an exclamation mark but placed in front of the sentence rather than at the end. "Mats, you saw the damage the lightning did to the church at Hamerton. You were correct that the whole wall needed to be reconstructed. I didn't want to take the chance that it would fall down before we could properly document it. I hired a firm. They numbered each stone and took pictures, mapping the entire wall. That has been done, but the crack went all the way down to the ground floor, necessitating the removal of the cover stone for the vault of the Knight of Hamerton. We had always thought that it contained Richard d'Hamerton, but a few years ago, Rodney's research indicated that it might be the grave of Alfred Hamerton, Richard's grandfather. It was too good an opportunity not to look into the vault."

"And what you found surprised you?" asked Mats with a smile.

"It was Alfred, grandfather to Richard. So we got that much right after eight hundred years. He was buried in 1218, when we think the church was expanded and the porch added."

"You might remember the inscription above *Knight of Hamerton* had been defaced," said Katherine.

"Inside the crypt were various items belonging to Alfred, along with a journal that we didn't know existed until yesterday," said Rodney, speaking for the first time.

"That is wonderful news for you," said Mats. "More than wonderful, actually, but why call us in with such urgency?"

"The journal is from the latter half of the nine hundreds. It predates any that are in our keeping. It was written in three different languages. The writer was Jarl Falkhand."

"Jarl Falkhand!" exclaimed Suzanne. "The journal I discovered in Turkey was authored by Jarl Falkhand. How is this possible?"

CHAPTER 26
HAMERTON, ENGLAND–945 AD

Jarl watched from the courtyard as Lord Watley left the castle keep. Watley stopped halfway across the drawbridge, looking at the work that had been done in the moat since his arrival. The bracken had been entirely cleared and the ditch had been deepened more than a man's height for five yards starting underneath the gate. Men were working in the hole while women carried the dirt toward the river. After observing the activity for a minute, Watley rode off.

Longtree was longer in leaving. Jarl reentered the great hall as he was quizzing Lord Hamerton and the priest about the Danes and how they had died. The priest kept to the story that the Danes were drunk, and that he, the servants, and his acolyte had been lucky. He said nothing about the packs. Jarl– his cowl still up and covering his face, stooping to disguise his height–stood behind where Lady Bridget was seated. He leaned over just long enough to whisper, "Lord Watley has gone."

"I would see these dead Danes," said Longtree to the priest.

"I am a stranger in these parts, Lord," said the priest. "I might be able to find the spot. There was a tree …"

"Lady Bridget knows. She can show me," said Longtree, sharply cutting off the priest. "This will also give me time to convince her to accept my proposal." He looked as if it were settled.

"It would be inappropriate for her to go with you unescorted," said Hamerton, his tone echoing Longtree's.

"The priest can accompany us," snapped Longtree.

"It would surely be a shock for her to be taken back to that place," said the priest.

"And it would be of little value," said Lord Hamerton. "Yesterday I sent men to bury the bodies. I did not want them found on my land."

"They had no belongings?" asked Longtree.

"Only the weapons Father Giacomo brought back," said Bridget, moving to the fireplace to warm herself from the fall chill she had been feeling since she oversaw the work on the moat. The hem of her dress was still wet and dark with dirt.

"Lady Bridget," said Longtree in an assertive voice. "Would you show me where these Danes attacked you?"

"Certainly not. I am vexed that you would ask such a thing. I would be frightened all over again."

Jarl was glad that his face was hidden and that the grin spreading across his face could not be seen. Her fearlessness was what had first attracted him to the lady. She had shown no fright, even as the Dane's sword was at her throat. Jarl's amusement was a contrast to the anger that was plainly visible on Longtree's face.

"Then I will leave you to repair your defenses and hope that my help will arrive in time if you are attacked by the Danes. What else do you plan to do beside cleaning the ditch? I would suggest studding the underside of the drawbridge." Longtree turned, and without acknowledging either of his hosts, strode from the room in a controlled state of rage.

Jarl went to the door and watched Longtree leave, followed by his retainers. He stopped at the midpoint of the bridge as Watley had, looking pointedly at the work being done in the ditch, but unlike Watley, he hardly hesitated before riding on.

"Well, that went rather well," said Lady Bridget from behind Jarl's shoulder.

Jarl turned and looked at her as the drawbridge was raised. Together they walked back to the great hall, where Father Giacomo was conversing with Lord Hamerton.

"What do you make of our two neighbors?" asked Lord Hamerton as Jarl and his daughter joined them.

"Both said and did enough to raise suspicion as to their being the Danes' destination. It is hard to choose between them," replied Jarl, lowering his hood. "Lord Watley was more interested in the repairs to the moat, and Lord Longtree was more interested in the Danes and the possible papers. Neither seemed worried about their own safety from the Danes, but Lord Longtree was particularly interested in the safety of Lady Bridget."

"He is not interested in my safety. He is interested in my hand and the lands it brings with it," spat Lady Bridget. "I despise the man."

"Does it really matter which lord is untrue?" asked Father Giacomo. "Except for a slight difference in proximity, which made no difference in their arrival time today, there seems to be little to distinguish which is the traitor."

"Longtree has the most men-at-arms, but Watley is a tested warrior and has fought Danes before," said Lord Hamerton, taking a seat.

"Both are jealous of your wealth and the production of your lands, Father," said Lady Bridget, moving to his side. "Both are aware that you have neglected your defenses in order to increase your productivity."

"I agree with Father Giacomo," said Jarl. "It matters little which one you must fear, except to know whom to turn to when the other betrays you."

"Is there nothing to be done then? That hardly seems like an answer," asked Lady Bridget before her father could respond.

"That is not what I meant," said Jarl quickly. "I could find out which one is harboring Danes by watching them, or I could ask Soren the White. As to what to do, you should continue to improve your defenses and train more men-at-arms to guard your walls. Longtree gave a suggestion that would help. Stud the underside of the drawbridge so that it is stouter when raised. You should also embed sharpened stakes in the moat when you have finished deepening it."

"I could send to Londinium to hire mercenaries," said Hamerton," but they might prove as untrustworthy as Danes."

"It's good that Lady Bridget has already started to improve your ditch," said Jarl, getting a look of surprise from Lord Hamerton.

"I set some of our serfs to clearing the brush and deepening the moat, as Lord Falkhand suggested at last evening's meal, Father," interjected Lady Bridget. "With the harvest in, there were idle hands. I thought you would approve."

"What else?" asked Hamerton, regaining his composure.

"Dig a small ditch to the river upstream to fill the moat with water," said Jarl. "On the far side, dig a trough back to the river, but leave a dam gate directly under your wall to stop the moat from being drained. Also, set your masons to build higher walls on either side of the gate two steps into your courtyard. Then have your smith forge another gate to hang on the two extensions so that anyone forcing the drawbridge will have to contend with another, which will offer a killing field for archers on your walls. Do you have archers among your serfs?"

"We do," said Lady Bridget. "Many of them are quite good."

"Bring as many of them as you can inside your walls to live and practice. Have your fletchers produce bails of arrows. You can't have too many. Danes seldom use armor other than mail. But bodkin arrowheads are preferable, if your smithy has time and the ability."

"You make it sound as if an attack is a certainty," said Lord Hamerton.

"If Blood Axe is involved, it is a certainty."

"How long do you think we have to prepare?" asked Lady Bridget, having paid close attention to Jarl's assessment of their defenses.

"That is what I will try to find out. I will leave for Soren's tonight after I examine the Danes' packs."

CHAPTER 27
LONDON–THE PRESENT

The Florist was driving his new rental car. He'd turned in the previous one after wiping both the interior and exterior clean of fingerprints and cleaning the blood stains from his wound off the driver's side as best he could. It would take someone really looking to see it as anything more than a smudge.

He was heading east on the ring road outside London proper, going to the emergency flat he had secured at the start of the mission. It was further out than the Florist would have liked, but the botched attempt to kill the brewer had necessitated that he move that day. He didn't know whether Abdul and Hasan were alive or dead. It seemed to him that Abdul had been moving slowly on the pavement, holding his throat, but maybe it was only an impression. It would be better if they both were dead. He'd been careful. They knew nothing about the attack he had planned, other than that it would include a royal and that the Irish would be blamed. Of course, his phone was compromised, but that had been taken care of.

He'd bought a newspaper, the *Metro*. It was lying on the passenger's seat. He glanced at it as he drove. There it was, at the bottom right corner of the first page–the news he had been waiting for the past two weeks. Now his mission had a time frame.

He came to the A1 turn-off, took it, and immediately came to a stop light. There, in front of him, was a billboard extolling the benefits of Brexit. This was the core of his mission. Whether he went through with the plan or not depended on whether Britain exited the European Union. The stupid English had voted to leave the EU, but almost half the politicians opposed the vote and were doing everything to prevent Britain from leaving. The whore of a woman prime minister had vowed to follow the voters' mandate and was doing everything to negotiate the withdrawal. Ironically, the biggest sticking point was the border crossing between Ireland and Northern Ireland. It was not just the Irish border that would close but the borders between the EU countries and Great Britain.

The light turned green and the Florist continued up the A1. It was afternoon. He saw groups of schoolboys on the sidewalk as he neared Borehamwood. It reminded him of his own youth, before his father's death. He had been born in Iraq. His father was Shiite, quietly opposing Saddam Hussein Al-Majid Al-Tikriti, who had come into power on the death of General Ahmed Hassan al-Bakr. Saddam had formed a well-armed and loyal security force, the Republican Guard. It had gained control of the armed forces and given power to the Sunni minority, holding sway over the eighty percent of Iraq's population that was Shiite. The Florist's father had died in an act of repression against the officials who ran Iraq's water supply, where he was a manager. The Florist–or Ali Chalabi, which was his given name– had just turned fifteen. He had fled, while his brother and two uncles were taken to confinement, never to emerge. Ali fled to Syria and joined a group that carried out border incursions against Israel north of the Sea of Galilee. After four such forays, he sensed the futility of their operations in opposing the much more organized and sophisticated Israeli defenses. He'd taken some of what was left of his father's hidden savings and enrolled in the Lebanese American University in Beirut. His choice of schools was based on the desire to learn English, as well as on the high level of engineering and computer science courses that were available.

He pulled into a residential street and stopped his car. The unbidden memories had evoked emotions he'd been unaware he still possessed. His father's death and Saddam's ties to the West were reason enough for his hate. What Israel was doing to Syria only fanned the flames. He'd poured his energies into his studies, living in a two-room apartment with three other students. His efforts were rewarded. He graduated near the top of his class.

Just before entering his final year, Ali was visited one evening by a man who knocked at the door of his room. Ali recognized him as a member of the group that had organized the raids on Israel from Syria. He had never spoken directly to the man, seeing him only as a silent observer as he and others were given their orders. The man had not offered his name then and did not do so now.

"You have been chosen. Be at this address in an hour," said the man, handing Ali a slip of paper. "Do not say anything to anyone." Without waiting for a reply, he turned and left.

That was the beginning of Ali's immersion in a small circle of intellectuals who met on an irregular basis; sometimes they saw each other weekly, sometimes more than a month passed before they reconvened. They seldom planned tactical attacks but discussed strategy more broadly–where the Europeans and the Americans were most vulnerable, how those weaknesses could be exploited. When occasionally they did plan attacks, Ali was given a leadership role. He saw it as a test to determine whether he had qualms about taking a human life.

A car went by, its windows down, the people inside laughing. He looked at his phone. He was only three blocks away from the new flat. He thought of how his family's home in Taji, just outside of Baghdad, resembled this suburb of London, and how his father's death had brought him to this point. He leaned the car seat back, which caused his arm to hurt until he stopped. He closed his eyes and remembered how he had been given this assignment.

It was over six months ago. Because of Ali's role in the group, he was told not only the task but the reasoning behind it. The actual act was of little importance, but the consequences would affect the Muslim cause for years to come. There were so many unknowns, factors out of their immediate control, that the ultimate act was hard to predict. Plans might have to be modified at any moment. It was one of the reasons he had been selected. He might not even have to complete the task. For that reason, it was necessary for him to know which events would trigger action and which would make it necessary for him to stay undercover.

Ten years had passed since he had joined the clandestine group. Still Ali didn't know which group of the divided Muslim brotherhood he was serving. He'd initially believed that it was an arm of Osama bin Laden's al-Qaeda, mostly because of the sublime nature of the tactics that were discussed to exploit the West's weaknesses. Almost always the strategies were long term, conceived of in terms of years, sometimes decades. One tactic that was constantly discussed for both its immediate and long-term effect on Western governments was the use of righteous terrorism. When Ali was sent into the field, which was becoming less and less frequent, terror was his undertaking.

Late in November of the previous year, a meeting was called. When Ali arrived at the secret meeting place, there was a newcomer there in addition to the three men who usually made up the group. From the deference that the others showed the man, Ali surmised that he was from the parent organization. If he'd hoped to learn who was funding the group and the missions they performed, he was disappointed.

"You are well thought of," the man said without introducing himself by name, rank, or affiliation. "Your planning and recommendations have been most useful and have been implemented into our overall strategies." The Florist could still hear the words in his head, could recall the feeling of pride he'd had upon hearing them. "You have written, in a number of your reports, of the disruptive effects of the migration of our sect to the European nations. This has been our long-term goal. When the Europeans created open borders, it was like giving us a weapon. It took almost twelve years of immigration before they realized what was happening. Sweden was the first to stop our migration, but it might be too late even for them to reverse the outcome. Others are now aware of their increased Muslim populations and the increased birth rate, which will likely give us a majority in two generations." The man straightened, holding his hands in his lap. It was a sign that he was finished.

Murmurs around the table broke the silence.

"I've brewed coffee," offered the leader of Ali's group, and received a nod from the newcomer. Similar nods were given from the others, so he got up and quickly filled five small cups with thick dark liquid from an elaborate machine in the corner that contrasted with the spartan furnishings of the rest of the room.

Each man put the small cup to his mouth with both hands, sipping loudly, watching the new man and allowing him to finish first before lowering their own cups.

"I'm most grateful," he said. "Please forgive my lack of courtesy, as I have another meeting this afternoon. As you know, Britain has voted to leave the European Union. The vote was passed by citing fear of immigration across their open borders. We do not know how this will turn out. We do know that a good number of their lawmakers are actively working against the vote. We also know that the stupid whore they have as their prime minister has vowed to make sure it is done. If she is successful, there is sure to be a disastrous effect on our placing people in that country. She must not succeed in her efforts. We do not know what the result will be as the expiration date approaches, but we want you to stop her, using force if necessary. It will be your plan and your operation. Am I clear?"

Having received nods of acknowledgement, the man stood. "Good. May Allah be with you." Turning, he left without another word.

CHAPTER 28
LONDON, ENGLAND–THE PRESENT

Mats and Suzanne were getting used to having breakfast in Katherine's office. The soundproof meeting room held a table and chairs for ten. There was plenty of room for the six of them and for the sausage, eggs, and potatoes that were set out with plates and utensils. When they finished, with the obligatory cup of tea or coffee, all eyes turned to Margaret.

Mats watched as she carefully unwrapped a small package. It looked to be six by eight inches. It was a journal, leather bound, not as thick as the one they had brought back from Turkey, but of the same construction. She put on a pair of cotton gloves and handed pairs to Mats and Suzanne.

"I only opened the first two pages. The spine is brittle, as are the pages. The first gives the name and dates the book was written, and the second is in three languages. I did not attempt to go further." Margaret picked up the book, using the wrapping that was still underneath it, and carried it around the table, placing it gently between Mats and Suzanne.

Mats put on the gloves and gingerly opened the book three or four pages deep, showing the contents to Suzanne. He watched as she took her iPad from her purse and opened the secure file that held the two journals she had photocopied. Opening the journal from Turkey that she had yet to translate, she held it up to the page visible on the table.

"Mats! The handwriting is the same! Even the languages are the same three used in the Turkish journal. Go to the flyleaf. Let me see the dates."

Mats did as she asked. She made note of the inscription and went back to her screen. "The dates are continuous with ours. This means all the journals were written by the same man. He sailed down the Dnieper River to Constantinople, to Corsica, and then to England."

"Falkhand came from Constantinople to here," said Mats, shaking his head, trying to absorb the significance of what they were learning.

"The journal my father gave me might also be of interest," said Rod. "It covers time spent in Corsica. The dates are much later, but it mentions that his ancestors arrived on the island from the east, generations earlier."

Margaret asked cautiously, "Can you translate it?"

"I can," said Suzanne. "I've just scanned the one I found in Turkey, the one you put on the secure site. There hasn't been time to really go over it. Part of it, the part written in Latin, can be translated fairly easily. The problem is the other two languages." She carefully opened the book again to the middle. "This uses runes much more extensively and what looks like Greek, along with Norman French. I'm proficient in Norman French but not Greek, which is one of the reasons we haven't translated the Turkish find yet. I would have to ask an outside expert for help."

"Would you be willing to do that?" asked Margaret of Katherine and Rodney.

"If we must," said Katherine.

"I do have a colleague who could do it," said Suzzanne. "He's discreet, and we would only show him the Greek passages. We could show them out of sequence, or even mix up the two volumes. It could be done."

"And the runes?" asked Katherine.

"The runes are not a problem," explained Suzanne, taking on the authority that she'd assumed when she first met Mats. "They look confusing but they're actually just an early form of half-writing, half-pictograph. It wouldn't take very long to decipher them with a reference text in hand."

"So that leaves only the Greek text," said Rodney.

Mats was about to suggest a timeline when he realized that Brian was raising his hand like a schoolboy. "Yes, Brian."

"At school we're required to take two languages. Most take English and one other. I'm Irish and you know what they say—the English invented the language, but the Irish showed them how to use it. That would be easy, and I wasn't looking for easy. I took French because of Suzanne, but I was assigned Greek as my second language. I've been taking it for almost two years now, and I'm first in my class. Our teacher mixes in sentences of ancient Greek to show us how the language has changed. I might be able to help."

Mats closed his mouth, while Suzanne suppressed a giggle at her husband's reaction.

"I mean, I was hoping to work out with Ramondo in karate, but you sent him away, so it's not like I won't have time," said Brian.

"Then the journal is yours to translate," said Margaret. "I only ask that you share the translation with us, since it obviously pertains to both our families." It sounded like she was indulging the boy. At the same time, she made sure he felt that he was part of the team.

"Of course," said Mats, realizing why Katherine had so much respect for her grandmother.

"Brian," said Katherine. "Perhaps you don't have to miss your exercise. Rodney could work you out. Won't you, dear?"

"Better martial arts than golf," laughed Rodney. "I'm sure Brian can show me some techniques I don't know. I use a dojo not two blocks from here when I'm in London."

Mats looked again at Rod Stoner and saw for the first time all the indications of a very fit man. He was almost certain that Brian would get more than a casual workout.

"Could you use your photography equipment to take pictures of the journal's pages?" Suzanne asked Katherine. "Then you can add them to our secure site, like you did for the Turkish one, and return the journal to a safe place."

"While you do that," said Brian, "maybe I can go back to the hotel and get my gi? That is, if Mr. Stoner has time this morning."

"I have all morning, Brian. And you don't have to go back to the hotel. There are plenty of gis at the dojo. Is it all right if he works off those three helpings of breakfast this morning, Mats?"

Mats nodded. "It looks like our wives will be busy photographing and preserving the journal this morning. Could I come along and watch? I'm not trained, but it would be interesting to see how Bri has been progressing under Herr Schmidt and Ramondo."

"Take it easy, boys," said Katherine, who had seen Rod work out with his adopted little brother, Kena Williams, in Washington, both drenched in sweat by the end of the session. Rod had the entire spare bedroom covered in tatami mats for when the young man came back on college breaks.

Mats saw the crinkle of her eyes and the slight upturned corner of her mouth. *This is going to be interesting,* he thought.

It took only five minutes to walk to the dojo. In America, there would be large windows to enable people to look in and watch, but there was no such thing here. Mats didn't know if it was the general custom here in England or if this was a private club. Once inside, he suspected the latter. They passed a counter where a small Asian man sat, merely nodding as the three men walked by and went to an open set of cabinets with various sizes of gi, pants, and belts. All the belts were black. Like in Schmidt's dojo in Frankfurt, the entire floor past the small counter was made of stretched canvas over thick rubber mats.

Rod and Brian came out of the dressing area and started warming up. Mats took a folding chair and sat next to the small Asian man. The difference between the two was immediately apparent. Both started going through katas, but Rod's were in slow motion while Brian's were at a much higher speed and intensity. Over a five-minute period, Rod increased his speed, and Brian began kicking and punching—short, quick, explosive motions with the heel of his hand rather than his fist. As if on a pre-arranged signal, they both stopped, faced each other, and bowed. Brian threw the first punch.

CHAPTER 29
HAMERTON, ENGLAND–945 AD

Jarl learned nothing from the packs of the dead Danes about their intended destination–just clothes, food, and drink. A sack of coins in each pack attested to the fact that they had raided successfully this year. Before the evening meal, he returned downstairs to the great hall. Lord Hamerton and Lady Bridget were still there, discussing the suggestions he had made about the defense of the castle.

"Did you discover anything?" asked Lord Hamerton.

"Just clothes, extra weapons, and coins that you can use to bolster your defense." Jarl gave two of the purses to the lord, having left the other two in his room.

Hearing Jarl's voice in the great hall, Father Giacomo came in from the small anteroom he had taken for his own.

"We have been discussing Lord Falkhand's suggestions," explained the lord as the priest sat down.

"It would greatly help if you knew when the attack would come, and also from what direction," said Jarl. "Do you have a gamekeeper for your lands?"

"Of course."

"Send for him. Ask him to name the two best poachers he must deal with. Bring them in and order them to watch the two lords. Have them stay out of sight and report back if they see any Danes or preparations for a raid. They should each bring a boy as a runner to carry word back to you. I would put Father Giacomo in charge of these spies, as I suspect he has done this before in his duties for the church."

"Your daughter has a talent for getting people to work on projects. It is a skill that you should use to see to the moat, the inner gate, and the building of the ramparts. You, Lord Hamerton, should bring every man who is skilled with a bow inside the walls. You will need at least fifty men to protect the castle if the Danes attack. Some can be spearmen, but archers would be most effective. I've already mentioned the need for arrows; you cannot have too many. The men will all need to be fed and lodged. It will take organizational skills."

"And you, Lord Falkhand?" said Bridget. "What will you do?"

"I will go to Soren the White's camp. When I have answers, I will return."

Lady Bridget moved to Jarl's side, placing a hand delicately on his back and looking at him with wide, concerned eyes. "Return safe, sir. You are more than welcome here."

Jarl heard her words and wondered if it was more than the Hamertons' need for help that was keeping him here.

Jarl left Hamerton after the evening meal. He took a different route than the one suggested by Lord Hamerton. Within a mile, the swiftly flowing stream that passed the castle flowed into flat lands, where it joined others, widened, and slacked its pace. At the base of a sharp bend, it entered a pond, not really a lake, but enough of a broadening to allow a longship to turn. If there was a drought, it was possible that a ship might be caught without enough water to regain the sea. But certainly now, as it had started to rain, that was not the case. He followed the flowing water. The rain soaked his clothing. Lord Hamerton would be glad that it had come after his crops were in. Walking two more miles, he noted only one slight stretch of water where a bed of knuckle-sized rocks might cause a crew to portage through a short shallow.

Jarl knew he could never pass for a Dane. His height would be enough to give him away even if his speech didn't. He would not give his name. If Soren was with Blood Axe, it might mean his life. He would claim he was a Norseman trying to get back to Red Hand. When he began to smell the Dane's encampment, he left the river and took a trail through the trees, walking with the gait of a wet, weary traveler. He had not gone half a mile before he was challenged. Holding his arms out at his sides, he continued walking toward the sentry, who was joined by another as he drew near.

"Halt. What is your business?"

"I am Erik Karlsson. I seek Soren the White."

"You were told to state your business."

"I come from Red Hand. That is enough for you to know. Take me to Soren." Jarl could see that his use of Red Hand's name had shaken the sentry.

"Take this man to Soren," said the sentry. "Make sure two others are at his back when he enters."

Within two hundred paces, they emerged from the trees into a large area that had been cleared around a castle that looked like it had been standing for a hundred years. Although the castle was old, its defenses looked new. Many of the improvements Jarl had suggested to Hamerton were already in place. The moat was filled with water and wider than a horse could jump, and the walls stood three men tall. They moved through a triple-gate complex into a large courtyard. Jarl turned and saw that ramparts had been placed chest high below the top of the wall. The yard was crowded with men. He quickly estimated at least forty individuals, with almost as many as he had seen outside the walls. A dock had been made out of timber at the riverbank and two longboats were tied up there, their bows pointed downstream with their figureheads stowed, showing their intent to trade rather than raid. All three gates he had passed through were substantial, made of thick oak and backed by iron straps riveted at right angles to the seams of the planks. Murder holes were evident for those who passed the first gate and were stopped by the second or third. Two men-at-arms stood at the entrance to the castle at the base of a series of three steps leading to another strong door.

"This Norseman would see Lord Soren."

The man with the spear grunted but made no move to let Jarl by.

"I am with Red Hand. Tell that to Soren," said Jarl, taking a single step toward the guard. He did not want to look like he was threatening the man but was not one to be put off by an underling.

The guard raised his spear, and when Jarl didn't step closer, asked, "Your name?"

"Erik Karlsson."

The guard flicked his head, a sign to his fellow on the steps, who opened the stout door and moved inside.

Jarl was unsure what he would see as he was motioned up the stone stairs and inside. The two guards flanked him as he entered, while the man who had come with him from the sentry stayed outside at the bottom step. He had half expected the great hall to be converted to resemble a Norse long hall, with dragon boards proclaiming that the interior was for men only. Instead, it was furnished like Lord Hamerton's. At the end of the hall was a rise of one stone and a great chair, on which sat a man. A fire at each side of the hall provided warmth.

Even the man, if he was Soren the White, was not what Jarl had expected. He was dressed not like a Dane but like an English lord. An ankle-length light-green tunic covered his shoulders and chest, falling to one side as it passed his waist and revealing hose that covered his legs to his leather boots. Jarl wondered if this was an attempt to look like a local lord to put his neighbors at ease, or if Soren had lived on the land long enough to have adapted to the dress and customs. Jarl had expected to find a fair-haired Dane, justifying the nickname "the White," but the man on the high seat had a crown of dusty brown hair that he wore long to his shoulders, free of braids.

"Welcome, Norseman. You told my men that you wanted an audience with me."

"Yes, Lord. I am Red Hand's man. I was left in Londinium to die, but I recovered, as you can see. A moon ago, I heard that there might be a need for fighting men here, and even if there was not, a Norseman would be treated better by the Danes than I was in that town." It was hard for Jarl to lie. Even giving a false name was difficult, against the culture in which he was raised.

It helped a little that some of what he had said was the truth.

"I have no need for fighting men. As you have seen, I have many."

"Then I am sorry to have disturbed you, Lord. In truth, you were mentioned in praise. The word was that men were needed in the area, not by you specifically. Regardless, this place is nearer to my own land. Perhaps you have a ship that is going north?"

"My ships are for trading these days, and there is little to trade for in the north, other than furs and amber, and they are controlled by Red Hand. I might be able to see you to a town that has ships going north, but it would be some weeks."

"Would it be possible to stay with you till then, or do other ships stop here?"

"I would offer you hospitality, Norseman, but I fear that any number of my men would wish to test you. There is another man, a Danish chief with four ships, who is raiding to the south. He is due back here next moon. He has spoken of establishing a place to winter two of his ships and half his men down river, but he might just as easily sail home, as in the past. Either way, you might earn passage."

"His name, Lord Soren?" asked Jarl.

"Blood Axe."

Jarl was hesitant to ask more for fear of arousing suspicion. Soren gave the impression of intelligence, unlike the brutish manner of Blood Axe. He wondered at the relationship between the two chiefs and if the accommodation given to Blood Axe and his crews was due to fear. Hamerton had said that Soren had at no time shown aggression in the three years since he had fought and defeated the lord whose castle he now occupied. It would explain the new additions he had made to his defenses.

"Lord, I would ask for the courtesy of spending the night. I have traveled far this day, and in truth have not eaten well. Thank you for the recommendation of your fellow Dane. I will go down river and wait for him."

"You may stay the night. Blood Axe may not be sailing north. He should have little trouble overcoming the defenses of the lord to my west, which I suspect he will do immediately upon arrival here. If that is the case, then he will stay here for the winter."

Jarl spent the night. His purpose was to talk with as many of Soren's men as possible to gain any information that the lord might not have mentioned or thought important. The first knowledge he gained was how it was that Soren had earned his name, Soren the White. His men were happy to tell the tale, obviously one of great pride in their leader. Soren's uncle had taken over after his father's death. His father had been hale, and there was thought that he had been poisoned. Soren had been next in line to become chief, but his uncle had warned him off, telling him he would die if he attempted to regain his father's ships and land.

It was the dead of winter, and a blizzard had blanketed upper Denmark with a thick layer of snow. It was so cold, and the winds so violent, that all the men were holed up secure in their lodges. During the worst of the storm, Soren had thrown open the entrance to his uncle's lodge. He was completely caked with ice. The few men between Soren and his uncle thought him an aberration. Three steps into the lodge brought him to his uncle's sleeping furs. His sword, covered with ice crystals, thrust hard into his uncle's chest. The men in the lodge recognized Soren, still covered in snow and ice, and lay down their weapons. The uncle had not been a popular leader. One of the men yelled, "Soren the White!" and the name stuck.

After the fourth tankard that Jarl bought for him, one of Soren's men-at-arms talked about the four Danes who had left five days ago.

"They were a foul lot," said Soren's man. "Our lord only tolerated them, and he was pleased when they left."

"Where did they go?"

"They were going to watch the castle that Blood Axe has in his mind to capture," said another, who was also drinking on Jarl's purse. "I heard that Lady Bridget was the payment Blood Axe had agreed to for gaining the help of a neighboring lord."

All agreed that Blood Axe was due back in three weeks, and unless he had suffered great losses in raiding, he would have upwards of two hundred men.

The next morning, Jarl took his leave at daybreak, heading west along the trail toward Hamerton. As soon as he was out of sight, he turned north. Crossing the river and staying close to the woods, he moved downstream, not to Hamerton Castle but to the coast.

CHAPTER 30
BOREHAMWOOD, ENGLAND–
THE PRESENT

The Florist's new safe house was smaller than his previous one. It was more like a large studio than a house, but it was a stand-alone with no common walls with another dwelling. Its furniture was new, and it had a good-sized desk and thick curtains that could be pulled shut.

Once inside, the Florist looked again at the newspaper. There on the first page were two articles that made his heart beat faster, which made the wound in his arm throb. One article announced that the prime minister had concluded a second negotiation with the officials of the EU, one that gave Britain more concessions in leaving the European Union. Reports stated that Parliament was likely to agree to the new arrangement. The second story took up the entire bottom half of the page. Seven members of the Labor Party, one of the main opponents of Brexit, had quit Parliament. Either article would have been enough to trigger the Florist's assignment; together, they left him no choice but to instigate the plan.

The assassination of a member of the royal family had been the Florist's suggestion. It had little to do with the overall goal of the plan, but it would ensure that the Irish came under first suspicion. However, there were other ways to point the blame at the Irish if he was unable to take out a royal as collateral damage. He had, in fact, planned several scenarios that he thought would work, though with less certain results. Now, down two members of his team and with the police undoubtedly having his description, it had become almost impossible to include two marks. One might have to do–the one individual whose death would ensure the overall goal of the mission.

The prime minister would die and with her Brexit– at least in the short term, quite likely permanently. He had contemplated several methods for the murder. He had favored a high explosive charge in a drone, until that scheme had been thoroughly thwarted in the Netherlands. He was still not sure how exactly that had been accomplished, so he didn't know if he could cir-cumvent the measures the French police had used. His preferred method of killing was with a knife, which was almost always possible, but not with a head of state. There was something satisfying in taking a life with a blade. Beheading aside, a knife kill was as much a statement as it was a kill. A long-distance rifle shot or a bomb had several advantages, however. These methods were the most likely to offer an escape, which was an absolute necessity in this case, and they allowed for the placing of small hints, evi-dence that would point toward the Irish.

Both men who were left to the Florist were excellent marksmen. Two excellent sniper rifles had been brought in from Amsterdam over a month ago. They were hid-den in the town of Dry Drayton at the home of a Muslim contact. Being overheard by the delivery boy had been unlucky. Plans often turned on luck, and his had not been good. He was apprehensive about going back to pick up the rifles himself. At first Dry Drayton had seemed the perfect place to hole up until the assignment was approved: a rural town, almost no police presence, and several of their sect who were willing to help. Then the delivery boy had heard enough to get himself killed. The Florist would send Bashar to the village to retrieve the weapons while he worked out the logistics.

The Florist's plan called for two snipers, each with a different angle for their shot, no chance to be taken on the kill. It would have to be accomplished when the target was outside, and over the past month, he'd done enough surveillance to identify the perfect place. Two hours before each presentation to the parliament, the prime minister met with her closest advisors. They met away from the Palace of Westminster at the offices of a barrister on the western side of Big Ben. The office was three blocks away from Parliament and belonged to the son of a member of the House of Lords. Regardless of rain or shine, she would meet there for an hour, then take a government sedan that dropped her off in front of the Palace of Westminster. There she would wave to the inevitable onlookers and greet a small delegation of supporters on the steps before entering. Each appearance was well orchestrated, taking on the average only fifty-two seconds from the time she exited the car to the time she entered the building. Fifty-two seconds, during part of which time she would be obscured by the car, her guards, or supporting members. It was likely only one of his men would have a clear shot. The plan would be that the first one to be sure of a kill would take the shot, and the second would fire as insurance as the woman hit the ground.

The CheyTac M200 rifle was accurate at 2,000 meters, over a mile in distance, but neither Bashar nor Habib would have more than 1,500 meters to shoot. One of them would have to cover the 1100 meters from the vantage point the Florist had selected. He had only been able to obtain one CheyTac. As for the other weapon, the McMillan TAC–50 he had purchased was more than adequate for the shorter of the two distances. Although the use of rifles removed the problems associated with handguns and knives, it created others. Their weight and size made for difficulties with transportation and removal. Movies that showed assassins snapping together a sniper rifle in seconds out of a briefcase were pure fiction. The rifles themselves were prohibitively expensive, as was the ammunition, and only available from a few sources.

He had bought the two weapons in Amsterdam, using an Irish arms dealer for the purchase. The dealer had insisted on a very high premium that unfortunately he was unable to collect, because Bashar's knife took his life and that of his bodyguard. Their bodies, well weighted, were dumped in the English Channel. They would leave the weapons at the site of their firing, both because it would make Bashar and Habib's escape easier and because they would create a trail back to the Irish dealer.

CHAPTER 31
LONDON–THE PRESENT

Brian's first punch was blocked, with Rod slipping under his arm and grabbing the front of the boy's gi. He fell, drawing the boy with him. Once on the mat, Rod moved with incredible swiftness, stretching Brian out in an arm bar that would either break the arm or more likely dislocate the shoulder. Brian quickly tapped out and got to his feet, bowing low to Rod.

They circled again, Brian being much more cautious this time. Both feinted with a series of blows and grabs until Brian brought Rod to the ground with a leg sweep, followed by a series of blows that stopped inches from Rod's chest and head. For the next half hour, they engaged in moves and counter moves, Rod gaining the advantage in most but not all the encounters. Finally, both sweating and breathing hard, they stopped and bowed deeply to each other.

"What was that first move you used on me?" asked Brian as he wiped off with a towel.

"Most bouts are won not with punches or kicks but with submission holds," said Rodney. "I was originally trained in Bok Fu. It's a form of Korean boxing. It's very aggressive, as are most of the Korean forms. It saved my cake a couple of times in D. C., but, when I'm in London

I study jiu-jitsu under Mr. Hioshida." Rod nodded to the small Asian man who had let them in and supplied them with the towels. "The style is well suited for one-on-one situations, but Bok Fu would still be my choice with multiple opponents."

Brian turned toward the Asian man, who was smiling, and bowed, placing a fist into the palm of his right hand as he did so. The man reciprocated with a slight bow.

If Mats had been impressed by what Brian had learned from Ramondo and Schmidt, he was equally stunned by how good Rodney Stoner was. There were times when Rodney looked to be holding back, but as they progressed in their workout, those moments became fewer. Mats wondered if it would be wise for him to study martial arts as well, then remembered his innate ability with a knife and axe, obviously bred into him from previous generations of Falconi.

"You are really good," said Brian, turning his attention back to Rod. "Have you competed?"

"Only once, years ago. I keep my training secret and would ask that you don't discuss it, or these sessions, with anyone but your sensei. Someone not knowing that I was trained saved my life two years ago."

"Ramondo says the same thing, that keeping your skills a secret can give you an advantage, especially in the early stages of a fight. Herr Schmidt thinks differently. He thinks that if someone knows you are trained, it tends to stop them from starting something."

"They are both correct," said Mr. Hioshida, coming to their side. "In casual disputes, a reputation can forestall most bullies, but in serious confrontations, it is best to have the element of surprise. This Herr Schmidt you speak of, is he in Frankfurt?"

"Yes. He and Ramondo have been my teachers for the last two years."

"I know this man," said Hioshida, more to Rodney than to Brian. "It is good that you were cautious with this boy if Herr Schmidt took him as a pupil."

"Sensei, I ask respectfully if you would take me as a pupil and teach me jiu-jitsu while I am in London," Brian said. "Mr. Stoner has said he will find time to work out with me. Could we use the time to study under you together?"

Hioshida turned to Rod. "Is this true? Would you be willing to train with the boy?"

"I can be free for a couple of hours each day and would look forward to having a training partner," said Rod. "It might not always be at the same time. Would that be all right with you, Mats?"

"It's a deal. Mr. Hioshida is most gracious."

Mats thought it would be good if Brian was occupied at the dojo, rather than exposed to danger in Dry Drayton. Couldn't he even once buy a brewery without a murder preceding his offer?

"Mats, you wouldn't believe what a great time I had today," said Brian over his salad. "Mr. Stoner is really good, not as good as Ramondo, but really, really, good."

Brian had arrived at the hotel just before dinner. He'd showered at the dojo, but his face was still flushed with the exertion of the workout.

"Rod and I sparred hard for over half an hour when we first got there. I thought Hioshida was just a caretaker when I met him, but it turns out he's a tenth-degree black belt in jiu-jitsu and a six-degree in three other disciplines. Rod asked him to take me on as a student. He worked Rod and me out for three hours. I'm so beat."

Brian continued in the same vein, reciting the various techniques, their advantages and where they might be used, through two orders of short ribs and two desserts.

"Well," said Mats, when the boy had taken a breath after attacking a major mound of three flavors of sorbet. "I hope you aren't too tired to translate a little Greek for us. Katherine has sent us digitized versions of both the notebooks–the one from Turkey and the one they just found in the church at Hamerton. We were going to start translating tonight. Are you ready to test your Greek?"

"Oh, I forgot," Brian said, stifling a yawn.

After dinner they took the elevator to Mats' and Suzanne's suite, pulling up chairs on one side of the low coffee table. Katherine had placed copies of both journals on their secure website and had also printed out and enlarged each journal on single-sided paper, placing them in ringed folders. Ever efficient, she'd numbered the enlarged copies and interspaced each page with a blank lined page to hold the translation. It was similar to what Suzanne had done to make the ongoing translation of the Bougainville library more efficient.

All three had their computers open to reference texts– Suzanne to a dissertation on runes, Brian to his Greek textbook, and Mats to a Latin dictionary. They decided to tackle the Hamerton journal first, even though it was almost surely the latter of the two works. Suzanne reasoned that it would be the one most apropos to their present situation and certainly to their apparent connection to Katherine Radcliff and Rodney Stoner.

Suzanne, either because of her skill in translating or because runes were the easiest to convert, was the first to complete a page. She began work on the next page, which was partially covered with apparently randomly skewed rod-like pen strokes. Then she changed her mind. She moved closer to Mats, seeing that he was only half-finished with his Latin translation. She worked with him, occasionally suggesting a different translation, until he finished his page. They looked at Brian, surprised to see that he was nearly finished as well. Having read their own pages, it was easy to guess what the Greek portion would tell. The boy's translation of the Greek was better than either had expected; they noticed a few possible mistakes, but only because they knew the content of their own pages.

"You did that really well," said Suzanne. "I'm not sure many of the translators at the Bibliothèque could have done it as quickly."

"Thanks," said Brian, smiling at the praise. "I just finished midterms and part of the test was translating a piece of ancient Greek. I think I aced it."

"Well, let's look at what we have so far," said Suzanne, taking the lead and gathering the three pages of translation. "It's a lot like your journal, Mats—composed in three languages. The runes and the Latin are the same, but Greek is added instead of Norman French. It's also unlike your journal in significant ways."

"How so?" asked Mats.

"First of all, it is written three hundred years before your father's. The handwriting and even the rune strikes are different, as would have to be the case," said Suzanne with a soft chuckle at the obvious. "The major difference is that your father's was more of a day-to-day journal in the traditional sense, whereas this one is divided by location rather than time. In this journal, the runes seem to give locations and place names. Mats' Latin translation describes events, and Brian's Greek gives the writer's thoughts. It will be interesting to see if this partition continues as we continue."

"What we know already is that Jarl Falkhand, the captain of a group called the Varangian Guard, escaped from Constantinople and went west in a dragon ship after taking revenge on the vizier who murdered his wife," said Mats. "Quite a start. Let's do another section."

The three continued as before, Suzanne assigning new pages. They worked until two in the morning.

"As exciting as this is, we need sleep," said Mats. "I suggest that we not put the last translations together until morning, because I for one would have trouble getting to sleep."

Suzanne, who had been placing the various pages in order, knew the story, as she had not been able to keep from reading what Mats and Brian had translated. Mats was right. Sleep would come hard for all of them tonight.

CHAPTER 32
DRY DRAYTON, ENGLAND–THE PRESENT

Inspector Small placed the call and identified himself to the Paris central police, asking for Inspector Medau. Medau answered, but merely asked for Small's name and station, saying that he would call him back. Small had called on his cell phone, but in less than a minute, his intercom buzzed, and his desk sergeant informed him that a Frenchie Inspector named Medau was on the line.

Small picked up the receiver with a positive opinion of Medau's security measure. He looked around his small office, his desk cluttered with papers, and wondered how Medau's office might differ.

"Inspector Medau, thank you for returning my call."

"You're welcome. What can I do for you, Inspector Small?"

"I have a Frenchman here who is involved in a man's death. He has given you as a reference. He tells me that he was a member of the FIPN for five years. His name is Ramondo Guibega–that's spelled G-U-I-B-E-G-A. Do you know him?"

"I know him. I didn't when he worked in the FIPN, but I know his record there was excellent. What is he involved with in England?"

"On his first day of work for a brewery here, three men attacked the owner with revolvers. One is dead, one has a crushed larynx, and the other fled with a wound in his arm from a knife thrown from at least thirty feet away."

"And what would you like to know?"

"You do not seem surprised," said Small, his own surprise evident.

"Actually, I am surprised," said Medau. "I'm surprised that all three men aren't dead. Ramondo Guibega is a most lethal man. He is a legend in the FIPN, both for his ability to infiltrate terrorist groups and his skill in dispatching them."

"He no longer works for the police, then?"

"No, not for two years. He left on very good terms, though. From what I understand, the FIPN tried to have him stay."

"Do you know what he does now?"

"I believe he works for his family, or possibly an American named …"

"Falconi?" said Small, interrupting Medau.

"Yes. Is Falconi involved as well?"

"Falconi had just bought part ownership in the brewery. Guibega was hired to replace a delivery man who was murdered last week, and to protect the owner."

"Falconi is an interesting man," said Medau. "I trust him. He helped shut down a major drug operation here two years ago, and just a few months ago he helped stop an attempted bombing and an assassination plot in the

Netherlands. In all instances there were deaths, but they were not his or Ramondo Guibega's doing, at least that we could establish. I would say that both he and Falconi are, as you English say, good chaps. Although they both seem to step in a lot of bad-smelling stuff."

"So, you would trust them?"

"Absolutely. One other thing–about the man who took the knife in the arm?"

"Yes?"

"Don't assume that he was lucky and that Ramondo missed and hit the arm."

"Oh, he's that good, huh?"

"He's that good."

"Well, thank you for the information, Inspector Medau. You have been most helpful and have saved me from going down unproductive paths."

"You're welcome, Inspector. I do have a request of my own, though. When whatever is going on over there is finished, I would like to sit down in person with you and compare notes in detail. I think it would benefit both of us, or at the very least, amuse us."

The phone rang, waking Mats from a sound sleep. He looked at his phone. It was just before nine. Both he and Suzanne had slept in, neither of them having set their alarms. His phone screen said "Ramondo."

"Mats, you know how it was the murder of Brian's parents that resulted in the Harp and Hawk being put up for sale?" said Ramondo.

"Yes …"

"Was there a circumstance like that surrounding this purchase?"

"No. Not at all." Mats related the story of Nickolas Rigsby touring the Harp and Hawk with Cathal's nephew, stealing the bacteria, and copying the process after finding the recipe on the internet. "Rigsby was desperate to turn a profit and thought a good non-alcoholic might do it for him. After I thought about it, I realized that a partnership with him would be to my advantage. He checked out as an alright guy who was just overextended. Why?"

"You didn't hear about the attempt on his life yesterday?"

"No. I turned my cell phone off while I was watching Brian work out yesterday afternoon. I'm looking now. I have three messages, two from Inspector Small and one from Rigsby."

"Three men tried to kill him yesterday morning," said Ramondo. "Rigsby is fine, a little shaken, but otherwise okay. Inspector Small was over here most of yesterday—seems competent. I gave him Medau as a reference, so I suspect it will get back to you pretty soon."

"Three men tried to kill Rigsby? What happened to them?"

"One got away with a knife wound in his arm. One is dead, and the third will give his answers in writing, as he will not be able to talk for quite a while. I don't suspect Small will get much out of him, though."

"I don't think the murder or the attack on Rigsby has anything to do with the brewery," said Mats. "Rigsby's troubles seemed to start with him seeing a man outside a pub, the same pub his driver was delivering to the night he disappeared. Rigsby is the only one who can identify the guy who lived next to the pub."

"You're right," said Ramondo. "Rigsby identified the man who tried to shoot him today as the same one he saw in the alley outside a pub. "

"It looks like you got there just in time," said Mats.

"You were right in sending for me," said Ramondo. "The two guys the police took look Syrian to me, maybe Iraqi. I've asked to be in on the interrogation of the one with the crushed larynx. Could you apply a little pressure for that to happen? I don't think it will take much of a push. Inspector Small didn't seem averse to me sitting in."

"I'll do that as soon as we hang up. In the meantime, stay away from Suzanne and Brian. Mainly protect Rigsby and the brewery."

"I understand," said Ramondo. "Would you mind if I went after the guy with the knife wound? Get him and the threat is gone." He hesitated, awaiting Mats' reply, then thought of something. "Did you say that Brian is working out?"

"Yes. It turns out the husband of the woman who helped us with security is very good at martial arts. He took Brian to a private dojo, where he's working him out. Brian is also learning jiu-jitsu–four hours a day. As to going after that guy, protecting Rigsby is your first responsibility. If you do go after the man with the knife wound, bring one or two men from Corsica to help you look after Rigsby. Bellino and Nicolo did well in France last month, and I'd like for Brian to meet Nicolo."

CHAPTER 33
EAST COAST OF
ENGLAND–945 AD

Jarl moved purposefully toward the coast. The morning sun was visible through the overcast sky like a shimmering silver orb. Although his pace was steady, his stride long and confident, his mind was not at peace. His thoughts kept racing between the plight of Lord Hamerton and his daughter, and his obligation and the purpose of his journey. As he walked, the memory of Bridget laying her hand on his arm kept intruding on his thoughts. The gesture had been strangely moving, and now, as he came closer to the coast, it seemed disturbingly intimate.

He'd set out to inform Red Hand of his daughter's death and to make sure her share of the treasure from Miklagard was given to him. His crew had marooned him, thinking he was dead. This didn't relieve him of his mission. While with his brother Jan, he'd learned that at least three of his original crew had taken berths that would carry them north, but he could not be sure if they would contact Red Hand. Since those three were going north, he could only assume that his ship and the rest of the crew was returning south with the bulk of the treasure to Corse, along with the women they had purchased in La Havre.

One thing Jarl could be certain of was that Hamerton and his daughter were in danger. Even if Soren the White did not join Blood Axe, the preparations for the defense of their household would not deter Blood Axe, who was likely to bring as many as two hundred men and to have the allegiance of one of the neighboring lords. Hamerton would be killed, and his daughter, Lady Bridget, given as a reward to Lord Longtree, whom Jarl was now certain was the traitor. The priest would survive, as priests always did. Even Danes thought it unlucky to kill a priest, in most cases.

Past mid-day, but still with plenty of light that shone though the diminishing haze, he came to a village located on the widening of the river where it emptied into the sea. It was merely a cluster of huts on the north side of the river. There were no boats, but there were two slip-ways in the mud on the shore, both empty but showing signs of recent use. Poles with lines stretched between them, festooned with strips of fish drying in the weak sun, confirmed that this was a fishing village. Jarl scanned the sea, not detecting either hull or sail. He moved silently into the scrub and bracken some ten paces off the trail and hid.

Just before sunset, from the concealment of his hiding place, Jarl watched as two fishing boats made tacks against the westerly wind and with skill beached their crafts on the shore. They were met by a handful of women and boys from the huts, who helped pull the boats up the slips until they were clear of the water and secured by lines to posts that were driven above the high-water mark. The women unloaded straw baskets of fish from each of the boats, while the fishermen secured their nets, lines, and sails. It was a domestic scene that he'd witnessed many times at his own sted, and he envied the group their simple chores and happiness.

As darkness fell and the village ate a portion of the day's catch, Jarl remained hidden in the bracken, content with the smoked meat he'd taken with him from Hamerton. Soon, the activity in the village stopped and a hush fell, broken only by loud snoring from one of the huts to tell that the place was occupied. No dogs confronted him as he crept out of his nest and down the beach toward the larger of the two fishing boats. He grabbed several fish strips off the lines and moved to the larger of the two boats. Slipping the knots, he put his shoulder against the bow and felt it move slightly. He increased his effort and the movement quickened. There was a slight gurgle rather than a splash as the stern entered the water. Thinking about the domestic scene he had witnessed hours before, he ran up the slip and placed a gold coin on the thwarts of the second boat, then pushed the vessel the last few feet into the rush of the river. He let the current take him toward the sea, using the oar only to steer, afraid that a squeak from the oarlocks would awaken the people of the village. When he could no longer see the village, he raised the sail, taking advantage of the wind that had headed the fishermen eight hours previous.

The wind that helped him leave the river proved fickle, turning cold and coming from the north as the first rays of morning sun lit the clouds above him. Jarl had thought hard about his obligation to Red Hand and to the Hamertons. He hoped he could honor both. If he got to Red Hand and managed to keep his life after failing to protect Gun, he would be able to gather a crew and return to the island, hopefully arriving before Blood Axe. He'd hoped that the westerly breeze would allow him to sail north around the tip of the Danish peninsula. The fishing boat was smaller than he would have liked for such a journey, which would take him at least five days, but if it had been much bigger, it would have been hard to handle alone.

The north wind he'd been expecting when he left Jan's land weeks before now pushed his boat southward; it was likely to predominate until spring. With it, Jarl abandoned his original plan and cut southwest across the channel, back toward Le Havre. When the sun was at its highest point, he passed through the narrows, where he could see land to both port and starboard. He was being pushed southeast toward where he'd departed less than a moon before. As he was driven toward the Frankish coast, he felt the threads of his life twist as the Norns applied pressure to the fabric they spun for all men.

He slept at the tiller that night, catching only brief moments of rest, for although the wind remained steady, the waves changed from directly behind his stern to quartering from the steer board, causing the small boat to twist from its heading. At noon the next day, he spotted a smudge of smoke that was Le Havre over the larboard rail, and he thrust the tiller and tightened the sheets to achieve the landfall.

Ashore, his small vessel did not attract attention. Jarl tied to a wharf and made his way to the inn owned by

Arne. The innkeeper was surprised to see him. He sat down with him and called for a tub of mead.

"Arne, I need two fast horses to take me to Jan," said Jarl after he had related what had happened after he and the priest had left a fortnight before. "And I need them now."

CHAPTER 34
LONDON, ENGLAND–945

It was becoming a regular thing. Mats called Katherine and asked if they could have another breakfast meeting on Thursday. She was quick to say yes, not even asking for the reason, but moved the time up by half an hour to accommodate a previously scheduled meeting on her calendar. Mats asked if Rodney and Margaret would also attend, and Katherine said that her husband would be there, but she would have to call her grandmother.

The English breakfast of the previous meeting had been replaced with porridge and a bowl full to the brim with grapefruit sections. There was also a platter of scones piled high. Mats expected that this was in response to seeing Brian eat his three helpings at the previous meeting. He was disappointed that Margaret was not there.

"The night before last," began Mats, "the three of us started translating the journal. I printed out what we've completed so far. I thought it important that we share what we've learned, as the next translation portion might be slower."

Mats looked over at Brian, who was finishing off his second bowl of porridge loaded with raisins and brown sugar, and was surprised to see Rodney Stoner following

Brian's example, his plate containing three scones. Both had gym bags on the floor behind their chairs. Mats was about to tell the story of Jarl Falkhand when the door opened and Margaret entered, slightly out of breath. Mats was glad to see her. She was obviously the matriarch of the family. It was Margaret who kept the family history, and the respect Katherine and Rod felt for her was evident.

"I'm truly sorry I'm late." She was dressed casually in a flowered dress and a cardigan sweater that matched the color of the predominant flower in the pattern. "I hope you started without me."

"Not to worry," said Katherine. "We just had a bite, and Mats was about to tell us about the journal translation. Would you like a scone, or a nice bowl of porridge?"

"A scone with some preserves would be nice, dear," said Margaret, as she took her seat at the head of the table.

"I'm glad you're here," said Mats as Katherine brought out two scones and a large spoonful of strawberry jam with a spreading knife for her grandmother. "We've translated the first part of the journal you found."

Margaret waved her hand, refusing the sheets of paper that were offered to her. "Why don't you just tell us what is important, as I suspect it concerns us all."

"All right," said Mats, taking another drink of coffee and looking at the papers he had offered Margaret. "First, this appears to be a continuation of the journal that Suzanne recently found in Turkey. The dates are consecutive with yours. The handwriting is the same, so we can assume it is written by the same individual–Jarl Falkhand, the captain of the Varangian Guard–the emperor's personal bodyguards.

"It starts with Falkhand's slaying of the emperor's vizier. The vizier was the man responsible for the death of Falkhand's wife. After killing the vizier with a bow and arrow, Jarl escaped in a longboat with twenty of his warriors. They were to sail back to their home, which seems to be modern Sweden or Norway, but they stopped in Rome after rescuing a Roman galley. The writer is a little vague, but it seems he was given land on the island of Corsica as a reward for saving the galley. He and his band stayed there for a year, then left to continue the journey north. From what he writes, he planned to return there after fulfilling his obligation to his father-in-law to inform him of the murder of his daughter, Gun, by the vizier."

For the next twenty minutes, Mats related the story of Jarl's travels through France to England, and how he was attacked twice and forced to land on the island with a priest. Sometimes he was interrupted by Suzanne, sometimes Brian, when they thought he had left out an important detail.

"He writes that he and the priest walked from near London to Hamerton," said Suzanne. "They mention being taken in by Lord Hamerton and his daughter, Bridget."

"We stopped translating as Falkhand left the island in a stolen boat," said Mats. "I suspect his year in Corsica is the connection to my family. Obviously, his coming to Hamerton is the connection with yours. We'll finish translating the journal tonight."

"Lord Hamerton was about to be attacked by Danes," piped in Brian, the excitement in his voice mirrored in his agitated hand motions and the widening of his eyes. "And Lady Bridget was a pretty girl. We wanted to continue working, but Mats made us go to sleep because it was late."

"This brings several questions to mind," said Margaret, her eyes narrowing. "First, since you say the journal continues past where you've translated, this Jarl Falkhand must have returned, or at least the journal returned. Second, what happened with the Danes who were about to attack? Lastly, exactly how does this Viking figure into our family history?"

Suzanne was almost sure Margaret knew the answer to her last question, and she suspected that she and Katherine did as well. They had all met and married men with similar traits.

"I'm sure those questions will be answered in the remaining parts of the journal," said Mats. "Maybe we'll even get the answers in tonight's work. When would you like the next update?"

Margaret looked at Katherine and Rod. It was obvious that they wanted the rest of the translation as soon as possible.

"I think we will let you decide that," said Margaret. "You will know when you come across something significant. Rodney, when do you return to Washington?"

"I've booked a flight two days from now at 2 pm," said Rodney, looking at his wife for confirmation.

"Then the day after tomorrow? The morning before you leave," offered Mats.

"Fine," said Katherine. "I'll have breakfast ready again. That will be Saturday, so we might meet later—say, nine. That will give Rod more than enough time to get to Heathrow in weekend traffic."

"One other thing," said Mats. "I have a man acting as security at the brewery. His name is Ramondo Guibega. I thought it necessary, with the delivery lorry having been stolen, the driver murdered, and the attempt on the owner's life. Ramondo has met with an Inspector Small, who runs the police station that includes Dry Drayton. Ramondo thinks Small is quite competent, but he'd like to make sure Scotland Yard knows he is at the brewery as protection for Rigsby. He was with France's anti-terrorism unit, so I value his opinion. We think the trouble has nothing to do with the Whistling Pig itself, but rather with the owner's ability to identify a man he saw in the alley across from the delivery entrance to the pub where his delivery boy disappeared. We know the apartment in that alley was occupied by a group of men when the boy was taken. They disappeared the next day."

"I'll contact Inspector Bawkin with your suspicions and give him Ramondo Guibega's name," said Katherine. "Do you have any thoughts as to why they would kill to avoid being identified?"

"Ramondo thought they were probably using the apartment as a deep safe house for a unit waiting for a particular job. Their leader must be a higher-up and possibly could be recognized."

"Interesting," said Margaret, "Let me know what Gerald Bawkin thinks, will you, dear?"

Standing, Stoner grabbed his workout gear and turned to Brian. "Ready to get your butt kicked?" he asked, moving to the door.

Brian joined him, turning back to the group. "Not by him. Sensei Hioshida eats both our cake." They left, laughing.

CHAPTER 35
GAUL–945 AD

Jarl arrived at Jan's castle on the third afternoon after taking the boat. The horse the innkeeper had given him in exchange for the fishing boat had been exchanged for others of diminishing quality as he raced inland. Jan's castle was situated inside a sharp bend in the river. It was late in the year, and the crops that surrounded the castle had been harvested, making a sharp contrast with what he'd seen thirty days before.

Jan listened in silence until Jarl finished. "I felt something had happened to you," said Jan. "What will you do now?"

"When I left the island, my intent was to get passage from Soren the White and find Red Hand. Soren would not send one of his ships to sea for half a moon. By then, Blood Axe might have returned. That is why I took the fishing boat and tried to sail north on my own." Jarl stopped, knowing that his brother would understand what was driving him on his return. "I left the river with a wind at my back that would have delivered me to Red Hand without touching the sail. Within an hour, it shifted directly into my face. I could actually feel the Norns spinning their threads. Instead of north, the winds brought me here without my needing a single tack. When I left the English lord, I was of two minds: finish my obligation to Gun and report to Red Hand, or help Lord Hamerton and his daughter, who had given the priest and me shelter. Fate has chosen for me."

"And the lady, does she figure into your decision?"

"I would not lie to you, brother. She is unlike Gun and my Corsican woman, but she has an inner strength about her. I do think about her, but mainly I think of taking revenge on Blood Axe for his role in Red Hand's separating us four years ago."

"What would you have me do?" asked Jan after a moment's hesitation. He looked at the ground. He already knew he would help, but he wanted his older triplet to voice the request.

"You said you had a shipload of wild young Vikings who were restless. I saw, when I rode up, that there were now two longboats at your dock. Would they follow me to fight the Danes of Red Hand and save an English lord? I am not sure what booty will come of it, though if Red Hand is defeated, I will request that your men be offered land on the island."

"Some of them know you, and those who don't have heard stories of you and your fighting luck told many times over winter fires. Bjorn Strongbow is their leader. He is young but has leadership skills. He is also restless and craves to make a name for himself. He will follow you even if I forbid it. Come, I will take you to him."

None of the buildings around the castle proper were large enough to hold the crowd that assembled outside Strongbow's lodge. Jan had not exaggerated either the mood or the eagerness of his men. It took no Thing to discuss Jarl's request. The thirty-eight who crewed the second longboat were joined by fourteen others from Jan's older hands, pledging their loyalty to Jarl. Since the longboat had arrived just two days ago without much to show from their raiding, it took little preparation for either it or the men to be ready. The men pounded their shields with their swords and axes as Jarl explained what was to be done. Most had not unpacked their sea chests. All were as eager as Jarl to leave for the island. Jan laughed at this lustiness as the men prepared their weapons and sea chests.

"If you are successful, brother, I would seek an alliance with the English lord, in case one of my boats should ever need to weather a storm on that coast."

"Done, without saying," said Jarl, grasping his brother's forearm.

"You know I would go with you," said Jan, as Jarl moved toward the rapidly filling longboat. The dragon prow had already been set. Women were packing food and clothes for their men beneath the stern platform as the men carried their sea chests to the longboat.

"And I would have relished having you at my side," said Jarl. "It would be like old times, but Red Hand is still a power, and it would go against his wishes, especially if we joined to defeat Blood Axe, which he specifically forbade. If Blood Axe attacks the English lord, and I happen to be there, Red Hand cannot hold the Falkhands responsible."

"The Norns are for certain weaving your thread, as the wind has even now changed direction. You might need luck with the woman, though, so that I will wish for you," said Jan with a grin, as his brother climbed over the gunnel of the longboat and took his place on the stern platform.

The last of Jan's Vikings climbed into the boat and took up the oars, propelling the vessel downstream with the current toward the saltwater of the channel. As they left the dock, a loud cheer came from the men who were doubling at each oar. It was answered by the crowd that surrounded the dock, women and children, and the remainder of Jan Falkhand's men.

Jan was correct: the wind had veered a hundred and eighty degrees. It had directed Jarl straight to his brother, and now it filled the blue-and-white striped sail, sending them back toward the island, slipping through the small rollers with ease. Even the choppy waves that had pushed him ever faster toward the land of the Franks had abated to a gentle swell from the south. It was unlikely weather for this season. Jan was known for his weather luck, and Jarl wondered if somehow his brother had been able to extend it to his passage.

On the second day at mid-morning, they moved into the mouth of the river, passing the fishing village from which Jarl had stolen his boat. He was happy to see the frame of a new boat already rising on blocks above the high-water mark. The river current was strong, but the men were fresh, having had the ship under sail during the crossing. With the oars double manned, they moved rapidly upstream.

The river narrowed rapidly as they approached the land of Soren the White. Jarl was concerned with what they would find when they came to his dock. Much would be determined by what he discovered there. He became tense, motioning for his men to keep quiet. He'd already instructed them that they might have to turn the boat in the narrowing stream. If he remembered correctly, Soren's encampment was just beyond the next bend in the river. He moved to the bow so as to be the first to see what was ahead.

As the Dane's landing came into view, Jarl almost gave the order to turn the ship. There were four longboats–Soren's two at the dock and two new ships pulled high on the muddy bank. What stopped him from giving the order was the lack of activity on the shore. He saw what he had observed when visiting the previous week. There was no sign of Blood Axe's men, who must have crewed the two new vessels. The best news was that just two of Blood Axe's fleet were in evidence. It meant a hundred men rather than two hundred.

"Keep moving upstream," said Jarl to the man at the steer oar. "Wave to those on shore. They are not our enemy."

They moved quickly out of sight of the settlement into the constricting stream. At the gravel bar, Jarl ordered the men over the side. There was just enough water to float the boat without the weight of the warriors aboard. Across the bar, they climbed back in and in less than a mile came to the pond. As they turned the bow around, Jarl thought he could hear the sounds of battle in the distance, faint, carried on the wind but muffled by the trees. The Vikings took their shields from the gunnels and followed Jarl toward Hamerton's castle.

CHAPTER 36
LONDON, ENGLAND–THE
PRESENT

"Damn English! Damn politicians!" The Florist was beside himself as he read the paper. Every day there was some new development with Brexit. Three times the EU's conditions had been rejected. Still the bitch of a prime minister had kept her job. Twice she had asked for an extension, and now the EU had given her another one. With each development, the timing for his own actions changed. He rose and paced the small room. His arm ached from the knife wound with each movement. All the newspaper and telly accounts focused on the economics of the move, not the migration of Muslims, which he knew was his leader's strategy. They would populate Europe, take over politically, then bring all of Europe under Sharia law. All of this politicking, this changing of sides and selling of one's position for favors, would never happen under the rule of a Faqih. There would be a decision made, and all would follow.

The Florist read the newspaper account again. Now the PM was seeking an alliance with the leader of the Labor Party. The PM, who was a Conservative, had worked for the Bank of England prior to entering politics, cooperating with Labor was unheard of. If she was successful, his target would stay the same. If she was forced to abdicate, as was the rumor last week, then she would live.

Inspector Small was not sure exactly what Scotland Yard's reasons were for requesting that the Frenchman be let in on his investigation, but Gerald Bawkin had made it clear that the man's background could offer a valuable perspective. Small told Guibega that he would consider letting him watch the questioning of the man with the crushed larynx, but he was thinking more of letting him view it from behind the two-way mirror. After seeing the results of his protection of Rigsby, there was no doubt that the man was competent, but he was still French, and no longer a policeman at that. But orders were orders, even if they were framed as a request.

The injured man had been medically cleared for interrogation. His larynx was crushed. There was a possibility that it could be somewhat repaired, but he would probably never be able to speak properly again. The questioning had not gone well, since the man professed that he could neither read nor write and could understand only basic English.

The prisoner shrank back as Ramondo entered the interview room, taking a seat beside Inspector Small. It was the first sign of emotion the inspector had seen.

Small watched Ramondo rather than the prisoner as his aide, Officer Winthrupt, who spoke Farsi, asked the same questions that had been asked the day before. The prisoner, as he had the day before, shook his head and raised the palms of his hands.

"May I try?" asked Ramondo in a low voice that only Small could hear. Receiving a nod, he spoke loudly in Farsi. Taking the notebook from in front of Small, he tore two pages out and wrote YES on one and NO on the other, placing them on the table in front of the prisoner.

"What did you say to him?" asked Small

"I told him I would personally put pig fat in all his meals and smear it on his bed sheets and clothes if he lies," said Ramondo. "If he can't write, which I suspect he can, he can point to the yes or no sheets in front of him."

Without waiting for a comment from Small, Ramondo spoke again in Farsi. The prisoner again shook his head and started to raise his cuffed hands, but before he had taken them above the table, Ramondo leaned across, obscuring the camera's view of the prisoner, and with a flick of his finger hit the man on his Adam's apple, in the center of the bruise on his neck. The man recoiled from the slight touch, croaking and raising his hands to protect himself from another blow. Tears flowed down his cheeks, although Ramondo looked as if he had barely touched the man.

"Hey, hey! We don't do that sort of thing here." Small laid his hand on Ramondo's, but with his head turned away from the recording camera, he smiled.

Ramondo asked his question again in Farsi. This time the man pointed to the paper with YES printed on it.

"Good," said Ramondo. "He is Shiite."

It was more than Small's team had gotten out of the man in two days. Again Small smiled at Ramondo and with a gesture urged him to continue.

"He will answer your questions now," said Ramondo. "He suddenly understands English."

The interrogator switched to English from the Farsi he had been using. Small was pleased, as he could not do the questioning without relying on Winthrupt. He decided he would ask the Frenchman to evaluate his assistant's language abilities at the end of the session. One question after another was posed, his assistant going down a list that had been prepared. All of these questions had been asked before and had gotten no response. Every now and then, the prisoner hesitated, but with only a slight shift in his chair or movement of his hand, Ramondo was able to instigate a response. His eyes opened wide, leaning as far back in his chair as his cuffed hands would allow, the prisoner was in utter fear of the Frenchman.

After Small's assistant had exhausted his page of questions and added a number of his own and Small's, Ramondo again asked for permission to interrogate the man.

Getting approval from Small, Ramondo put down the pen he had been using to record the man's answers. He asked in Farsi, "Have you or your group picked up or made any explosives since you have been in England?"

The man looked relieved as he pointed to "NO."

"Have you obtained any weapons, besides the revolvers you used at the brewery?"

The man hesitated for just a second, glancing at Ramondo's hands before pointing again at "NO."

"You lie," said Ramondo in English. "Inspector, would you please leave me alone with this pig?"

Small could see what the Frenchman was doing. There was no way he was going to leave him alone with the man, but that didn't mean he wouldn't look like he was leaving. "Officer Winthrupt, this has made my throat dry. Let's get some tea." They pushed their chairs away from the table and stood. The prisoner shook his head and threw himself back against his restraints, shaking from side to side. Small and Winthrupt continued toward the door.

"What guns did you get besides the revolvers?" asked Ramondo, pushing a paper and pen toward the prisoner.

The man looked at Ramondo, then at Small, who had turned as he reached the door as if to look at the man one last time. He reached for the knob.

The prisoner let out a croak, then grabbed the paper and wrote something, holding the paper up at Small, who returned to the table, accepted the paper, and read the words scribbled there. He handed it to Ramondo.

"Being with this pig has made me need to use the toilet. Please continue with him, Inspector, now that we know he can write. I'll be back. Tell me if he fails to answer any of your questions, and I will see that he understands what lack of cooperation will bring him." Ramondo got up and left as Small and Winthrupt returned and sat back down.

Ramondo slammed the door to the interrogation room behind him, then went directly to the viewing room, where two officers sat behind a video camera and sound recording equipment. The one-way mirror showed the prisoner scribbling frantically in response to questions posed to him by Small. After every question, the man looked fearfully at the door, as if expecting Ramondo to barge back in. After half an hour, Small was convinced that the man had no more to give.

"What happened to our colleague?" asked Small of his assistant, expecting the answer they had rehearsed before entering the room.

"I suspect he is trying to obtain a warrant that will allow him to bring this man to France," said Winthrupt, watching the prisoner shake his head and again struggle with his restraints. "Do you think it's true, what we heard about his last prisoner?"

"I hope not. Have the sergeant bring this man back to his cell."

After the prisoner was led away, Small and Winthrupt sat down with Ramondo in Small's office.

"Very through interrogation, Inspector Small," said Ramondo, his compliment genuine.

"It was easy once you scared the life out of him. The FIPN must have a fearful reputation among terrorists."

"The ones who do not fear death do fear violating their religious rules before standing before God. I don't know why they wouldn't be afraid of blowing themselves up but be frightened of doing it smeared with pig fat. That was the best good cop, bad cop routine I have ever been part of."

"These two weapons?" asked Small, showing the paper to Ramondo.

"The CheyTac and the McMillan are both long-range sniper rifles. Both are expensive and considered among the best," said Ramondo. "It suggests that this man is part of a group that intends to assassinate someone."

"Gerald Bawkin will not be thrilled to hear what we've learned," said Small to himself.

"The prisoner says he does not know what the guns are for," said Winthrupt, looking at his notes.

"He might not know the target, but he was chosen for the operation," said Ramondo. "He might even be one of the marksmen. Next you should concentrate on where the guns were obtained, from whom, and whether they have scouted any locations."

"You were most helpful. I don't think he would have broken for us. I'll give Inspector Bawkin a call and thank him for suggesting that you join us," said Small, shaking Ramondo's hand. "I will let you know if we obtain any further information, and I ask that you keep us informed as well."

CHAPTER 37
DRY DRAYTON, ENGLAND–THE PRESENT

Ramondo returned to the small cottage in Dry Drayton that he'd rented after his rather eventful first day at the brewery, and he found that Bellino and Nicolo Guibega had already arrived from Ajaccio. Bellino was typical of the Guibega clan, just under six feet tall with broad shoulders and brooding brown eyes, hard focused under dark brows. Nicolo had the same coloring but was slight, even accounting for his youth. At seventeen, he'd not yet found it necessary to shave more than once a week. Even then, it was more to hide an accumulation of fuzz than to remove the dark beard that Bellino shaved every morning.

Protecting Rigsby was to be Bellino's assignment, one that he was more than capable of handling. Nicolo had other talents. He was an expert hacker, a genius of sorts.

"Nicolo, would you be able to locate a phone used at a particular spot in the last week?"

"Probably. I could access the phone company records if I knew the phone number. Then I could give you a record of the calls and where they were made from."

"What if I could give you a partial number?" asked Ramondo. "Could you do it then?"

"Yes. It might take some time, depending on how many digits I had to start with and how much traffic there was in the area."

Ramondo took a small notebook from his back pocket. "I took information from the cell phones of the two men at the brewery before the police arrived. The first five numbers were the same, and the sixth just one off. I think that a number of burner phones were bought at the same time. There is a possibility that the leader who got away had the same sequence, though he has probably discarded the phone by now."

"Let me see," said Nicolo, taking the numbers from Ramondo.

"There's another job as well. Two sniper rifles were bought in Amsterdam and brought to England. That is all I know about them, though I expect that they were bought fairly recently. They're rare, highly specialized weapons. I want to find out everything I can about those guns–who sold them, who bought them, how they got to England, who picked them up, and if possible, where they are now." Ramondo tore a second page from his notebook with "CheyTac and McMillan TAC–50" written on it.

"All right," said Nicolo, seeming more interested in the gun search than in the hacking of the phone service.

"Can you do it?"

"If they are as unique as you say, and either text or email was used, I should be able to find something. I take it that terrorists are at one end?"

"I believe so, yes. Is that important?"

"It helps. They tend to use dead drops and messages in chat rooms. It's cute, but they rely on trying to look normal, without passwords, so once you know the sites, if there's enough content, I can isolate it. The items will probably be found on the Dark Web if they were for sale. Do you think they were bought from the same supplier?"

"I don't know," said Ramondo.

"I only brought my computer, the one I used in Paris. It's pretty good, but I wonder if Mats would let me buy another one. The work will go a lot faster and have less chance of being detected."

"I'm sure he'll approve. Would you need me to drive you to London?"

"That isn't necessary. When we drove in, I saw a sign for Cambridge. That's a university, isn't it?" asked Nicolo.

"Yes. Quite an important one here in Britain."

"I'm sure I can find what I need there."

CHAPTER 38
HAMERTON, ENGLAND–945 AD

Jarl led his men from the pond and their longboats. He moved along a path that followed the bank of the stream, then angled away from the water toward the woods. They would be concealed as they approached Hamerton's castle. As they passed through the glades of oak, the sounds of battle increased, and with them Jarl's anxiety. He'd hoped to arrive before Blood Axe. He might not have enough men to defeat the Danes if he were isolated outside the castle's walls. Jarl noted with interest that he could hear no clash of weapons, the singing chime of metal against metal–only battle yells and the muted sounds of metal against wood. It meant that the walls hadn't yet been breached.

He held his band just inside the tree line and crept forward, separating the branches of a bush to observe the scene in front of him. He could only see the backs of the Danes, halfway from where he was concealed and the walls of the castle. Notching them off in his mind in groups of ten, he estimated ninety to a hundred, all holding their round shields in front of them and shouting insults. There were spaces enough between the men that he could see the changes Lady Bridget had managed in the time he'd been gone, and he felt a sense of pride in what the woman had accomplished. The area before the moat had been completely cleared of brush and was now populated with the bodies of at least eight Danes, all with arrows protruding from their inert forms. Several were crying for help, but none of their comrades seemed to wish to risk their own lives to rescue them.

The Danes had felled a tree and sharpened one end of it, and they were busy tying ropes around it every three feet. Their intent was obvious: to storm the gate, using the tree as a battering ram. Others were fashioning a walkway consisting of lesser trunks bound together to drop across the moat and provide access for the ram.

Jarl couldn't see the moat itself from his position, so he could not ascertain if it had been deepened, but looking at what had been done to the walls and knowing Lady Bridget's efficiency, he suspected it had been done. Likewise, from the heads that occasionally appeared above the walls, he was sure that the walkways had been added as he had suggested. It was quite an accomplishment in the five days he'd been gone.

The noise of men moving to his right prompted him to withdraw further into the trees. The men making the sounds were not attempting to keep their weapons silent or did not know better. Jarl lay on his stomach and inched his way from the protection of the woods. It took only a moment for him to see that another group was hiding in the woods. Jarl's angle was bad, but he could see fifteen, with perhaps a like number behind them, deeper in the trees. There were three in armor who led, giving hand signals to those behind, urging them to crouch and be quiet. Most did not look like warriors, at least not those that Jarl could see. As the men at the rear settled, a figure in full armor moved to the front and raised his visor. Jarl recognized Sir Roger Longtree.

"Lady Bridget had the measure of the man," murmured Jarl as he inched his way back into the brush. "Now the only thing is to find out which side he fights for. I suspect it will be for whichever one is winning."

Seconds later his question was answered as a Dane spoke to Longtree and then left the woods, going to Blood Axe's men, who were preparing to attack the gate. After a short discussion, he turned and made his way back to the woods.

"We stay until they breach the gate!" Jarl heard Longtree yell the command to his three men-at-arms. "Then we add our weight to their attack."

Jarl inched back to his own troop. "Take four archers through the woods and kill the men in armor," whispered Jarl. "There might also be some Danes in the band. Kill them as well but wait until I attack the men who threaten the walls."

Jarl watched his archers move slowly through the woods, first going deeper, then disappearing among the trees as they moved silently toward the other band.

Jarl could tell that his men–Jan's men–were eager. He hoped the four he'd sent to Longtree's band would do as he'd commanded. If they shot too early, before he attacked, Blood Axe's men would be alerted and turn to face them. If they did so while still out of range of the archers at the castle walls, Jarl's men would be outnumbered, with Longtree at their backs.

The ramp and ram had been completed. Half the men picked up the two devices while the rest grabbed shields and held them in front and above those with the ram. Slowly they moved into bow range. Jarl had seen attacks like this before. The men with the bridge would place the front sharpened ends into the ground in front of the moat, then flip it over the ditch. The men with the shields would protect them from the side, while the timbers of the bridge would do the same from the front as they lifted it into a vertical position. Only after it dropped into place would they be vulnerable, but as soon as it fell, the men with the ram would use it to cross the moat. Those Danes who had carried the bridge would then add their brawn to the ram.

Jarl waited until the ram had struck once, the bulk of the Danes crowding behind and waiting to force entry. He motioned his men forward, using hand signals, as he wanted his approach to go unnoticed. He placed his five remaining archers in the front, telling them, probably needlessly, to target the rearmost Danes first. His men would have known, but this was his first action with his brother's warriors, and he could not take anything for granted.

Jarl saw four of the Danes drop, arrows in their backs, followed almost immediately by shouts of alarm from Longtree's men in the woods. A few of the Danes at the bridge turned and were rewarded with arrows to their chests. In all, eight Danes were down. He heard an alarm from the woods and hoped the archers had done their job. He couldn't turn, having to rely on Jan's men to do as he had instructed.

Standing on the castle walls, the archers shot with terrible effectiveness at the unprotected Danes swinging the ram and into the backs of the men who had turned to face Jarl's charge. With a war yell, Jarl led his men at a run across the cleared expanse in front of the moat. His archers still were sending their arrows over their heads toward those still standing beside the ram. The effect was devastating. No more than twenty-five of the original ninety lived to meet them. Those at the ram, deprived of their own shields, ran toward the protection of the forest.

Jarl looked for the brutish form of Blood Axe but could not find him. Instead he saw one man rallying the Danes into a defensive position, having them lock shields in a wall. Unless they were joined by Longtree's band, the maneuver would be fruitless, as Jarl had enough men now to flank the ends. They wouldn't be able to reach the safety of the forest. It would only be a matter of time before they were all killed by the archers.

Jarl strode directly toward the leader. He was a large man, his arms covered by rings of gold and silver, attesting to his fighting ability and wealth. He wielded a sword but had an axe in his belt and a round shield over his left forearm. A question crossed Jarl's mind: was Lady Bridget watching? He trusted his battle luck. The two came together in a crash of wood and metal.

CHAPTER 39
LONDON, ENGLAND–945 AD

Sitting in front of his computer in his safe house, the Florist reflected on the planning sessions that were held in Syria. The Florist was told that there were two main obstacles the politicians would have to overcome in moving Brexit through the vote in the British Parliament. One was obvious–the disruption to trade and tariffs. The second was the movement of people freely across borders. The whole point of the Florist and his team being there was to ensure that the borders were kept open. The British Parliament wanted control of the borders, but they had a major problem in that they couldn't close them without closing the border of Northern Ireland. If that was done, it would almost certainly lead to a resumption of the "Troubles," something neither Britain nor Ireland wanted. Now, if the papers could be believed, the clever Irish had come up with a solution that seemed so logical that even the stupid bitch of a prime minister could sell it to the EU and her own governing body. That done, it was almost certain that Brexit would pass, no matter if she remained in power or not.

The Florist checked the two chatrooms every hour, hoping he would get instructions that would clarify not his objective, but the means of achieving it. He had been so self-satisfied when he was included in the inner circle of planning and strategy. Now he realized that leadership came at a cost. He was being left on his own. His success would mean an advancement; failure might mean his death.

The news told of an upcoming meeting between the Irish representative, John Fitzgibbons, and the member of the British Privy Council. If it resulted in an agreement, it would be hard to stop the vote to leave the EU. If he switched his target to them, there would be chaos, and as had originally been planned, and the radical Irish would be the obvious focus of the investigation. He would have to scout the new location, as the meeting would certainly not be held at Parliament. He knew he could get the location of the meeting with a single phone call. In his mind, it was done. All he had to do was work backward from their deaths to the present.

Checking the two chat rooms again, he left a message about an upcoming wedding being canceled, the flower arrangements no longer needed for the event but sure to be needed in the future. His handlers would know that his plans had changed but the objective would still be met. Putting his computer aside, he called a number from memory.

"Yes." The male voice had no accent. The Florist had spoken to him twice before and had no knowledge as to whether the man was English or Muslim, or how old he was. The only thing the Florist knew about the man was that he was in England, and his superior.

"I am arranging flowers for Pamela and Barry, her Irish friend. Where exactly should I send them, and when will he be arriving?"

"They make a cute couple. I'll let you know." The man hung up.

The Florist's objective was to stop Brexit, not necessarily to kill the prime minister or a royal. His superior would understand the change of target and hopefully approve. If he did, the information he needed would soon be left in the chat room.

CHAPTER 40
DRY DRAYTON, ENGLAND–THE PRESENT

Ramondo looked over Nicki's shoulder as the boy's fingers flew over the keyboard. He'd been at it all morning while Ramondo made breakfast, then lunch. The boy had been overjoyed to find that the house Ramondo had rented had fiber-optic internet service. The FIPN had trained Ramondo in computer use, and he considered himself more than competent, but the boy went far beyond competency. Last night he had taken less than an hour to set up his new computer, adding peripherals and programs that Ramondo had never heard of.

"It wasn't hard to hack into the phone company's database," said Nicolo, not taking his eyes from the screen. "The real trick is to not leave any trace that you were there. Those two numbers you gave me were located just down the road in Dry Drayton, for six days. One of them called a number that had all the digits but the last one in the partial number you gave me. You can be reasonably sure that that was the phone of the leader. It was easy to find out who he had called and who called him."

"Is he still using the phone?"

"No. It's been dead for four days now. Its last location was halfway between Dry Drayton and Cambridge. What's interesting is that when I cross referenced its calls with the three dealers you gave me who could have supplied the rifles, I got a hit for one in Amsterdam. Three calls going both ways. I don't have recordings of the calls, but I think I can get them for you if the Brits' intelligence captured them. It might take a day or so, though."

"Don't," said Ramondo. "The British are very sophisticated with data transfer. They use most of the same software as the Americans. They might detect you."

"We might not need to," said Nicolo. "I came across a police account that the owner of a gun shop in Amsterdam was murdered in a robbery two days after the two guns were sent across. I'm sure it's the same dealer."

"Zut!" murmured Ramondo. "Oh, I forgot to mention that the prisoner said the leader was known as the Florist. Obviously a code name, but it might be useful."

Nicolo's fingers continued flying over the keyboard, navigating through multiple tabs on the flat screen. "I looked into the dead dealers' financial records," said the boy, not stopping his tapping on the keyboard. "It seems the arms dealer keeps two sets of records. One was hidden quite cleverly with a BOT password. It's where he hides his black-market transactions. The guns were placed on a coastal fishing boat, then transferred mid-channel to an English yacht. One of the dealer's men accompanied the shipment to this address." Nicolo clicked on a spot on the screen, and the new printer on the desk spit out a sheet. Ramondo grabbed it.

"A store on the north side of London. Nicki, you are a wonder."

"I couldn't have done it without the partial number you gave me. Would you like me to search for possible targets?"

"How can you do that?"

"Well, there are two guns. You said powerful sniper rifles. Is that correct? It suggests that there are two targets, probably related in some way."

"Do it," said Ramondo. "I'll be back after I talk with the police."

Ramondo called Inspector Small from the brewery. He did not want to disclose the presence of Nicki.

"Inspector, I have some information that might be of value to you and Inspector Bawkin. Can I meet you at the station?"

"I'm in the car. If you are at the Whistling Pig, it will be faster if I meet you there."

"I'm here. I'll wait for you."

They used Rigsby's private office. The brewmaster was with Bellino in the front, showing him the operation as he started a new run of the non-alcoholic offering.

"I was able to call in some favors in Paris," said Ramondo, hoping to offer a bit of a smoke screen to hide Nicki's involvement. "Here is the name of the dealer who supplied the two sniper rifles and the address they were delivered to in London. They came by small boat with a mid-channel transfer. I was only able to get the name of the vessel leaving Amsterdam, not the one that brought them ashore."

Small looked at the paper and raised his eyebrows.

"Oh, and I was able to get the phone the leader used in the transaction, but it would appear to have been destroyed." Another slip of paper was passed to the inspector.

"How sure are you of this information?"

"Reasonably sure, but it would be good if you checked. The delivery was made to a store." Ramondo passed another paper to Small. "I haven't had time to do much research on it. I would appreciate your sharing information with me, too, as it might save time if we were covering the same ground."

"If this is as good as it looks, I'll see what I can do," answered Inspector Small, half meaning it. The information on the two slips of paper went beyond what his own men had been able to come up with. If the same was true with Bawkin and Scotland Yard, he would get a few feathers in his cap for letting them know.

On the way out, Ramondo introduced the inspector to Bellino.

"Bellino will be splitting Mr. Rigsby's safety and the brewery's security with me. He is licensed to carry a firearm, as am I, but I seriously doubt that he'll have to use it," said Ramondo as they exited the building.

Ramondo was not about to tell the inspector about the conversations Mats and Katherine had had with MI6. Let him wonder. So much the better if he thought there were even higher levels involved. It might make sharing information more palatable to him.

CHAPTER 41
HAMERTON, ENGLAND–945 AD

Jarl was taller than the average Norseman. In the years he had spent as captain of the Varangian Guard in Miklagard, he'd been a full head taller than the soldiers of the vizier. His many training sessions in protecting the emperor had been instructive for facing the quicker fighting style of those southern warriors. The Varangians, being exclusively Norse, would normally win with their sheer size and brute strength, but that didn't mean there was nothing to learn from their opponents.

The leader of the Danes who now approached Jarl was much larger than he was–not as large as Lars, who had built the Dancing Horse, the ship that he had sailed from Corsica, but still a full hand taller than Jarl stood. In Miklagard, Jarl had adopted a slightly longer blade, along with many of the southerners' techniques. He had paid a smith in Miklagard to fashion a sword in the Viking style, but slightly longer and lighter in the blade to maintain its balance. It was forged in the blue veined steel that held an edge and would never break. In facing the Dane, it gave Jarl an additional reach that countered the man's longer arms.

The Dane separated himself from the shield wall behind him, recognizing Jarl as the leader of those attacking his band. As he approached, he swung his sword overhead in a great arc, hoping to shatter Jarl's shield with a single blow. Instead, the blade met Jarl's sword with a clang of steel that sounded above all the other sounds of battle. Jarl felt the power behind the Dane's blow and flexed his knees to absorb the shock. A spark flew from their weapons, and the second they disengaged, Jarl noticed a large chip in the Dane's blade, as well as a slight bend. He assumed the fighting stance he had learned from the smaller southerners. Instead of trying to stand tall to match the height of the Norsemen, the southerners crouched low, taking advantage of the smaller round shields used by Jarl's men. They went after the legs of the Varangians with swift cuts and thrusts of their longer, lighter weapons. It had taken several wounded men to devise a defense against this tactic, but once practiced and perfected, no further injuries had been sustained by his men.

The Dane was not so schooled, and Jarl's first thrust cut deep into his calf. The Dane's second overhead blow lacked the power of the first, further bending his blade against the blue steel of Jarl's sword. Jarl feinted at the man's unprotected legs, and the man's shield dropped. Jarl reversed his lighter weapon and swung parallel to the ground, just above the rim of the lowered shield. The Dane's bent sword only slightly deflected Jarl's, and it cut deeply into the shoulder that held the shield. It was not a fight where the outcome was in doubt. The Dane's men watched from the shield wall as Jarl thrust the tip of his sword into the exposed throat of their leader, separating the links of mail and allowing the spurt of blood to rise as high as the man's helmeted head as he sank to his knees and died.

The archers on the wall kept launching arrows into the backs of the men who now clashed with Jan's young band of warriors. In less than a minute, the Danes drew back and threw down their weapons in surrender, keeping their shields raised against the threat of more arrows from the walls.

"Give them quarter!" yelled Jarl over the cries of the Danes.

From behind him, Jarl heard yells and saw Longtree's band running from the woods toward his men. It took a moment for him to understand that they were not attacking but rather fleeing the woods and his five archers. A single command and half his men turned to face the oncoming group. Confronted with Norsemen from the front and arrows from behind, Longtree's men dropped their weapons and knelt in surrender.

Jarl looked from front to back, afraid the two groups that had surrendered would realize that they greatly outnumbered his forty men. He was about to shout another order when the gates of the castle opened and twenty men, led by Lord Hamerton, poured out and over the lowered drawbridge. At the same time, his archers from the woods came out, their bows at the ready, two of them dragging the armored form of Sir Roger Longtree.

Jarl gave orders to disarm Longtree's men, then went to Hamerton as the old man raised the faceplate on his helmet.

"Well done, Lord Falkhand," said Hamerton. "We were holding our own but could not have prevented them from storming the gate if their ram had been given another hour. Your arrival was timely."

"The repairs to your moat and the height of your walls bought you time," said Jarl, now able to see the full extent of the repairs to the ditch. Just above the surface of the water were the tips of sharpened stakes.

From the open gate, unseen by Jarl, Lady Bridget ran out, dressed in a hunting outfit that did little to disguise the fact that she was a woman. He felt movement and began to turn his shield as she hit him from the side, throwing her arms around him and kissing him on the cheek.

"M' lady!" was all that he could muster before forgetting the English he had learned and reverting to his native Norse.

Jarl's men stripped the dead Danes of their weapons, arm rings, and purses, then relieved the living of the same. The Danes had been raiding the southern coast for four months and were rich with plunder, which now filled the purses of Jan's young band. Jarl was certain there would be more in the chests aboard their longboats at Soren the White's docks.

As soon as the remaining Danes were constrained, Jarl had four of his men mount Longtree's horses, sending them after those who had run. He suspected the Danes would try to make their way east to Soren's protection. Lord Hamerton lent his gamekeeper and several of his poachers-turned- archers to guide the Norsemen. Just before they left, Jarl took Bjorn Strongbow aside and gave him a message for Soren the White.

"After you overtake the Danes, go to Soren. Tell him that I value his friendship and that both Jarl and Jan Falkhand are allied with Lord Hamerton. I will come to him soon. We'll assist him with Blood Axe if there is any trouble. Lord Hamerton wishes to live at peace with Soren and knows that this attack was not his doing."

"Will he let us take the ships we passed?"

"I believe he will, but before you bring them upriver, give him a third of the treasure they contain."

Bjorn looked at Jarl, questioning the command.

"The offer will help ensure his friendship to us and Lord Hamerton. Also, it will put him at odds with Blood Axe in the future."

Bjorn jumped on the gray stallion Longtree had ridden and followed the guides out of the gate. Jarl had Longtree dragged into the courtyard. The archers had done more than Jarl had asked of them. As soon as Jarl had attacked, the three armored men-at-arms had been shot through their necks. Four Danes had also received two shafts each, and an arrow had found a small opening in Sir Roger's plate and was embedded high in the man's thigh. Without leadership, the rest of the band, composed mostly of serfs, sought refuge further in the trees, where the archers took them before they ran forward and surrendered.

"What is this outrage?" yelled Sir Roger as he was placed in front of Lord Hamerton, who stood next to Jarl. "I come to your aid, and I am attacked?"

"You came to our aid?" asked Lord Hamerton, looking at Jarl.

Jarl smiled, seeing the disbelieving look of disgust on Lady Bridget's face, then stepped forward.

"An outrage!" yelled Sir Roger again as he recognized the priest's acolyte.

"You lie." Jarl's words came softly. "I heard you order your men to attack with the Danes as soon as they had forced the gate."

"You are mistaken. I said no such thing."

Jarl reached behind him, and taking his axe, tapped Longtree on the back of the head. The man went down on his face, unconscious. Lord Hamerton's aged eyes looked at Jarl, forming a question.

"He lies. Others heard his words as well. His men will confirm it. Keep him restrained and without weapons until this understanding with Soren the White is completed. Then we can discuss his fate."

CHAPTER 42
DRY DRAYTON, ENGLAND–THE PRESENT

For Brian, work on the journal was exciting. Back in the hotel room after his workout, he couldn't wait to begin translating the Greek. This morning's workout with Rodney and Sensei Hioshida had stretched an extra hour. Tired beyond belief, Brian had decided to shower at the hotel. He spent fifteen minutes under the water– five minutes washing the sweat and salt off, and ten letting the hot, pulsating stream of water massage the muscles of his back and arms. It was still before three, and they wouldn't start translating until after supper, but he had the impatience of youth. Ordering a sandwich and milk from room service, he sat down at Mats' computer.

He opened the file on the secure computer. He had almost completed a rough translation of the first Greek section when his food arrived. His hunger overcame his curiosity, forcing him to put his efforts on hold. Sitting down on the couch, he turned on the TV to the AT&T Byron Nelson golf tournament, which was in its second round in Texas. His stomach, full of sandwich and milk, combined with the soft tones of the television announcers to soothe him to sleep.

Suzanne and Mats came back to the suite before dinner and found Brian sitting on the couch, his mouth open, sleeping. They soon saw that his nap hadn't blunted any of his enthusiasm for translating Greek. He rose from the couch, surprised at the stiffness in his shoulder and left hip. Exercise had never left him stiff before, but he'd never had a workout like the one he'd experienced that morning.

"I'm glad you guys are back," he said. "I couldn't wait. I translated the next section of Greek. Jarl returns with a boat full of men, but I don't know where he got them. They attack and beat the Danes of Blood Axe, who are attacking Lord Hamerton. Longtree also has a band of warriors, but I don't know what's happening with them. Could we translate first–fill in the sections around the Greek I've already translated–and then go to dinner?"

Suzanne smiled and Mats laughed; Brian looked dismayed. "I think we can wait until after we shower and eat," said Mats, reaching giving Brian's shoulder a rub. "After all, things haven't changed in nine hundred years, and they're not likely to change if we wait a few more hours."

Brian winced at Mats' touch.

"Are you all right?"

"Yeah, I didn't tap out quite fast enough on a technique Rodney and I had just been taught. I'll know better next time. I'm just a little stiff."

"Let's take a quick shower. There's an Italian restaurant around the corner that will feed us faster than the hotel's dining room. Will that suit you?"

"Brilliant. I can't wait to find out where Jarl gets his Vikings and what he does to Longtree."

"Okay, get to your room and let us get ready. We'll knock in about fifteen minutes," said Mats. Suzanne was still smiling at the boy's impatience.

The meal was served promptly, as Mats had promised. As Mats paid the bill, Brian sprinted the block back to the hotel. When they got to their suite, they found that Brian had already spread his translation out on the table next to the computer and had printed out both Suzanne's and Mats' sections, double-spaced and enlarged to notebook size. It was Suzanne's translation that had Jarl leaving Soren the White's holding and stealing the fisherman's boat, but Mats' section provided the information about the arbitrary winds and Jarl's belief that it was the Norns who were weaving their web and sending him directly back to his brother. A short section in which Norse, Greek, and Old English alternated almost every paragraph brought Jarl and his band of Vikings back past Soren to Lord Hamerton's lands, where Brian took up the translation he'd already completed.

"We only have a quarter of the journal left," said Brian. "We could finish it tonight."

"Probably not," said Mats, scrolling through the remaining pages on the computer. "It looks like the rest of the pages are mostly Old English, with small sections of Latin between them. I see only two short parts in Greek. That means Suzanne will have to translate the majority of it. There's no way she can do that much in one sitting."

"Aw, I'm sorry, Suzanne. I'm just excited to finish the story."

"I'm curious as well, Brian," said Suzanne. "Why don't I finish one section more and teach you what I'm doing and how to use the reference text? With your knowledge of Gaelic, it should be easier for you than for Mats."

Brian brightened, and the two of them started the translation. The next morning was Saturday, and they had much to tell Margaret, Rodney, and Katherine about their shared heritage.

CHAPTER 43
DRY DRAYTON, ENGLAND–THE PRESENT

Ramondo was discussing the significance of the two sniper rifles and the possibility that the prime minister might be one of the targets with Inspector Small. Small had already contacted Gerald Bawkin, but Ramondo had not been privy to that conversation. Rigsby was making enough noise out on the brewery floor that Ramondo felt his cell phone's vibration before he heard its soft ring.

"Sir!" Nicolo's voice sounded excited. Ramondo looked at Small, and with a shrug of his shoulders, excused himself, leaving Rigsby's office.

"Yes, Nicolo," he answered, knowing the boy would not have called without having some important information.

"I have two possible targets, and there are other things I don't want to say over the phone."

"Stay put. I'll be there in twenty minutes."

"Something important?" asked Inspector Small as Ramondo reentered the brewery's small office.

"I might have more information for you. It's being checked now. How long will it take for you to verify the information I've already given you?"

"We should have something by this evening," said Small.

"I'll be in touch then," said Ramondo. He went out to the brewery floor and spoke to Bellino. He saw Small watching him from the back, obviously wishing that he had shared what he'd been told on the phone.

Nicolo was at his desk, hunched over his computers, headphones on. He hadn't heard Ramondo come in the front door. Ramondo touched him lightly on the shoulder. The boy flinched.

"Sorry," said Ramondo, sitting down next to the boy. "You sounded excited."

Nicolo held up a finger as he typed furiously on the keyboard of the new computer. Ramondo looked at the screen and saw a string of numbers and figures separated by occasional words. Nicolo's typing paused as he used the keyboard to issue several commands; there was a period of stillness, the boy in deep concentration. He took a deep breath and removed his headphones.

"Sorry. I just wanted to make sure of something." Nicolo tapped a key, and the printer to his right began making grunting noises.

"I gave the police the phone number and the gun information, including the Albanian store location," said Ramondo. "They're checking on it now. I take it you have something more."

Nicolo smiled, which made him look younger than his seventeen years. "Lots, but I may have made a mistake."

"Always the good news first, unless we're at risk," said Ramondo, putting a hand on the boy's shoulder.

"This is the leader's new phone number and two local burn phones he's called."

"Great! You'll have to tell me how you did this."

"I might also have your targets, or at least two who are very likely. I can't guess the locations of the hits, but the police should be able to supply those."

"Fantastic. And the bad news?"

"I think I screwed up and was discovered accessing the FIN database. I know you warned me, but I still thought I could hack it. I think they detected my presence. If they did, they could trace my computer's location. We should dump it and the printer in some lake just to be safe."

Ramondo didn't bother to ask why. He was already working out the logistics of buying new units, this time in London, in case they could track the computer's signature to the place of purchase.

"Okay. Do you have to copy anything before we dump it?"

"Already done," said Nicki, holding up a small external drive. "It would be best if we changed hotels too."

It took less than five minutes to pack their clothes and the computer in the car. It took an hour and a half to travel sixty-five miles to Grays, just off the eastern aspect of London and hard against the northern bank of the Thames, but only a minute to dump the computer and printer into the outgoing tide of the river after wiping them clean. The drive south gave them the opportunity to call Bellino, whom they told to rent a new apartment and not to return to the old one. Nicki was also able to explain his theory of where the sniper rifles might be used.

"When you said that having two rifles most likely meant there were two targets, it actually made things easier. I put a flag on any announcement of individuals who might make a difference for Brexit. At first I thought the prime minister would have to be one, but she might be stepping down and it didn't make sense. Then I saw a communique that the president of the United States was coming, a natural target, except for the security that goes with him. Unlikely that any assassin would be allowed to get a shot off, let alone two. And then this showed up in the *Times*."

Nicolo handed Ramondo a press release from the previous day. It read, *A representative from Ireland with the power to negotiate is meeting with the head of Labor.* "They hope to come to an understanding about the border crossing between Ireland and Northern Ireland, independent of Brexit. Both of them are determined to make a show of it. You said that border was a real hang-up for the PM." Nicolo handed Ramondo another paper. Ramondo glanced at it before turning his attention back to the road.

"The other possibility is weaker," said Nicki. "That's a report that a representative of the EU is coming to London if the PM steps down. It's unknown at this time exactly who he'll meet with. At least the papers don't seem to know, which doesn't stop them from speculating. That leads me to believe it will be done with secrecy, meaning less chance of catching the two outside."

"Nicki, you're amazing. I don't know if you're right, but it makes as much sense as anything the police have come up with. I'll call Inspector Small. Now, let's get you a new computer."

CHAPTER 44
LONDON, ENGLAND–THE PRESENT

Waiting for their meeting with Katherine was hard on Brian. He was virtually bursting with what they had learned from the journal.

The meeting was set for 7:30 AM. Katherine had come in early to cook breakfast for the group. They arrived to a huge platter of scrambled eggs, fried tomatoes, mushrooms, and bacon, with sticky buns from a nearby bakery. Rodney had his briefcase and a small carry-on packed and set against the wall.

"There's been a change in plans. The president is coming in this morning," said Rodney. "I'm to meet him at the airport and stay with him for the duration of his stay."

Mats watched Brian shovel in his second helping of eggs and said, "I think Brian should tell the tale, as he pushed the translation forward."

Brian swallowed what was in his mouth, took a swig of orange juice, and began. "You remember that Lord Hamerton was going to be attacked by a bunch of Danes, and Jarl had left." His voice rose in pitch. "Well, as soon as Jarl stole the fishing boat, the wind changed and took him straight back to his brother." It escaped him that everyone was as much entertained by his eagerness as by the story itself. "He brought a longboat full of his brother's men back from France and attacked the Danes as they were storming the walls of Hamerton."

Brian related the details of the battle and the aftermath, finally taking a deep breath and concluding with the imprisonment of Sir Roger Longtree.

"Brian, you will continue in the long-standing tradition of great Irish storytellers," said Margaret, the first words she had spoken all morning. "How much of the journal is still left to translate?"

"We probably have only one more session," said Suzanne, getting an enthusiastic nod from Brian.

Mats' phone vibrated, his screen showing Ramondo's name.

"You won't be able to use that in this room," said Katherine. "It prevents the use of all sound devices, except for the notice of incoming calls."

Mats excused himself and stepped out of the room.

"Our boy Nicki is a wonder!" Ramondo gave Mats the new information concerning the phones and the possible targets for the snipers in short bursts of sentences. "We should be careful to keep the boy's name out of it. He did some serious hacking. I've told Inspector Small that I got the information from my contacts in France. With the U.S. president coming in tomorrow, I think Bawkin is invested in finding the two rifles and, more importantly, the shooters."

"Undoubtedly! But there's been a change in plans on that score. It seems the president is arriving today. Keep that quiet, though. I'm not sure if it's known yet. Keep me informed of your situation." Mats clicked off and reentered the conference room.

"That was Ramondo. He thinks he's discovered the possible targets of the two snipers. He's spoken to the police."

"The president's security detail came in yesterday. I'm to meet POTUS at the airport. He has speeches for me to work on. He thinks I have a special feel for the English people," said Rodney, smiling at Katherine. "I'm sure Bawkin will inform them of the threat, but I'll warn the Secret Service as well."

"From what Ramondo said, I don't think it's the president they're after, but he is too tempting a target to ignore completely."

"Ramondo can't be sure, can he?" Rodney stood, grabbed his bag, phone, and computer, and went to the door. "Katherine, would you take me to the airport … now?"

"Let me drive you," said Mats. "You and I have things to discuss." Katherine nodded, giving her assent to her husband. "I'll take Suzanne back to the hotel. It will give us some girl time together. I take it Brian is still going to work out. I'll give him some money. He can take a taxi back from the dojo."

Mats exited the private lot behind Katherine's offices in his rental car, while Rodney turned in the passenger's seat, placing his duffel bag in the back seat along with another case, which looked like it might hold a collapsible pool cue. For some reason, it made Mats think of the axe that was still in the trunk of the car. He'd bought it after the attempt on Rigsby's life. He could not carry a gun in Britain, but he would not be without a weapon.

"You probably know the way as well as the GPS, so just tell me where to turn," he said to Rodney.

"Why is it you wanted to drive me?" asked Rodney, looking at Mats across the center console.

"I wanted to talk to you about what we call 'the Gift–Regalo' in my family." Mats took a deep breath. He'd been warned not to discuss the "Gift" with anyone, not even the Guibega. He hoped he was doing the right thing. "I am guessing you have a version of it as well and have been warned of the need to keep it hidden from outsiders."

"From what you've said about the journals you've translated, I suspect you think our abilities are related," said Rodney.

"Exactly," said Mats. "But not only our abilities. It's something I've been unable to discuss completely with either my Guibega helpers or Suzanne. But I think we will find that we are related genetically through Jarl Falkhand when we finish translating the journal we're working on."

"And you believe it is trying to tell us something we should apply to our present situation?" asked Rodney.

"Yes," said Mats, risking a quick look at Stoner in the passenger seat.

"It's something I thought about when the journal was discovered in the church," said Rodney, fingering the outline of the glovebox on the dashboard. "I was forewarned of danger to Katherine by a journal that Margaret gave me. She insisted I take an antique knife with me back to Washington. It had been in the family for hundreds of years. At the time I thought it was an unusual request. It was that knife that I used to kill the man who threatened Katherine."

Mats almost swerved out of his lane. "Three years ago in France, I killed a man with an ancient sword that had belonged to my ancestor. I too was warned by my journal and by dreams. It seems we have more in common than we could have imagined."

"Are you getting any warnings now?" asked Rodney as they neared the offramp for the airport.

"No. Are you?"

"No, but I haven't read a journal in a while. In the past, though, I've felt compelled to if there was a need."

"I suspect the bringing together of our two families was enough. That, and the translation of the journal from the church. Will you be riding with the president from the airport?"

"I don't know yet," said Rodney. "It depends on how prepared he feels for the visit."

Mats had not been directed to Heathrow but to Northolt, a short drive northwest of London. He saw the first of the airport signs on the overhead lane display. It was just after 9 AM. They had eight more kilometers.

CHAPTER 45
LONDON, ENGLAND–945 AD

Sitting on his sofa in the safe house, the Florist confirmed the new targets with his superiors through a private chat room. It was not stated, but he could tell by an unnecessary comment or two that they were pleased with his selection of new targets. He also knew that their approval would change in an instant if he failed. His status would be greatly diminished—he could even lose his life. Because of his foiled attempt at killing the brewery owner, to remain in England was impossible. He was sure that Abdul was dead, and probably Hasan too, but either way, they knew nothing of the plan–only that it involved a murder. They didn't even know his real name.

He closed his computer and called his remaining two men, telling them to meet him at the restaurant at noon.

"We'll strike in three days," said the Florist, sipping his tea. They had taken a table against the far wall but were not conspicuously separated from the other diners. All had ordered soup and sandwiches, which they ate as they casually discussed murder—just three friends having a quiet lunch together.

"It will coincide with the American president's visit, which is good, as most eyes will be on him and the royals.

Our targets are meeting in a manor house just outside London. Because of the president's arrival, most security will be drawn away for him, but it will make it more difficult for us to leave the country. We'll leave by boat to Ireland, then return home. I need you to buy different clothes– casual pants, polo shirts, pull-over sweaters. Brown or green. Avoid bright colors," he added, he hoped unnecessarily. "Oh, and buy a small spade, the kind the military use."

"How will we transport the guns? The CheyTac is particularly big and heavy," said Bashar.

"We might not have to. I'll have an answer after I scout the location. I'll know more this afternoon. We will meet here tomorrow, but one hour later." The Florist took the last bite of his sandwich and stood up, putting enough money on the table to cover all three lunches and a moderate tip–not big enough to make the waitress take notice or small enough to make her mad.

It took forty minutes to drive from the restaurant to the site where the meeting would take place. He assessed the situation. The city gave elevations and sight lines from numerous structures. The area was made up of rolling hills, open with scattered trees, houses, and a small village well over a mile in the distance. The manor house where the meeting would take place had a formal garden in front, mowed grass, and a clinker driveway and paths. On one corner was an outbuilding, probably for the equipment of the staff who took care of the grounds. The Florist felt sure that it would be used by security.

He drove past, parked the car in the village, bought an ice cream bar at a creamery, and then walked back down the other side of the road past the house. He picked up a plastic bag he found discarded by the roadside and began picking up other trash, which gave him time to observe the front entrance to the house and driveway. Just out of sight of the house, there was a fence with a gate. On the other side of the fence, in the direction of the house, was a stand of trees, beyond which was what looked like an open field. The trees ended in a slight hill. The lock on the gate was unhinged. He went through it and up the small hill. It was perfect. The elevation gave an unobstructed view of the front of the house, about half a mile away. He had started to leave when he heard a sound, followed by a voice from the field behind him, and saw two men walk by some hundred yards away.

The Florist saw them stop, one man obscuring the other, and then heard a metallic sound and the nearer man shouting "Fore!" What he had taken for a field was a golf course. If there was a fence on the other side, he had his escape route, as well as the perfect way to conceal the weapons. Staying perfectly still, he waited until they had passed, then entered the woods, finding a large oak that would provide excellent cover for a shooter. In his mind, he had made his plan. He would need bolt cutters, in case the gate was locked, but he had his plan.

He walked back to his car and drove around the golf course to the other side of the hole where he had seen the men playing. It took longer than he expected; the club, Frilford Heath, consisted of three separate courses. There was a fence but no gate. It didn't matter. Bolt cutters would open a way out for his men. It would also take considerably longer for anyone to reach that point in a car. His men would only have to cross the fairway. They would be gone long before security could reach them.

It took him five minutes less to return to his apartment than it had taken to arrive at the killing site. He slept soundly that night.

The next afternoon, he again met with his team. He brought with him a pencil drawing of the manor house, road, and adjacent golf course.

"You are to put on the clothes I had you buy yesterday. They will be your camouflage. You will also buy two golf bags. Get them at a pawn shop or secondhand store. They should have a rain cover to go over the clubs. That will hide the guns."

The waitress brought lunch. After she was gone, the Florist placed his drawing on the table in front of his men.

"There is a gate here." He pointed to a break in the fence next to the road. "It is out of sight of the house. I'll drop you off just before dawn. After you go through the gate, secure it with this lock, then take your positions—Bashar, you on the hill, and Habib you in the tree. After you take your shots, walk across the course with your weapons in the golf bag. There's a fence but no gate. I will have snipped the wire and tied a red cloth at the break. There's a road just beyond the fence. I'll pick you up there. There is no chance of them getting to you from the house before I pick you up. I've been instructed to hide the weapons before we leave England. They can be used again."

CHAPTER 46
HAMERTON, ENGLAND–945

Jarl rode out of Hamerton's castle on horseback. He turned east, following a well-worn trail toward Soren the White's land. He arrived at Soren's gate before Bjorn Strongbow, who had gone after the last of the fleeing Danes. Arriving in his mail, he took off his helmet and was recognized as Erik Karlsson by the guard at the gate. It was the name he had given Soren weeks earlier. The gate opened for him.

Soren the White was coming out of his hall, still fastening his baldric, his sword sheathed. Jarl briefly worried that he should have waited for Bjorn, in case Soren was really allied with Blood Axe in the attack on Hamerton. A quick glance told Jarl that the warriors he'd seen on his first visit were still in the keep. Soren had not seemed like a man who would prove false, and the presence of so many guards suggested he was true to his word.

"Erik Karlsson, you seem to have risen in the world," said Soren by way of greeting as Jarl dismounted.

"I would have words with you in private," said Jarl, dismounting and giving his weapon to the man who grabbed the reins.

"Come then," said Soren, turning and moving inside his hall, followed by two guards.

"My true name is Jarl Falkhand," said Jarl as soon as they were seated. "It pained me to tell you false, but it was necessary, as Blood Axe is an enemy of my family, and I couldn't risk him finding out that I was here."

"I've heard the saga, as have my men," said Soren. "Knowing Blood Axe, I find it difficult to believe. I'd heard you were in Miklagard."

The two guards who had followed him into the hall unsheathed their swords.

"I was returning home to tell Red Hand about the death of his daughter, my wife, and the revenge I took on the man who killed her. I was blown off course with the priest to this land many days south of here. We traveled north, hoping to find passage to Red Hand. I killed four Danes who had captured Hamerton's daughter. The rest you know."

"And your use of black magic that is told in the saga?" asked Soren, tension tightening his words.

"Six years ago, I joined Blood Axe for a raid on the coast two days' sail north of here. As we were about to go ashore, I saw great numbers of warriors protecting the walls of the town. I told Blood Axe and suggested that if we quickly sailed to the town to the north, we would arrive before the men could return by land. He would not listen, so I left and sacked the town to the north. Blood Axe was repulsed and blamed me for his failure, sending skalds to sing his false saga. Four years ago, my brothers and I separated because of the distrust sewn by his lies. There has been no talk of dark magic since–just our victories. I've heard the tale of how you became 'the White.' You should well know the power of men's superstitions."

Soren chuckled, breaking the tension that had been present since Falkhand had given his real name. "I've not seen Blood Axe for two years. He sends his ship master, whom you must have seen at Hamerton's. He's a giant."

"I fought him. He is dead. What I need to know is whether you have any loyalty to Blood Axe."

"None, but I fear his strength. I have enough men to be secure from the English, but not from his numbers."

"Those who came in the longboats at your dock have been defeated," said Jarl, his tone accusing. "And Longtree captured. Most of Blood Axe's Danes are dead. A few ran and are being pursued by my own men. I think they will try to use their longboats to escape."

"I couldn't deny their landing. I refused my men. I'd told Blood Axe's man that months ago," said Soren quickly. "Blood Axe is likely to blame his defeat on my refusal."

"I regret that you have become part of this feud between Blood Axe and my family. I offer you alliances with my brother Jan, Hamerton, and perhaps Red Hand, should Blood Axe attack you." He left unsaid the threat that it would be held against him if Soren played him false.

"I would greatly appreciate such an alliance," said Soren. Then, trying to change the subject, he said, "Longtree! I wondered which of the two neighbor lords would betray Hamerton. Blood Axe did not trust me with the name. The dragon ship that went past us—they were your men?"

"They fought with me, but they are my brother's men. The Norns weave a strange pattern. I left here to seek Red Hand's assistance, but the winds blew me straight to my brother in the land of the Franks. He gave me one of his ships and crew."

Two women arrived with great horns of brown ale. Jarl had not eaten since he'd left the sea, and he downed the measure in three gulps. The younger of the two servers was quick to refill his horn.

"You say you married Red Hand's daughter?" asked Soren, extending his horn to be refilled as well.

"Yes. But last year she was murdered by the vizier of Miklagard. I was sailing back to tell Red Hand of her death."

"Tell me of the battle at Lord Hamerton's," said Soren.

Jarl was about to begin when there was a commotion in the yard. Both Jarl and Soren jumped to their feet, running to the door.

Four Danes were in the courtyard, surrounded by three horsemen. Other Norsemen on foot were being held outside the gate.

"Hold!" shouted Soren. At his command, the men on horseback stopped, directing spears at the four, one of whom was on his knees, holding his side.

"Lord Soren, we were attacked by an overwhelming force," cried one of the Danes, who was still standing.

Jarl stepped to Soren's side. "I led the defenders at Lord Hamerton's. You were not outnumbered, but you ran. Where are the rest of the cowards, Bjorn Strongbow?"

The central of the three horsemen dismounted. "These are all who are left, Jarl. The rest did not run as fast."

"Bring them inside," said Soren, motioning to the guards who had filled the courtyard. "And close the gate!"

"You were about to tell me of the fight," said Soren when all were in the hall.

"You saw our ship come by on the way upriver," Jarl began. "We rowed all the way to the small pond and went overland to Hamerton's castle. Blood Axe's men were already attacking the walls but had not breached them. They were caught between Hamerton's archers on the walls and my men. These men and about a dozen others ran, leaving their fellows to face us alone."

"And Longtree?"

"His men surrendered, and he was taken. The Danes who were with him are dead."

"What will happen to him?"

"That will be up to Lord Hamerton," said Jarl. "For now, he is locked up."

"Who is this man whom you believe over Blood Axe's men?" asked one of the Danes in a disrespectful voice, turning Soren's head.

"I am Jarl Falkhand," said Jarl, taking a step toward the Dane. Soren restrained him, placing a hand on his shoulder.

The Dane stepped back, cringing against his fellows. "Falkhand," he said. "How?"

The man beside him yelled, "Lord Soren, we ask for your protection!"

Soren walked to the three men. "What happened to the fourth man?" he asked the guard.

"He was bleeding. We didn't think you wanted him in your hall. We saw to his wound as best we could. He won't last till morn."

"These three have my protection. They will not leave these walls until I say or until Blood Axe comes for them.

Falkhand, you will honor my word. You and your men will leave my land. Take these men to quarters and feed them."

When the room cleared, Soren turned to Jarl. "I would rather avoid making an enemy of Blood Axe." He motioned to where the men had been led away. "He has many more men than I have. I have no wish to become the object of his wrath. I will return these three to him, with the information that I had no part in the fighting."

"I understand, but know that if he does attack you, you have my pledge of support. I would not treat further with Blood Axe." Jarl watched Soren. His broad face showed that he understood the threat. As much as he feared Blood Axe, the Falkhands' reputation, even without the use of dark magic, was more fearsome.

Jarl rode out of Soren the White's gates with Bjorn, joining the rest of his band of fifteen. They had killed thirteen of the Danes who had fled. They skirted the approaches to Lord Hamerton's castle and rode to the west, picking up the footprints of the men Longtree had led to aid the Danes.

An hour's travel brought them to a fine-looking stone castle with towers at the four corners of the wall protecting it. As they approached, they raised their weapons and shouted of victory in the Danish tongue. Those inside could not tell Danes from Norsemen, and the gate swung up. They rode unchallenged into the keep, with Jarl at their head. There were few inside the walls, barely enough to raise the gate. Jarl had two of his men stay on either side of the entry and rode toward the main keep, where a richly dressed man was descending a short flight of stone stairs.

"You were successful, then. Did the old fool Hamerton have the sense to die in the battle?" asked the man. "When will Lord Longtree be returning?"

"Who are you, sir?" asked Jarl.

"I am Roger Hornsby, the Lord's chamberlain. I am in command here until Lord Longtree returns. Did he get the wench?"

"It would be more accurate to say that the wench got him," said Jarl, dismounting and moving to the man before he could duck inside. "Your master is captured. The Danes are defeated, and now your castle is taken."

Jarl's men quickly overpowered the few guards who were left. Hornsby protested until Jarl brought the side of his axe down hard on his shoulder. Hornsby sank to his knees and would have gone to the ground but for Jarl grabbing his hair, keeping him on his knees.

"I am Lord Jarl Falkhand," announced Jarl, dragging the chamberlain by the hair into the open area where his men had herded the few men left behind by Longtree. "I've assisted Lord Hamerton in defeating the Danes of Blood Axe and taken Longtree's men as prisoners. I am now the lord of this manor. I'll leave my men here to instruct you in your duties, and to keep the peace."

Jarl threw the whimpering Hornsby toward Bjorn Strongbow. "Lock this one up. I will deal with him when I return." He strode to his charger, swinging easily onto his back despite the weight of his mail. As he rode out, the gates closed behind him.

CHAPTER 47
OXFORD, ENGLAND–THE PRESENT

Ramondo sat across from Nicki at a 24-hour Happy Chef roadside stop. It was dark. There was little traffic on the highway. They were waiting for Bellino to join them.

"It's not that I can't locate their phones," Nicolo was explaining. "I can, but I'm positive I was detected the last time I broke into the system. If I break in again, they'll know it, and they'll know the phones I'm tracking."

"And they could locate you?" asked Ramondo.

"Yes."

"What time is the meeting of the minister with the Irish ambassador planned?"

"That I can tell you. One in the afternoon," said Nicki, looking at his computer screen.

"Bellino should be here in an hour. That will be almost two AM," said Ramondo.

"What I can do is ping their phones, just for a second," said Nicki. "Just long enough to get their location. It will tell us when they're moving and when they become stationary."

"Do it," said Ramondo. "We assume the two followers will have the rifles. Bellino and I will go after them. Nicki, you will have to drive the car. I'll call Inspector Bawkin so that we are not shot by mistake if the security for the meeting is better than I suspect it will be."

"Uh, Ramondo …"

Ramondo looked at the boy. He was confident when hunched over his computer or with his thumbs flying over the face of his phone, but now he looked unsure, almost frightened.

"I don't know how to drive," said Nicki. "I tried once outside Vico. I kept stalling the car."

"Ours has an automatic transmission. It's a lot easier to drive than a stick shift. We have time. I'll take you out on the road after Bellino gets here."

Bellino joined them in his rental almost on the hour.

"We should eat, as I don't know when we will have another chance," said Ramondo. The Happy Chef was not what one would call haute cuisine. Nicki didn't seem to mind, eating two hamburgers in the time that the others finished one.

At 5:05 AM, Nicolo pinged the phones. They'd already moved from where they'd been the previous day. He repeated the pinging every few minutes. They were moving toward the area where the manor house was located.

"I'm going to call Gerald Bawkin as soon as we're positive that the Irish ambassador is the target. I don't want anything taken from the president's security detail unless we are absolutely certain."

Nicki's short pings showed that the phones were stationary and adjacent to where the meeting would take place. "Time to go," said Ramondo. "Bellino, leave your car here and come with us."

There was little traffic on the highway. Ramondo stepped on the gas, bringing their speed to just over the posted limit. They passed the entrance to the manor house just before seven. The front of the house and the approach were still in the shadows from the rising sun. Dew glistened on the grass in front of the manor. The driveway was dark, with a light covering of moisture. Two miles down Oxford Road, they came to the entry to the Frilford Heath Golf Club. Using the driveway to turn around, Ramondo gave the driver's seat to Nicki and told him to drive in the opposite direction past the manor house again.

While Nicolo was examining the controls and adjusting the mirrors, Ramondo asked, "What did you see on the first pass, Bellino?"

"There's a shed on the property. It is only fifty meters or so from the entrance. It's to the side, so unlikely to interfere with the sight line for a sniper. It's probably used to house part of the security detail. Across the road there's a fence and a group of trees on a small hill. It's where I would choose to shoot from."

Nicolo was getting the hang of driving the Volvo and was liking it. He drove past the house, somewhat slower than Ramondo had in the other direction. Ramondo told him to stop just out of sight.

"Ping the phones again."

"They haven't moved. It looks like they're almost on this road, just to the west of it, anyway," said Nicolo, looking at his phone.

"Then they are already in place in the trees behind the fence. Smart."

"Do you want me to drive by again?" asked Nicolo.

"No, we've already pushed our luck. See if you can loop around the golf course. Turn right at the next crossroad."

Nicolo was gaining confidence behind the wheel. He took two right turns, one onto Kingston Road and another onto Digging Lane, the width of the road diminishing until he turned on Abingdon Road, which cut through the golf course.

"Slow down. I think I see something," said Bellino. "Yes, back up."

The order was beyond Nicolo's ability, as he almost put the car in a ditch.

"Stop. Let me get out." Bellino opened the rear door and stepped out onto the shoulder.

"We'll come back and pick you up," said Ramondo, motioning Nicolo to drive on. He thought he had seen what had caught Bellino's eye.

A quarter mile down the road, there was a turnout, which allowed Nicolo to make a U turn without having to put the car in reverse. He drove back slowly toward where they had dropped off Bellino. As they approached the spot, a car came from the other direction.

"Drive past him. Don't slow down." Ramondo looked at the side of the road and saw Bellino standing with his back to the pavement, urinating against a tree. After the car passed, Ramondo said, "Now stop."

A few seconds later, Bellino was back in the car.

"I found their escape route," said Bellino as the boy moved the Volvo back onto the road. "The fence has been snipped, then placed back in position. Just beyond the fence is a mowed fairway. On the other side of it is the hill where the snipers are set up."

"It is too isolated here for him just to wait by the side of the road. He will come after the shooting." Ramondo checked the time on his phone, then pressed a number from his favorites list.

CHAPTER 48
OXFORD, ENGLAND–THE PRESENT

Mats was in the left lane of the M4, entering the offramp, when his cell phone rang. Glancing quickly at the screen, he accepted the call and clicked it on speaker, placing it in the cup holder.

"Yes, Ramondo. I'm in the car with Rodney Stoner."

"We are at the meeting site for the Irish diplomat and the Labor leader. They're scheduled to meet at 1300. We believe the Labor leader is already in the house. We've located the position of the two snipers, who are already in place, as well as their pickup spot."

"Have you notified Inspector Bawkin?"

"I did, just before I called you."

"Is he sending people?"

"Yes, but he doesn't know when or how many. I get the feeling they are really scrambling with the president's early arrival. He as much as said that the Irish thing might be a diversion to weaken security for the president. Bellino and I are going to take care of the snipers, but that leaves only Nicki to deal with the leader."

"How long will it take for you to get into position to take out the snipers?"

"It will be a difficult approach, as we can't be seen," said Ramondo. "Maybe an hour. We figure they will try to take out the Irish ambassador when he's greeted on arrival, between twelve-thirty and one."

"Leave Nicolo somewhere I can find him. He can show me where the pickup spot is. I'll be there as soon as I drop off Rodney."

"I'll leave him at the Frilford Heath Golf clubhouse. It's just ten minutes south of Oxford. It should be on your GPS." Ramondo looked at the boy, so eager, quickly learning to drive the car. As capable as Nicki was with computers, he wasn't trained like Bellino. He needed to be protected.

"Tell Nicolo not to leave. I'll be there in forty," said Mats.

Mats was already on the offramp and could see the airport in front of him.

"The next roundabout, take this road back out to the M4," instructed Stoner. "I'm coming with you."

Mats looked at Rodney, who was already clicking his phone. Mats could hear a strange ring, a shrill alarm rather than a dial tone. It was answered almost at once. The voice on the other end was loud, almost as if it was amplified. Although Rodney didn't have it on speaker, Mats could pick out the words clearly enough.

"Adam, have you landed yet?" asked Rodney.

"We're about fifteen minutes from touchdown. Looks like we're just over Liverpool."

"Good, you're with POTUS. I wasn't sure you were coming."

"As if they could keep Adam Kappe away from this one."

"Adam, I can't meet you at the airport. Make my excuses to the president. If everything goes well, I'll be at the residence early this evening."

"I'll do it, but he isn't going to be happy. He's already said that he wants your touch on the two speeches I've prepared for him."

"If he presses you, tell him it's as important as the situation in London when he was running for election. He'll know what I mean. I have to go. I'll see you tonight."

"Did you really just call the president's plane?" asked Mats.

"All the senior staff have satellite phones. Adam Kappe was the senior speech writer when I first joined the campaign, and now he's the press secretary. Turn left here, then it's a straight shot to Oxford."

They entered the Oxford Ring Road, passing a Rover factory below them to the left, looking for the Wootton Road offramp. They didn't see the offramp on the GPS. Looking at the screen, they saw that they had missed it and continued around the Ring Road until they again passed the Rover plant, taking the next offramp, A420. It was not the designation on the GPS, but was right as the car dot followed the GPS's blue guide line. Ten minutes later, they drove through the entry of the Frilford Heath Golf Club, a fifty-four-hole complex nestled in woodlands and crossed by streams and small lakes. Their cells showed 12:23. They were late.

They rang and were admitted to the clubhouse by the club secretary, a Mr. Preston.

"The boy you describe just left, not more than a minute ago," said the secretary. "He was left here by two foreign-looking gentlemen who are out on the course.

He ate two orders of fish and chips but departed in a hurry after scribbling a note for a Mr. Falconi."

"I'm Mats Falconi," said Mats with a smile, reaching for the note, which was now in an envelope. "Did Nicki leave an account?"

"No, the two foreign gentlemen left more than enough for that. Do you have some identification?"

Mats snapped his wallet open and showed his driver's license, then took the envelope from the secretary, who gave a small bow. He tore it open. Printed in heavy strokes were the words: "I had to leave. I'm on Abingdon Road, just off A338 (Oxford Road). Nicolo."

Mats quickly thanked Mr. Preston and ran after Stoner into the parking lot. Quicky opening the boot of the car, he took out the axe and stuck it in the space between his seat and the middle console. *Nicky should not have left,* thought Mats. *He is only seventeen and in danger. Ramondo should never have left him alone with the car.*

Stoner drove, explaining that he had seen the road just before they entered the club's driveway. He turned left onto Oxford and took another left onto Abingdon less than half a mile past the club gate. Ahead they saw the Volvo that Ramondo had rented moving slowly down the road. Mats, sitting in the lefthand passenger's seat, had a clear view of the area in front of the car. A hundred yards in front of the Volvo, a blue sedan had parked at the side of the road. The driver's side door swung open.

Mats had not expected the Volvo to speed up and slam into the front driver's side wheel of the blue sedan, just missing the open door. The car rocked back. Nicolo jumped out in a cloud of smoke and hid behind the

Volvo. The man who had just exited the sedan drew a gun from under his jacket and fired three rounds at the boy.

Stoner didn't hesitate. He gunned the engine, causing the back wheels to squeal, and accelerated at the gunman, who jumped out of the way at the last moment, rolling into the roadside drainage ditch. Stoner, unable to stop, hit the sedan at the rear wheel well, spinning the car into the drainage ditch, just missing the gunman. Mats dove out of the passenger's seat, clutching the axe, just as the airbag went off, momentarily trapping Stoner.

The Florist turned his gun on Mats as he struggled to his feet but was distracted by a loud yell from Nicolo, who threw a rock at him. The distraction allowed Mats to get to his knees as the Florist turned his weapon back on him. Mats was still on his knees, without leverage for a proper throw. Still, the blade of the axe hit the Florist on the inside of his left knee, causing it to buckle, which in turn caused him to lower the gun to keep his balance. As he raised his gun again, aiming at Mats, Rodney Stoner got out of the car. He'd opened his case, taking out a blade that shone in the sun. He threw it. A silver blur arched toward the Florist. The tip of the eighteen-inch blade embedded itself in his right shoulder, sticking between two ribs. It was not a death wound, but the man lost control of his right arm, his gun dropping to the earth at his feet.

Mats was first to reach him, grabbing the axe, bringing it back for a killing blow. The Florist sank slowly to the dirt. The fabric of his pants at his left knee was ripped and drenched with blood. Stoner ran to his side, moving behind the Florist, pulling the blade from the man's chest and placing it at his throat.

Just then a man came running from the woods, a gun in his hand. Stoner whipped the Florist around, placing him between himself and the onrushing gunman.

"Ramondo!" yelled Mats as he got to his feet. "Put the gun down! He's with us."

Ramondo slowed, dropping his gun to his side. As he walked the last few yards, Nicki peeked over the hood of the Volvo, letting out a whoop.

"You got the leader," said Ramondo as he reached them. "That's the man from the brewery."

"Ramondo, this is Mr. Rodney Stoner, Lady Katherine's husband. You're sure this is the man who tried to kill Rigsby?"

Ramondo moved quickly to Stoner's side, looking at the man on the ground, and gave a nod. He reached down and tore away the Florist's jacket and shirt, uncovering his right shoulder. The wound from Stoner's sword was still bleeding. On the back of his arm was a bandage, which Ramondo pulled off, exposing a two-inch puncture closed with a series of sutures.

"This is where my knife took him at the brewery."

"What happened to the two men with the rifles?" asked Mats.

"One's dead. The other is wounded. Bellino is watching him. The security at the house heard the shot and were alerted."

"Shot! We didn't hear any shot. Are any of the diplomats hurt?"

"No. One sniper was hidden in a tree, the other on the ground. We had to approach very slowly. It's hard to subdue someone in a tree, so I took him out with my knife. Bellino was in position with the other. The one in the tree fell on his rifle, which went off. Bullet went up through his chest, throat, and jaw and out the top of his head. A neat little round hole. Almost no bleeding. The sound was muffled, but Security heard it. It looks like you made plenty of noise on your own," said Ramondo, looking at the cars.

"Nicolo prevented the leader from escaping," said Mats in explanation. "I'd better call Inspector Bawkin to make sure Bellino is not accidentally shot."

Mats clicked on Bawkin's name, but before he could speak, Rodney Stoner reached for the phone. Ramondo changed places with Stoner, his gun pointed at the Florist's head.

"Inspector, this is Rodney Stoner. We have two crime scenes here. One is across the road from the manor house, and the other is on Abingdon Road, just off A338. One sniper is dead, and the other ..."

Ramondo mouthed the word *wounded*.

"The other is wounded and under the control of Bellino Guibega. The ringleader is wounded and with me and Mr. Falconi on Abingdon Road. We will need two ambulances, one to each site, and three tow trucks to the Abingdon site."

"We don't have enough security people to watch the conference and go to both sites," said Bawkin. "Two of the men assigned to the security of the house are entering the forests now. We're keeping the Irish ambassador away until we know it's absolutely safe. I'll have to call the local police to take care of your prisoner."

CHAPTER 49
FRILFORD HEATH, ENGLAND–
THE PRESENT

The local police arrived in force, just before the ambulance. They came in three cars, undoubtedly determined to show the Yard how efficient they were. Sergeant Westlake was in charge of the four others. He was a buff individual with a head shaved below his hat. Mats was sure it was shaved under it as well. His first words at stepping out of his patrol car were to Ramondo.

"Put the gun on the ground. The hatchet as well," he added, pointing a finger at Mats.

Ramondo complied but placed the gun to his right, away from the Florist.

"Now, let's see what we have here. Glove up and bag those weapons," he instructed one of his officers. He looked at Nicki, who was still holding the keys to the Volvo in his hand. "How old are you?"

"Seventeen," said Nicki, looking at Mats, then Ramondo, for assurance.

"Sergeant, I'm Mats Falconi and this is Rodney Stoner, an aide to the president of the United States. These two are my employees. Were you notified by Inspector Bawkin of Scotland Yard? This man is a terrorist, in charge of a group that was to assassinate the principals at the delegation meeting at the manor house," said Mats, pointing at the Florist, who was crouched, bleeding from his knee and back.

"Dispatch took the call. My captain is on holiday, so I'm in charge." Westlake was interrupted by the arrival of the ambulance, which if anything made more noise than the police vehicles. As soon as it pulled to the side of the road, the Florist began moaning and saying in perfectly accented public school English that he was feeling faint, like he was about to pass out. The paramedics rushed to his side just as he started to slide toward the ground.

"Take care of that man," said Westlake.

Mats took advantage of the diversion to hit Bawkin's number again.

"Sergeant Westlake. It's Inspector Bawkin," he said, handing the phone to the policeman.

"Sergeant Westlake here, Oxford district."

Mats could only hear one side of the conversation, but from the look on Westlake's face, he was not happy with what he was being told.

"Well, sir, let me tell you what we have here. Not least is an underaged foreigner, too young to have a license, causing a substantial wreck. We have one man severely injured both in his leg and shoulder. I have no knowledge that you are even who you say you are. I don't know how you do things there, but in Oxford District we do things by the book, sir."

There was a brief pause while Westlake listened.

"I'll tell you exactly what I'm going to do. I'm sending the wounded man to the hospital. I'm arresting the juvenile and taking the three men with me to the station for questioning. If you are who you say you are, you can contact me there." He turned off Mats' phone and pocketed it.

The ambulance was about to close its rear door when suddenly there was a moan from Ramondo. His right shoulder slumped in an unnatural position, and blood squirted from a gash on his left arm, soaking his shirt.

"Don't let the ambulance go without me," he cried, obviously in distress. "My shoulder! My arm is cut badly."

Westlake hesitated. He had not noticed the man's shoulder and certainly not the blood.

"Get the medic to look at this one," he shouted at the youngest of his officers.

The ambulance driver came around the lorry and gave Ramondo a quick exam. Ramondo cried in pain when he probed his shoulder, and he let go of his left arm so that the blood squirted the medic on his sleeve.

"Take that one too," said Westlake to the ambulance driver. "Bramby, you go with them. As soon as they're taken care of, call me. Is that clear?"

Now fully in charge, Westlake put Mats and Stoner into the back seats of different police cars, placing Nicolo with Mats, and drove off to his station. He was not prepared for the reception as he drove into his yard.

CHAPTER 50
OXFORD, ENGLAND–THE PRESENT

The two patrol cars followed Sergeant Westlake's cruiser to the Oxford precinct station. Mats and Rodney were led inside by officers on either side, while Nicki was grabbed by Westlake. He was half-dragged into the building and thrust against a desk where a young woman in uniform sat behind a computer and a number of phones.

"Book this boy for driving without a license, reckless operation of a motor vehicle, and causing an accident," said Westlake. "Then charge these two with the use of deadly weapons, aggravated assault, and abetting a minor."

This is not going well, thought Mats. *The press is going to have a field day, with Rodney being involved.*

Sergeant Westlake started to say more.

Probably thought of another charge or two, thought Mats.

The precinct doors flew open and a police captain came in, followed closely by two men in suits.

"Release these men, Westlake," said the captain.

"But sir," began the sergeant.

"You should have called me, Westlake." The captain walked across the room to where Mats and Rodney were standing. "Which of you is Mr. Stoner?" he asked.

"I'm Stoner," said Rodney, extending his hand for a handshake.

"Then you must be Mr. Falconi," said the captain, turning from one handshake to another. "I'm sorry for any inconvenience we might have caused."

"Do you still want me to arrest the boy?" asked the woman behind the desk.

"Boy?" said the captain, obviously confused.

"He's with me," said Mats. "He stopped the assassin from escaping."

"What's he charged with?" asked the captain.

Westlake saw his chance to regain some control. "He's too young to have a license and he caused a three-car accident."

"I think you'll find it's as Mr. Falconi says," said one of the suits. "He's free to come with us."

"No charges," said the captain.

"But, sir," stammered Westlake, but got no further.

"Sergeant Westlake," said the captain. "You must return to the crash scene and protect it."

"The ringleader was driving the blue sedan," said Mats.

The captain looked at Nicolo for confirmation, getting a nod. "Put it in the impound yard. We will need it for fingerprinting and DNA. Make sure it's secure."

One of the suits jerked his head toward the door. Rodney put his arm around Nicki's shoulder and followed the suit's direction. Mats stopped in front of the sergeant and held out his hand. "My phone, please."

Westlake obliged, saying weakly to his captain, "It's evidence."

It was the last thing they heard as they were shown to the back of a black Rover wagon. Mats briefly wondered about Ramondo, then smiled. It was Ramondo. He was the last one he had to worry about.

The group that assembled for breakfast in Katherine's office two days later was not very interested in the food laid out on the end table.

"Rodney will try to get here later," said Katherine. "The president is having him write yet another speech about how his staff thwarted a major terrorist assassination plot on British soil. Rodney keeps writing it and the president keeps sending it back, telling him to keep it true but spice it up."

"I know parts of the story, and of course, I've read what the press put out," said Margaret. "Mats, would you please tell us what really happened?"

Mats did, giving Ramondo and Nicolo full credit.

"What happened when you arrived at the police station?" asked Margaret.

"I should really let Rod explain that part when he gets here," said Mats, a grin spreading over his face. "Other than stopping the attack and catching the terrorist leader, it's the best part."

Margaret didn't say a word, just looked at him hard over her half glasses. She knew that both Katherine and Suzanne had heard the story from their husbands, so she was the only one, other than perhaps Brian, who hadn't heard the full account.

"Go on, tell it Mats," said Brian almost bursting into laughter, leaving Margaret in no doubt that she was the only one yet to hear it.

Rodney is a professional and a much better storyteller than I am, thought Mats. *I'd like to hear it from his perspective, but Margaret doesn't look like she wants to wait.* I told her what had happened, stressing Westlake's disappointment at not being able to arrest Rodney.

"We got into a car with the suits, who apologized for the local police's attitude," said Mats. "We came back here, where I met Inspector Bawkin. After we explained what had happened, he drove us back to the hotel and we joined Katherine and Suzanne."

"What became of your man, Ramondo?" asked Margaret.

"He seems to have disappeared. He was last seen at the hospital just after the M 5 agents arrested the man they're now calling the Florist," said Mats.

Like a schoolboy, Brian raised his hand to speak. It was an unconscious gesture, and he quickly brought it down, looking embarrassed.

"Ramondo came by my hotel room yesterday morning. He brought Nicki and asked if he could stay with me for a few days, but he was not to leave the room for any reason."

"Is he still there?" asked Mats.

"Yes, he's really a great guy. He's going to show me stuff on the computer, and I'm going to teach him some jiu-jitsu. He said he's going to school in America. We're hoping we can go to the same college."

"We can talk about that later. What else did Ramondo tell you?"

"He said he had nicked his arm so he could ride with the terrorist in the ambulance. It was good that he did, because the ringleader tried to jump out."

"What happened?" This time it was Katherine asking. She had not met Ramondo, only heard the tales of Mats' head of security.

"Ramondo said the guy must have slipped, because he shattered his left knee. The other one was already ruined by Mats' axe. He couldn't take a step."

"Yeah–slipped," said Mats.

"Well, Ramondo stayed with the guy until the police came and arrested him. Then he slipped out of the hospital, found out where Nicki was, and helped him disappear as well. Nicki isn't in trouble, is he?"

"No, Brian, Nicki isn't in trouble, but I wish you had told us he was in your room," said Suzanne.

"Ramondo said it was better that you didn't know for a few days so you wouldn't have to lie," said Brian, clearly worried that he might not have done the right thing.

"You did fine, Brian," said Suzanne, getting up and giving the boy a hug. "Now, why don't you tell Margaret and Katherine what we learned from the journal?"

Everyone was seated, the breakfast dishes stacked in the sink, and Brian was about to begin, when the door opened and Rodney Stoner stepped in.

"Sorry I'm late. Everyone wants to know who this mysterious French operative is, even the president. Fortunately, I could say I'd never seen him before he stepped out of the woods and subdued the terrorist leader. I had to write another speech for the president this morning. It was hard discounting your involvement, Mats, while stressing British Intelligence."

Katherine got up and kissed her husband. "I'll fill you in on Ramondo later. Brian was just about to tell us about the last entry in the journal."

"There's not a lot to tell. It was very matter of fact. Jarl Falkhand stayed. He took over Lord Longtree's lands and made an alliance with Soren the White. Actually, Mats' translation was the last one. The important thing is that Jarl stayed."

Yes, Mats thought. *I can add a few details. Not only from the journal but from the dream I had the night before they captured the man the press was calling the Florist.*

Jarl stayed with Hamerton the evening of the battle after he'd secured Longtree's castle with his men. He awoke the next day in his room to the sun throwing shafts of light on the covers over his legs. He swung his feet to the floor, reluctantly standing and moving to the basin of water that had been placed on the small table under the window. The water was cold, despite the sun hitting it, as he splashed it on his face, combing his hair with his fingers. Refreshed, he went down the circular stone stairs and found the others already at the table, breaking fast.

They discussed Jarl's meeting with Soren the White and whether the Dane could be trusted to keep his word. Then they went over the question of what to do with Longtree and his holdings. Here they were split in their opinions.

"He is a lord and should be treated with respect," said Lord Hamerton.

"Father, you are too trusting," said Lady Bridget. "Your shortage of warriors would have cost us our lands without the help of Jarl and his men. Longtree was willing to join with the Danes and would have killed you or had them kill you to obtain your lands."

"We do not know that for certain. The facts would seem to point that way, but no blow was struck against us by Longtree or his men. Only the Danes attacked. Bring him up and let him answer our questions." With a wave of his hand, Hamerton summoned a servant. "Bring Lord Longtree here."

When the servant had gone, Jarl spoke. "Lady Bridget is correct, m'lord. I can leave my brother's men here to help train your men and ensure your safety. Some of them might stay on with you with an offer of land. Without troops, you will always be viewed as a plum to be picked."

The conversation was halted by the arrival of Longtree, flanked by two of Hamerton's guards. The man was indignant, trying hard to contain his anger.

"This is intolerable. I come to your aid and receive an arrow as thanks? Then I'm thrown into your dungeon!"

"You were with the Danes before the battle and watched as they attacked Lord Hamerton," said Jarl, his voice even, containing no menace.

"We had a few Danes that we had captured. That is all," spouted Longtree, advancing toward the group.

"Yesterday, we were mistaken for Danes when we rode unopposed into your keep. Your chamberlain asked if Lord Hamerton was dead and if you had taken Lady Bridget yet. You lie through your teeth."

"I was coming to aid Lord Hamerton. My men will testify to that. I will tell my tale and you will be known as foresworn."

Jarl took a step forward, removing his axe from his belt, and with a single motion swung overhead, planting the blade of his axe in the center of Longtree's forehead. The guard, three steps behind, gasped and moved out of the way as the lord fell dead at his feet. Jarl moved to the dead man, placing a foot on his neck, wrenched his axe free, and wiped the blade clean on the man's tunic.

"He was right. He would tell his lie, and people who did not know you would believe him. You would never be safe with him alive," said Jarl to Lord Hamerton. "Blood Axe did the same to me and my brothers, but we were prohibited from taking revenge by Red Hand. Longtree was offered no such protection."

"Now it will be said that lords are not safe inside these walls," said Hamerton, shocked at Jarl's action.

"Not so, m'lord," said Jarl. "It is why I took his life while you had no part in it."

"Still," Hamerton protested.

"I am sorry to have distressed you, lord," said Jarl. "I will leave before my presence causes you further worry." Falkhand turned and walked to the stairs leading to his room. He would take what he came with. The priest would come with him or not. Jarl suspected he would stay.

In his room, he began stuffing things into his pack and into one of the dead Dane's. The door opened and Lady Bridget came in. She closed the door and barred it with her back.

"I don't wish you to go. And neither will Father, once he thinks about it," she said, moving to the center of the room.

"I feel I must, if for no other reason than to protect your father's honor. There is too much good in him, too much trust."

"That is why you must stay. All that you have accomplished will be undone if you leave. I don't want you to leave." She reached up and undid a row of buttons at her back, letting her dress fall to the ground at her feet. Her undergarment was made of bleached white linen. She moved swiftly to him, giving Jarl no chance to stop her. She pressed against him, lifting her head.

"I don't want you to leave. I want you." She stood on her toes, raised her hands behind his head, and drew him into a kiss.

Jarl felt his resolve dissolving in the sweet moisture of her lips. Without thought, he returned it. Then, using almost no strength, he lifted her, holding her at arm's length and looking at her small, perfect form. He felt himself giving in to her wishes.

Later, both having exhausted their desires, they lay and talked.

"The only way I can stay is if I take over Longtree's land. That will leave your father free of shame. If Longtree's intention was to claim you as a prize, none will think it strange that I have done so."

"And when my father goes to his reward, we will join our lands and our children will rule."

CHAPTER 51
LONDON, ENGLAND–THE PRESENT

The British press was all over the story of the attempted assassination of the Irish diplomat and the leader of the Labor Party. The tabloids were famous for speculating and dramatizing events, especially those concerning public figures like entertainment celebrities and politicians. In this case, they didn't have to exaggerate. They knew that the speech writer for the president of the United States was involved in the capture of the assassins. That in itself was enough.

Rodney was able to keep Ramondo and Mats' names out of his account. Nicolo was described as a teenaged driver who was recruited by MI6 on the spot. His name was withheld because he was a minor. Several reporters knew there was more to the story but could not get the answers they wanted. One of the more reputable papers interviewed Sergeant Westlake and learned that there was more to the taking of the assassins and their leader than was being revealed by the government. The president's speech, written by Rodney, coincided perfectly with that of Inspector Bawkin. It praised MI6 for acting quickly and decisively on information Rodney had uncovered when helping set up security for his own president.

Mats kept Nicki in the hotel with Brian. When Brian left to work out with Ramondo and Sensei Hioshida, Nicki kept busy with his new computer.

The greatest positive, other than having saved the lives of the head of the Labor Party and a lesser-known Irish diplomat, was the Whistling Pig. Bawkin, Rodney Stoner, and Inspector Small lavished praise on Rigsby, who, with his unnamed employee, had injured the mastermind of the attempted assassination, wounded another, and killed a third, using only brewery tools. Because of Rigsby's testimony, the police had been able to identify the assassins and their targets. The press stormed Dry Drayton and the Whistling Pig Brewery, making Rigsby a celebrity. The sales of the beer, both pale ale and non-alcoholic, skyrocketed. After the story began to die down, sales dropped only marginally. Rigsby hired two new employees, one to replace Ramondo and Bellino, and a second to help with the increased demand. Whereas before he had brewed twice a week, he was now brewing every day.

Mats had discussed an expansion of the facilities, as they had not yet begun exporting to the United States. Ramondo had even suggested that they export to Corsica, where the penalties for drinking and driving were harsh. The amounts wouldn't compare with those sent to the States, but the Guibega already had distribution set up for their wine, and adding a N.A. beer would not be much additional work. Coming to England prior to flying to California had turned out quite well for Falconi.

HAMERTON, ENGLAND–945

Jarl's move to Longtree's castle and takeover of his land was aided by the fact that Longtree had been disliked. He'd allowed his chamberlain to cheat his tenants and serfs. The first thing Jarl did was reverse Longtree's actions, awarding small parcels of his holdings to many of the more abused serfs. His most popular action was to make slaves of the chamberlain and four of his staff, placing them in chains on one of the two longships that had brought Blood Axe's men. Jan's men were already rich from plundering the dead Danes and their share of what they'd found on the two longships, but they were also offered small plots along the border of Hamerton's and Jarl's new land. Those who took the offer resided with Jarl and would stay with him until he received reinforcements from the north.

After ten days of arranging things at his new home, Jarl went down the river in one of the longboats. He stopped at the same village and was glad to see that a new boat had been built, somewhat larger than the one he'd stolen a month before. The fishermen were used to watching Viking ships row upstream, but the ships seldom stopped, and then only to steal the dried fish that were always hanging on the racks.

Jarl and a spokesman climbed over the bow into three feet of water and waded ashore, while the crew moved the boat further out into the stream. He explained that he was the one who had taken the boat and left the gold coin. He complimented the villagers' skill as shipwrights and asked if the coin had been enough.

The spokesman told Jarl in his native tongue that that was generous, but the village had seen hunger, having only been able to use the smaller remaining vessel while the new one was being built.

Jarl was used to living off the sea and had anticipated the answer. "Tell them I would use the new boat they've built, just within the moon. I'll give them more gold and provide food for them while my men use it."

The offer was unexpected, and after several questions were raised and answered by the interpreter, the headman nodded his acceptance. Jarl shouted to his ship, and they beached next to the newly built fishing vessel. His men carried two sides of venison to the village and two pigs that had been slaughtered and gave them to the headman. Two of Jan's men, whom Jarl had picked for the task, went to the new boat, examining it carefully and giving their approval.

Jarl gave the headman another coin and said, "I would have you build a beacon fire on that rise and light it when any dragon ship enters the mouth of the river. I will reward you for your efforts as well as for the use of your boat."

His interpreter explained what Jarl had said, showing them the height of the fire and when they should light it. He also told them that it must have both flame and smoke, so wet leaves and branches should always be at hand. If the flames were not seen, the smoke surely would be. The headman again agreed and explained the task to the small group of women standing just outside their huts.

Jarl had chosen the two men who were the best seamen in Jan's band. They would sail north to recruit men in Jarl's name and then sail back to the isle. Those who returned with them would replace Jan's men, who, loaded with plunder, were anxious to return home. He would have taken one of Blood Axe's longships and gone himself, but he was worried that Blood Axe might return, and he would have removed twenty warriors from the protection of his new lands, Hamerton's, and Soren the White's.

Arrangements made, the two pushed the fishing boat into the water with the help of two of the villagers. The men on the longship cheered as the others set sail, shooting out of the mouth of the river. This time the wind was favorable. Jarl hoped it would continue to be so. He had told the two men to sail past the lands of Red Hand and east to his own sted. He told them to use his name when they reached the northlands. He and his brothers had had no problem recruiting men to join them in the past, and the recognition of his name by the Danes they had killed led him to believe that this would still hold true. The main problem would be acquiring the use of a long-boat for the return trip.

Jarl waited until the fishing vessel was out of sight, then ordered his crew to return up the river. If the two were successful, he would have enough men to protect his castle and lands as well as those of Hamerton and still allow Jan's men to return home. Then he would be able to sail to Red Hand and fulfill his duty to tell him of his daughter's death and the revenge he had taken on the vizier. If Red Hand allowed him to live, he would return to his lands. But of which lands–those in Corse or those newly acquired on the island–he was unsure.

Since the attack on Hamerton and the taking of Longtree's castle, Jarl had been busy. First he'd had to repair the damage done to Hamerton's castle. The moat was filled with bodies that needed burying, the walls needed repair, and finally, he'd had to install a second gate of iron bars behind the drawbridge. Then there was the enhancing of Longtree's walls, which, while more substantial than Hamerton's, were still not adequate, in Jarl's opinion. Every few days, Bridget rode to Jarl to ask his advice on everything from her father's fortifications to the training of the field hands. Jarl's attention was freely given in his own compartments. Some of it was quite physical. Lady Bridget always returned satisfied with the advice she had received.

When Lady Bridget left, Jarl reflected on the three women he had loved. Gun, whom he had married, was beautiful, tall, and strong, a warrior in her own right. She was his first love and the strongest. Lesia of the Guibega was fiery of temperament. Strong like Gun and a leader, she was much shorter in stature than Gun but fearless. She had taken him by surprise one night, declaring that she was his woman, and slowly convincing him that love after the death of Gun was possible. Lady Bridget was completely different physically. She looked frail, delicate in form and stature, yet she had an inner strength of character. Their love-making was more tender, less physical, but every bit as satisfying. Both his lands on Corse and those on the island he had most recently acquired were far more valuable than his sted in the north. Still, much like his women, he couldn't decide which he would finally choose.

Ten days after the full moon, a guard announced that the beacon fire at the coast had been lit. Seconds later, the alarm was raised and a messenger was sent to Hamerton, where the signal could not be seen. A runner was also sent to Soren the White, who was downstream from Jarl. As his men gathered their weapons, Jarl wished he had thought to have the villagers at the river mouth build two distinct fires, which would tell him if a single vessel had arrived or several.

The man who was sent to Soren returned, his horse in a thick lather.

"Sire, it is a single ship, a knarr, and it bears no figure-head. They were waving to Soren's men as they passed. I thought I saw one of the men you sent north standing at the bow."

Jarl took a deep breath. If it had been Blood Axe, his and Hamerton's combined forces would have stood a chance against the Danish chief but only with luck on their side. He watched as the ship pulled against the current for the last twelve boat lengths and counted at least forty men rowing and another ten to fifteen standing in the hold. They moved upstream, turning the ship around before returning to the makeshift landing Jarl had begun to construct at the high-water mark. The boat was wider than a longboat, with higher sides and a deeper hold, more for carrying cargo or in this case, men. Jarl wondered how it had negotiated the shallow section downstream until he saw that almost all the men were wet to the waist. Jan's men cheered, as did the men on the longboat as it was fastened, its oars stored amidships. Almost immediately, the men began coming ashore, led by the two he had sent. By their dress, Jarl could see that they were northerners. One separated from the rest and walked directly toward Jarl. It had been years, but he recognized the man as one he'd left with the Varangian Guard in Miklagard. His name came easily to his mind and tongue.

"Bjorn. How good to see you," said Jarl, extending both his arms in greeting.

"Jarl Falkhand," replied Bjorn, taking both of Jarl's forearms in his hands. "We must talk."

CHAPTER 52
LONDON, ENGLAND–THE
PRESENT

Mats sat alone in the small flat they had rented in London. Suzanne was out shopping, the boys at Hioshida's dojo. If Mats was concerned about being responsible for an adopted son in Brian and a semi-adopted son in Nicki, he didn't show it. Rodney Stoner and Katherine had made a date to visit Mats and Suzanne in Sausalito late that summer. Mats still owned the house he'd grown up in with his father, which was large enough to accommodate the adults as well as the boys.

Mats had found it necessary to stay in England to help with the Whistling Pig. He purchased the lot next to the brewery for what he considered a reasonable price, allowing them to do an expansion. Mats brought over Cathal Magee from Ireland to help with the design of the addition. They decided to build an entire new plant hard up against the right wall of the existing building. Suzanne, with her sense of style, insisted that the outside design of the structure that enclosed the new equipment mimic the original. Two months after they broke ground, they finished removing the wall between the two buildings and installed piping to connect the new and the old. They had two separate brewing tanks, two mixing vats, both using the same bottling machinery. It would allow them to brew both the N.A. with a new bacteria fermentation element and the original IPA or pale ale at the same time with the addition of just a single employee.

Thinking of his house in Sausalito brought back memories to Mats, reflections on how things had changed for him in the four years since his father had been murdered on the steps of their restaurant. He had gone to Corsica to discover his father's past and had instead discovered his own future, the journals, the "Gift," and Suzanne. The "Gift" allowed him to understand more about his ancestors' past than what was written in the journals. His lineage was connected to Corsica, but here in England, he'd found Rodney Stoner and the Hamertons, to whom he was linked. He suddenly felt tired. He closed his eyes.

HAMERTON, ENGLAND 944 AD

Jarl welcomed the newly arrived warriors one by one. He was surprised that other than a single man, Bjorn, he knew none of them. They looked at him like he was a chief. *It was how I looked at Red Hand so many years ago*, he thought, as he led them into the keep.

"You are here well before I expected," said Jarl as he offered a chair to Bjorn and called for ale.

"The name and deeds of Jarl Falkhand," said Bjorn, "have inspired many sagas since your death at the hands of the vizier's fleet."

"My death? Who would tell such a tale?" asked Jarl, surprised to hear of his own demise.

"The captains and crew of the vessels the vizier sent to stop you as you left. They didn't spout their lie for long, though. They were all murdered within six days," said Bjorn. "Where have you been?"

"That is of no import. Now that you have arrived, I must go to Red Hand. There are enough here to hold this place until I return."

"More are coming. This is just the first boat."

"More coming? How is this?"

"The two you sent to find men told of the killing of the giant Holgraf, who had taken leadership of Blood Axe's fleet. They tell of your promise of good, fertile land. They tell of your leadership and battle luck. Many think you have returned from Valhalla."

"How many more are coming?" asked Jarl.

"A longboat of forty or fifty men. They should not be more than a few days behind us."

Jarl considered the number. Longtree's land was vast but mostly untended. It could easily support seventy-five Northmen, who were basically farmers who went a-Viking after the crops were planted. The rest he could assign to Hamerton, who could offer the same. They would provide the men-at-arms he sorely needed.

"That is not what I have to tell you," said Bjorn. "Do you believe that Gun is dead?"

Jarl tensed, the memory of Gun filling his mind. "Yes. The vizier sent me her shrunken arm, missing her hand. The emperor knew that one of us would kill the other. That is why the emperor sent me away. The trap the vizier set at sea cost one of his vessels before the other two turned and ran."

"At first our men didn't believe the captain's tale," said Bjorn. "Even three of their clumsy vessels are not a match for a Viking longboat. But we heard nothing of you, and after a year we accepted that you were dead. That's not important, though. Gun is alive."

No blow he'd ever received in battle hit Jarl harder than those words. "Don't jest," he finally managed to say.

"A year after you left and were supposed dead, I left the Varangian Guard. I had acquired wealth that would last me my life. Sven was well established as captain. I longed for a sted in the north and a strong woman. I went north up the Dnieper River on a trading vessel. We stopped to pick up some passengers from one of the local tribes a few days' row below the rapids. As soon as we touched land, my dog, Loki, jumped from the boat and knocked down one of their women. I reached him and pulled him off. It was Gun. Loki was licking her face. She told me to pretend I didn't know her. Obviously, Loki did, so I tied him to a thwart in the boat. Gun had dyed her hair black and wore a glove that hid the loss of her hand. I told her of your death. She made me take an oath that I wouldn't tell anyone of her existence, even her father. She said that doing so would put her in danger. She thinks that you are dead, just as you believed that she was murdered by the vizier."

"Gun lives!"

"Yes. We let her off just below the rapids. Her band went east. They were not one of the river tribes. I left Loki with her. She insisted I take a handful of jewels. It was as much as my total fortune."

"How long ago was this?"

"Almost three years now. I have a good sted and a fine woman. I would not have left but for hearing your name."

"I regretted not bringing you with me when I left," said Jarl. "Sven needed you with all the uncertainty after the vizier's death. Now I ask another favor. I must go to Red Hand and tell him this news, then travel south and find Gun. I would have you rule here until I return. I'll send your woman to join you here."

"I would come with you."

"You would serve me better here. It is important to keep order. I fear Blood Axe will attack in force. I've formed alliances with two lords adjacent to my lands, but still I fear his wrath after defeating two of his longboats."

"Blood Axe is dead, killed by your brother Kjell," said Bjorn. "Holgraf, his second in command, took his name and vessels."

"When did this happen?" Jarl's world was being rocked, his foundation shaken.

"Two years past, at sea, a day's sail up the coast. Blood Axe had set a trap for Kjell with three of his ships. Your brother defeated them and Kjell took Blood Axe's life with his axe. I was told that you killed Holgraf."

"I did." Jarl had been with Jan for over a moon. Why hadn't his brother told him of Blood Axe's death at the hands of Kjell?

It took fourteen days for Jarl to parcel out the land to the newcomers and settle matters inside the keep, establishing Bjorn as his second in command. Six days after the arrival of the knarr, the second boat of Northmen arrived with an additional forty-three men. The hardest task was telling Bridget that he had to leave. Jarl had sworn Bjorn to silence in the matter of Gun. Bridget understood that he must report to Red Hand but asked to sail with him. She was refused. When the day came to leave with Jan's warriors, who would take him north before returning to Jan on the river in Frankia, she stood on the battlements of Hamerton Castle and waved. As the ship passed and rowed out of sight, she rubbed the slight swelling of her belly, fighting the urge to be sick.

It took eight days of sailing at night and rowing during the day for the longboat to arrive at the wide fjord that led to Red Hand's land. As at their first meeting, Jarl could see sentries on the banks. By the time they berthed, there was a crowd of over a hundred, many of them armed, to greet them.

Red Hand had aged. His hair was nearly white, while his beard was completely so. He was still imposing, taller than Jarl, but now with a slight stoop. He opened his arms to Jarl with concern on his face as he looked for his daughter among those who had arrived.

"Prepare a feast," were his first words, sending his slaves and attendants scattering. As urgent as his message was, Jarl knew better than not to accept the welcome.

"I'm grateful for your hospitality," said Jarl. "While they prepare, could we speak in your chambers?"

Red Hand had heard of Jarl's return and the recruitment of men to the island. Without a word, he led Jarl to a large two-story log building behind the great hall. Red Hand moved to a shelf where there was a pitcher and two drinking horns.

"I expect that your tale will require ale to wet your throat," said Red Hand, filling the two horns and moving to the table and chairs that occupied the center of the room.

It took a full two hours for Jarl to tell his tale to Red Hand. The chief smiled and was pleased when he was told of Jarl's love for Gun and their marriage. Red Hand had lost both his sons in battle, and Gun had been his only surviving child. He'd raised her to be a warrior maiden until she was thirteen, when Jarl had severed her hand at the wrist as she tried to kill him. Red Hand had seen in Jarl the kind of man who might tame his daughter, not with force but with understanding. As part of the alliance, Jarl was given the responsibility of raising his daughter and continuing her training. Red Hand had hoped they might be attracted to each other during the trip south to Miklagard. It was why he had given control of the second long ship to his daughter—so that Jarl might see her as an equal rather than a responsibility.

Jarl continued with the events that had led to Gun's return to the north, going by ship up the Dnieper River, and the vizier's treachery. Red Hand slammed his drinking horn down on the table when Jarl told him of the vizier sending him the right arm without a hand and of Gun's death.

"I'd heard rumors of your death and that of Gun," said Red Hand. "As the years went by, there were sagas sung of your death while escaping Miklagard but nothing of Gun's fate. I kept hope until now." The old man shrank into himself, his great frame falling back against the pillows behind him.

"I avenged Gun's death. I killed the vizier with my own arrow and left the Varangian Guard on the emperor's orders. But, sire, Gun is not dead. I was deceived. I learned just a moon ago that she survived the attack and is hiding among the tribes along the Dnieper River. I wish to go south and find her."

There was a knock on the door. Red Hand said, "Enter."

"The feast is ready," said the warrior at the entrance.

"I suspect there is much more to tell," said Red Hand. "What you have done these last three years and what you would do now. It is a tale that will take longer than we should keep the feast waiting. We will talk later." Red Hand got up, pushing off the table as if his legs needed help supporting him.

We went into the great hall to the cheers of the men, more than a hundred strong. We sat next to each other at the elevated platform at the rear, a singular honor for me, and drank the first toast of the evening.

It was first light when Red Hand and I left the few men who were still standing and went back to Red Hand's lodge. I told of my trip home from Miklagard, of my land on Corse, and of being left for dead in the land of the Franks. I hoped that Red Hand would understand why I'd been diverted in his attempt to bring him the news of Gun's death.

When I finished my tale, leaving out the two women who had filled my life since I'd heard of Gun's death. Red Hand sat silent, staring at the wall. I knew the next minutes would decide his fate. After a minute, Red Hand's eyes sharpened.

"You thought Gun was dead, but why did she not return here or go back to you?" he asked.

"At first, she was waiting for me to sail up the Dnieper River and rescue her. She sent the one man to escape the southerners back to me, but he swore he saw her attacked and killed by five spearmen. He was telling the truth as he knew it, but Gun didn't die. She took refuge with a tribe that lives to the east of the river. Bjorn saw her as he was going north and told her what he thought was the truth, that I was dead. She had Bjorn swear an oath that he would not reveal her survival, not even to you, as she was still in danger from the Rus who controlled the river. She had colored her hair dark like the tribe she was with and she wore a glove that hid her missing hand. It was less than a moon ago that Bjorn discovered I was alive and told me his tale."

"Why didn't she continue north with Bjorn?"

"I don't know," said Jarl. "Bjorn said that she was steadfast about not leaving but glad for his dog. I ask that you loan me a ship and crew so that I can find her. My own men are most likely on Corse, believing the Franks have killed me. I've used my brother's crew to come here, but they wish to return to his land in Frankia."

"The time of year is not favorable," said Red Hand. "The rivers are low and there will not be snow for the portage for another two moons."

"Provide me with a crew plus ten and I will reach the Dnieper above Kiev. That river always has water. I will roll the ship on logs to make up for the lack of snow. I know the Rus that Gun is hiding from. I've beaten them once. I will bring Gun back."

"There are crops to be taken in," said Red Hand. "Wait until the rains come. You will have your boat and crew."

"I can pay for the crew and ship," said Jarl. "If you will trust me for payment until I return with Gun."

"You think I put coin above the safety of my daughter?" roared Red Hand.

"No, sire. I only say that it will be far more profitable for the men than having extra hands for the crops. There is a vast treasure hidden near where Gun hides."

Red Hand took several deep breaths, looking hard at Jarl, a man he had trusted with his daughter. "All right. You will have your boat and men in fourteen days. I only wish I was younger so that I might go with you."

CHAPTER 53
DRY DRAYTON, ENGLAND–THE PRESENT

Inspector Small knew he should let it go. Both he and his department had received commendations after the arrest of the two men responsible for the attempt on the lives of the Labor Party leader and the envoy from Ireland. But in Small's mind, things didn't add up, not even the praise heaped on his own unit.

Nickolas Rigsby seemed as confused as he was, but it could have been the rapid expansion of his production since Mats Falconi had become an equal owner of the Whistling Pig. That is where it had all started for Small– with the appearance of the American. Was it a coincidence that he had arranged to buy half of the Whistling Pig just after the delivery boy was killed? Falconi had done the same with his other brewery in Ireland. Then there was Ramondo Guibega, a trained killer, who had started work for Rigsby on the very day that four men tried to kill him. Guibega and Falconi were vouched for by the French police, who were reluctant to say why.

Neither the newspapers' accounts nor the government's seemed to add up. Two of their agents took credit for killing the two assassins, but there were too many gaps, too much unexplained. Small was sure that Falconi and his relationship with Rodney Stoner, the husband of Lady Katherine Radcliff, was at the root of the mystery. But with M5 controlling the published accounts, his instincts told him he should let it go.

RED HAND'S STED, NORWAY–OCTOBER, 945 AD

As Red Hand had predicted, it was moons before the winter rains would swell the rivers and provide snow on the overland route to the headwaters of the Dnieper. Jarl, in his haste to reach Gun, hadn't realized how difficult the trip south would be. He crossed the Baltic Sea and passed through the land of the Lats but soon came to narrowing streams with less than a third of the water he'd used before. Then there was the portage without benefit of snow. Most days they made less than five miles.

Jarl had trees felled and cut into stride-length logs. These were placed under the keel to roll over while those left behind were carried to the front. It took them almost eighteen days to reach the headwater of the Dnieper.

Jarl rested his men when they had finally completed their portage. He wanted them strong and alert when they arrived at Kiev.

"I cannot be seen in Kiev," Jarl said to his men. "I know many of you have heard of the delights of that city, but I ask you to understand that we cannot risk stopping there for any longer than to replenish our supplies. Our finding Red Hand's daughter and returning with a great treasure depends on secrecy."

"Listen to Jarl Falkhand," shouted Aksel Johansson as the men voiced their disappointment. Johansson was older than most of the crew, a warrior with a solid reputation. "We are Vikings, not traders. There must be no word of our true intent."

"Aksel will act as captain in Kiev," said Jarl. "He'll tell all who will listen that we plan to go back north to collect more furs. If any man speaks otherwise, he will forfeit his share of the treasure."

All the men agreed, and Jarl had the hold covered, hoping that it looked like it contained furs and pelts. In reality, it was empty except for the weapons of the crew— bows, axes, and swords, along with shields and mail.

Within hours of arriving in Kiev, pigs and great quantities of porridge started filling the space beneath the covering. Some of the younger men came back with the shiny cloth Jarl had gotten used to in Miklagard. He let them act like awestruck bumpkins, as it further disguised them as traders. The first night, he demanded that all sleep aboard. He would not risk a drunken word that could reveal their real purpose. After only one night, with all on board, they rowed against the current upstream, away from Kiev. After an hour, they pulled into a small cove and drank a keg of the ale they'd brought aboard. At midnight, in the dark, they would row past Kiev and down the length of the great river.

Jarl did not know how many of Olaf Olafsson's band were still with him or how many more he had recruited in the last four years. He knew in his heart that if Gun was hiding, it was Olafsson who was at the root of her fear. His plan was to pull ashore a day's sail from the head of the rapids, where Olaf had been before.

Jarl rowed the men hard. He knew that Olafsson would have spies in Kiev, reporting to him any and all traffic that left that great city. He hoped his ruse of rowing upstream had worked and that no one had seen them slip by at night. Still, there were many small settlements along the river that might have men loyal to the giant. They wouldn't catch Jarl's longboat, but they could reach the rapids before Jarl returned from the east with Gun. There was nothing to do about it except to expose only a maximum of twenty men above deck during the daylight hours.

Jarl recognized the river as they were a day's sail above the stronghold of the Rus. As often was the case, the trip down the Dnieper seemed much faster than it had on the previous trip, even with the reduced current in the river. He thought this was because he knew what he would see around the next bend, rather than searching the unknown. They found a small stream on the eastern shore, a half day's row above the Rus settlement, and pulled into it. Using the logs they had brought with them since the portage, they pulled the boat into the stunted trees and bushes along the stream's bank and hid it with branches and boughs. Jarl left Aksel Johansson in charge, with instructions to stay hidden and use absolutely no fire. With the ship hidden, Jarl and his band of ten Vikings started east on foot.

Jarl was concerned that they would be mistaken for Rus as they made their way inland. He'd seen how Olafsson had treated the tribes of the interior. There could not be good will between them. At the beginning of the second day, he had an idea. He cut two thin boughs and made a rude cross. He took off the shirt he wore under his tunic and stretched it on the sticks like a banner. He took a piece of charcoal and drew on the banner a woman with long hair and one hand missing. He carried it in front of his band as a banner. He hoped it would prevent an ambush as they traveled further from the river.

On the fifth day, toward evening, a man stepped in front of them. He was a head shorter than his warriors, but he stood without fear. He had a bow, but it hung in his hand with no arrow set. Jarl suspected that there were others around them in the woods who were far more prepared. The man motioned toward the banner and said something unintelligible. Jarl pointed to the drawing and then to his heart. He did it several times. Finally, the man nodded.

"Rus?" The word sounded more like "Rusk."

Jarl quickly shook his head. "No Rus." He pointed at one of his men, saying "Rus," then drawing his sword and pretending to strike the man down. He carefully replaced his sword and said again, "No Rus."

The small dark man in front of him seemed to understand. He gave a shrill whistle, and four men appeared on the trail behind them. Jarl heard more rustling from either side of the trail and saw the tips of several arrows extending from the undergrowth.

Jarl pointed again at the banner and then at himself, making a sign of walking with his fingers.

The man said in recognizable Latin, "Put your weapons down."

"Take me to the woman, Gun," answered Jarl in the same tongue.

The man pointed to Jarl's sword with the tip of his bow. "Down."

"Put your weapons on the ground," Jarl said to his men, placing his own sword and axe at his feet. His men seemed more inclined to fight than give up their weapons. Some started to shout until Jarl bellowed, "Now!" It was a sign of the trust his men had in him that one by one, they lowered their swords and axes to the earth.

Four more men, replicas of the one in front of them but younger, came from the bushes and collected the weapons. When they moved behind the ten Vikings, the leader said again in Latin, "Come. We go woman."

CHAPTER 54
DRY DRAYTON, ENGLAND–THE PRESENT

Inspector Small sat in his office at the precinct station. His door was open. His computer was turned away from the entry, positioned so that only he could see the screen. He read the articles from the Washington D.C papers for the third time. Stoner had killed a man who had threatened Lady Radcliff before they were married. The circumstances were too similar to what had happened with Ramondo at the Whistling Pig not to feel certain that there was some connection between the families.

There was no evidence that the families knew each other before Falconi bought his share of the Whistling Pig. Small had been unable to get any information from Lady Radcliff's security firm, his contacts at Scotland Yard, or Falconi. What was clear was that immediately after the firm was hired by Falconi, a bond had formed between the families. What the connection was exactly, he couldn't guess. He was sure Ramondo would be a dead end, even if he could find him, as would be the French, who had already shown their reluctance to speak of Falconi or Ramondo Guibega.

Small leaned back in his chair and looked up at the ceiling. No matter what he found, it would not make a difference in the outcome, which had been the prevention of a serious threat to England and recognition for himself and his unit. A feeling of unease clouded his mind with the thought that he might be working against his own government's self-interest. He shook his head. He would keep digging. It was what he did. Eventually things would become clear.

DNIEPER RIVER–OCTOBER 945

The leader of the group of bowmen guided Jarl's band for almost half a day. Jarl was sure the man had doubled back and switched trails in an effort to confuse them should Jarl ever try to find the village again. Finally, they arrived at a collection of thirty or more round dwellings scattered around a central clearing that faced a larger lodge.

The bowmen who had escorted them fanned out along the periphery of the clearing, arrows still notched in their bows. An elder emerged from the main lodge with a younger woman at his side and faced Jarl, his hand upturned. Jarl didn't know if it was a sign to stop or one of greeting.

The elder said something in his native tongue that Jarl couldn't understand, but it was translated immediately by the woman at his side, in Norse, with the worst accent Jarl had ever heard. It was so bad that Jarl did not realize at first that she was translating the man's words.

"Welcome, Norseman. Our chief asks why you are here."

"I come seeking a woman. A tall woman who is missing her right hand. A warrior woman. She is my wife."

At Jarl's voice, there was a commotion from a hut two away from the chief's lodge. Jarl looked and saw Gun. She had come out of the hut, holding the hands of two dark-haired boys. Their heads reached her mid-thigh.

"Jarl!" she yelled, running toward him. "You live!"

Jarl was unprepared for the swelling in his chest, the emotions filling his mind and body. Gun had been dead to him for over four years, but now she stood in front of him.

"As do you!" he cried. They embraced as the two boys lingered slightly behind her.

"These are your sons, Erik and Jarl," said Gun, parting from Jarl's arms to include the boys. Jarl looked at them. They were identical, their hair stained as black as Gun's, but their eyes were blue. If seeing Gun alive was a shock, seeing two children who were the image of his brothers when they were young brought him to his knees. He embraced the reluctant boys.

"There is much to tell," said Gun, "but first let me introduce you to our chief. If you have an axe of good quality, it would be wise to offer it as a gift."

Jarl called to one of his men, who he knew carried two axes, then remembered that they had been disarmed. He went to the bowmen and selected an axe that was slightly smaller than the others. He tested the sharpness on the hairs of his arm. The handle was of dark hardwood and the blade slightly inlaid near the hasp. It was an elegant weapon, despite being an axe. He gestured to the guard that it was to be a gift to the chief, slowly picked it up, and returned to Gun. She said something to the chief and then told Jarl to present the weapon to him. There was much excitement among the tribe members as Gun spoke loudly in their tongue, clasping Jarl on his shoulder and placing her hand on the heads of the two boys.

As Gun spoke, a number of women and children came from the surrounding huts. Many of the women were lighter skinned than the men, many taller as well, but none were as tall as Gun. Some were fair haired. The children who clung to them were a mixture. Indeed, there was much to talk about.

The feast the chief insisted on to welcome Jarl and his Vikings was no more than a mid-day meal by Jarl's men's standards. It consisted primarily of rabbit and one deer flavored with pine nuts and many root vegetables that were unfamiliar. Gun spent most of her time translating between the chief and Jarl. Jarl asked about the strength of the Rus encampment on the river, and the chief asked how Jarl had come to find his village. Any conversation between Jarl and Gun was postponed until they would be alone. When the chief tired of questioning Jarl, Gun took him aside and introduced him to two women and the man who had stopped him on the trail. The older of the women was the chief's wife, the younger the apprentice healer who had helped Gun with her boys. As the sun set, the women started to remove the bowls and cups, and the men began to disperse. Gun explained that the village lived by the sun, unlike Vikings, who often ate and drank through the night. She led Jarl along with her two boys, who were already yawning, to her hut.

Inside, she put the boys on two small palates against the far wall, then motioned Jarl through an opening to a room off the main chamber. The space had obviously been added to the main structure and was rectangular, like a Norse hall, rather than round. It held a larger sleeping palate covered with pillows, much like the ones the people of Miklagard had used. On one side of the doorway was a rack that held a bow, several axes, and three of the devices Gun used to replace the hand she had lost. There was no sign of a man. Jarl chided himself for looking, feeling a deep guilt over the two women he had loved since he'd been told of Gun's death four years before.

"Your boys are strong and smart," said Gun as they settled on the edge of her bed. "Already they help me gather herbs in the forest. They even trap small animals on their own."

"How old are they?" asked Jarl.

"They've seen four winters." Observing the look on Jarl's face, she added, "I was with child when I left you in Miklagard. I'd not bled for two moons. I knew if I told you, you would insist on going with me. I was the one who was expelled, not you. The emperor needed you, more so after I killed the vizier's brother. It was your sworn oath as the captain of the Varangian Guard."

"I was told you were dead. The vizier sent me your shriveled arm in a wine amphora."

Gun looked confused, and then she nodded, her eyes wide. "A day after we left you in the Black Sea, we found a wrecked vessel filled with a rich man's harem. Our men saved them before their vessel went under and took them as mates. We went up the river and made a winter's camp below the rapids. The vizier's men, along with Olafsson's men, attacked us and killed everyone but one man and me. I sent him on a horse to tell you what had happened, and I ran and hid in the cave. The arm must have been from one of the slaves who also had lost her right hand, but she was a small woman."

"I thought it had shriveled in the wine," said Jarl. "The man came to Miklagard and swore he saw you being speared in the tall grass."

"I saw a bear with her cub as I ran through the tall grass to hide in the cave," said Gun. "She attacked the vizier's men as they followed me. It must have been that which he saw. I'm so sorry. I thought you knew I was alive and would come to me."

"Nothing would have stopped me, had I not believed you dead," said Jarl.

"I waited for you in the cave until I couldn't climb the cliff," said Gun. "I was so large. I needed help with the birth. I killed a Rus and used his boat to cross the Dnieper. I knew the eastern tribes had no love for the Rus. They took me in, and our boys were born. I waited for you still. Then Bjorn came and told me of your death. The rest you know."

"Why didn't you go north with Bjorn?" asked Jarl.

"The boys were infants. They might not have survived the trip, and the Rus were still looking for me. It would have been foolhardy. I had Bjorn swear that he would not tell anyone of my hiding place."

Gun lit a small oil lamp and sat back down on the edge of her bed.

Jarl's tale took less time, as he did not mention the women he'd left in Corse or on the Island of the Angles. He spoke at great length of the sinking of one of the vizier's ships and the running of the others back to port. Of his journey home, he excused his crew for thinking him dead at the hands of the Franks, but not the Danes who had stranded him on the Isle of the Angles with the priest. He told of Bjorn hearing his name and coming to him with the news that she lived, and his sailing to Red Hand to ask for a crew. He told her that the bulk of his men and his ship were hidden just above the Rus settlement.

"Then we can sail north without Olafsson even knowing you were here," said Gun, kissing Jarl. There was joy in her face, knowing that she and the children were finally safe.

"After what he did to our men and after forcing you into hiding for the last four years?" said Jarl, his voice rising in anger. "He will pay with his life. Will the chief lend me his bowmen?"

"But there is no need," said Gun. "You heard what the chief said. Olafsson has more than a hundred warriors with him now."

"I would not be a man as long as he lived," said Jarl, and the subject was closed. There was a scratching at the door to the hut. Jarl grabbed his axe. Gun smiled and went to the door, which was made of interwoven branches. She let in Loki, Bjorn's dog, who was holding a large rabbit in his jaws. The dog dropped his prize and jumped on the bed with Jarl, recognizing his scent. They pushed Loki off the narrow bed, and between long and tender kisses, proved that they were both very much alive.

The next morning Jarl convinced the chief that with the help of his bowmen, they could completely wipe out the Rus above the rapids. What finally decided it for the chief was Jarl's claim that he had enough warriors to attack and defeat the Rus by himself, though some might escape into the woods, as they had last time. With the help of the chief's men, there would be no Rus left to rebuild.

Over the course of the four years since Gun's arrival, the chief had become, if not in name, certainly by reputation, the headman of the area. The neighboring villages were also eager to see the threat of the Rus eliminated.

On the morning of the fourth day, they left the village—ten of Jarl's own men along with ten village bowmen. The chief watched as the women of the village surrounded the men, offering hugs and kisses. The chief wished them success. Gun, dressed as a warrior, went with them. Her two boys, who were carried as often as they walked, stayed alongside Gun and their father. His men all vied for the honor of hoisting the boys onto their shoulders.

As they moved east, they were joined by another fifteen native bowmen from nearby villages. The man who had first stopped Jarl on the trail led the way. He took a much more direct route than he had taken when he led Jarl's men to his village. Since Jarl's arrival, Gun had been washing her hair and her sons', but she'd only been partly successful in removing the beetle-juice dye. Her hair was now light brown, shading toward its natural yellow. If she were to fight the Rus, they would know who she was. She carried her bow, sword, and axe, as well as her shield and the devices she'd created to let her use them. The boys thought it was a great adventure. They insisted on being let down, and then, each holding a small knife, they would run past the line of men until they tired and raised their hands to be hoisted again onto the shoulders of Jarl's men. Loki insisted on leading the group, looking back at the guide to make sure he was right behind.

It took only three days for the band to reach the coast, arriving at the exact spot on the river where Jarl's crew had hidden their boat. Jarl strode next to the man who had guided them. As they neared the river, a voice rang out.

"Halt! Jarl, I see you. Are you free or a prisoner?"

"I'm with Gun, and with friends who will help us against the Rus," yelled Jarl, glad to see that his men were diligent.

His crew appeared from the surrounding growth. The twenty-five native bowmen seemed afraid until they saw Jarl's men grasping the forearms and slapping the backs of the new Norsemen. The boys demanded to be let down, and Gun's introduced them to the new warriors. The youngsters still maintained possession of their knives and clearly considered themselves part of the band. Gun suddenly wished she had brought a woman with her who could take care of the boys while she fought the Rus.

Introductions were made, Gun translating for both groups. A meal was prepared and eaten. Then Jarl sat down amongst the ever-growing band of warriors, now numbering 75, and started going over his plan.

There was a commotion at the edge of camp, and Jarl thought he'd lost the element of surprise. His sentries escorted two women–the young healer and the woman who had helped Gun with the children–and the elderly chief into the circle of men.

"We knew you would need a healer," said the young woman in passable Norse. "The boys must also be watched."

The chief said something, which was translated by the woman. "He says you left a trail that a blind man could follow."

Their guide laughed and said something in return. "He says it is so his men can find their way home." The translation elicited laughter from all the natives.

Jarl detailed his plan. Twenty-five Vikings would take the boat and beach it at the Rus settlement. He suspected that the Rus, as they had previously, would offer their hospitality prior to attacking the boat's crew. This time they would not wait until the Rus offered a feast, as they had four years ago. The morning of the second day, all twenty-five would form a shield wall and advance toward the Rus lodges. That direct threat would cause the Rus to mass in strength, sure of a victory. The rest of his band would be hiding to the back of the Rus camp. None of those groups would show themselves until the Rus challenged the shield wall. Then they would attack the Rus from both sides and from the rear.

Jarl figured that his men were still outnumbered by almost three to two, but he thought the first two volleys from his own archers and those of the natives would more than even the odds. He selected the best bowmen among his men to go with him to the rear and the strongest to sail the ship and form the shield wall. Gun was as good a shot as any. She would go with Jarl, and her children would stay with the woman and be protected by the chief. The plan decided, each man knowing his role, the band went to sleep. The boat would leave when the sun was high the next day.

CHAPTER 55
DRY DRAYTON, ENGLAND–THE
PRESENT

The further Inspector Small looked into the two families, the more obsessed he became. Katherine Radcliff's grandfather had been an important figure for the British in World War II. In documents that had been released after fifty years, Small noted that Radcliff, Lord Hamerton, was offered as the liaison between Montgomery and Eisenhower. Had he taken the position, there might have been more cooperation between Montgomery, the head of the British forces, and General Patton. Instead, he had asked to be assigned to the effort to liberate Corsica, a much less important role but one that gave him control of the British in the theater.

Small closed the Radcliff file and put it in the cabinet to the right of his desk. The light in the office was fading due to the hour. The small window at his back faced away from the setting sun. He opened the file on Falconi. Falconi's father had emigrated from Corsica to the United States four years before the war and had done well for himself. Then, two years into the war, he had disappeared without a trace, only returning to California to run his fishing fleet and start a restaurant after the Allies freed his island birthplace. Some thought he had hidden from the draft, but Small discovered that the time he was gone coincided exactly with the appearance of the mysterious Marquis, the leader of the Corsican resistance. Even de Gaulle had failed to unmask the man's identity. For Small, it might be a coincidence that one man had disappeared just as the another had appeared, but if it was, it was a strong one. Just like Falconi and Stoner being the same age and living within ten miles of each other, yet not meeting until Falconi's wife had hired Katherine Radcliff to do some work in regard to the purchase of a brewery.

Lady Margaret had passed the title on to Katherine. The old woman was almost a recluse, but she had come down from Hamerton Hall in the north to meet Falconi and his wife. Whatever connected the families was rooted in the past, with Corsica likely being the focal point. Mats Falconi had visited Corsica, then France, but what he'd done there was still clouded in secrecy by the Paris police, and the same was true for what Stoner had done in the U.S. It was driving Small crazy. The only thing that stopped him from starting an official investigation was that there had not been crimes committed. That, and MI6 and the American Secret Service would have been at his throat.

A series of robberies at three computer stores near Cambridge was taking his full attention. He had to let his infatuation with the Radcliff-Hamerton-Stoner-Falconi-Guibega story recede to the back of his mind. He was zeroing in on a gang he'd long suspected was responsible for a chain of golf club smash-and-grab robberies, and now computer store thefts. He was sure he'd discovered a shipping company that was being used to transport the stolen items overseas.

DNIEPER RIVER–945 AD

Jarl wanted to be with Aksel Johansson, who would lead the men on the boat. They would have the most dangerous job, facing the whole of the Rus band in a small shield wall. He couldn't be part of it for fear of being recognized by Olaf. If he was, the plan would certainly be seen as a trap by the giant Rus. Instead, he joined the group that would travel inland and around to the east of the Rus encampment. It was essential that they not be detected and that they be in place prior to the boat touching shore.

The boat was to leave just after midday with its twenty-five men, its cargo hold covered with sail cloth. The rest of his men and the tribe's bowmen would leave at first light. They would be in place surrounding the rear of the Rus compound by the time of the longboat's arrival.

The twenty-five bowmen, many of whom carried long knives in addition to their bows and over-filled quivers, accompanied his fifteen Vikings. They were led by their original guide. Jarl was amazed at how quietly the tribesmen moved through the woods. His men, although quiet, sounded like cattle compared to the smaller, dark-skinned bowmen. Not one word was spoken, even when the guide signaled to the group to stop well past mid-day. With hand signals, he had the group stay while he led the first band to their spot on the north side of the Rus encampment.

331

Returning, he led Jarl, Gun, and the bulk of their band to the trees directly behind the small village. Then he went back to head the remaining group to the south and their place of concealment. When the longship arrived, the Rus encampment would be completely surrounded.

Jarl wanted to see what the Rus had done with their camp since he had burned it four years before. He edged to the border of trees and saw that they had cleared an area away from the river and planted crops. It prevented Jarl and his men from approaching as close as they needed to be for the optimal range of their arrows. Between the field and the river, there were many new dwellings that barred him from seeing where the ship would come aground. He moved back, chose a large tree, and started climbing, leaving his weapons at the base. He climbed high enough to see over the dwellings to the shore. There were men and women working in the field below him. He counted twenty-two. They were tethered two by two at the ankle, their hands left free for the tending of the crops. Two Rus watched them, both with axes.

To the north side of the field was a well-used path that led to the woods, fifty steps from where Jarl was perched. Jarl climbed down the tree and had Gun instruct one of the villagers to climb it and keep watch on the beach. Jarl took a man and went north to where he had seen the path.

They smelled their destination long before they crossed the path. Just inside the woods there was a pit with several planks spread over it at different heights. This was where the Rus disposed of their waste. Vikings had long ago learned to cover the whole pit, leaving it uncovered only over the planks used for standing or seating. The

Rus were lazy, or perhaps just ignorant of basic hygiene. Jarl had noticed during his previous trip that the Rus, despite being next to a river, didn't bathe like Vikings, who above all cherished cleanliness.

The path was likely to be used frequently. Jarl would post men to watch and make sure that any Rus relieving himself did not wander further into the woods and discover his men. Looking back at the Rus buildings, he saw that he would need to move his bowmen into the field to be in range of where the Rus would meet his crew's shield wall. The two guards who oversaw the prisoners would have to be dealt with. Leaving a man to watch the pit, Jarl made his way back to Gun and his bowmen.

As soon as Jarl was back, he called the guide to his side. He told him to go to the other groups and bring back a Viking and a native to meet with him. The guide left, and Jarl again climbed the tree.

There were three ships drawn up on the beach of the river. Two were of the build that the Rus favored. They were like longboats, but squatter, without the elegant lines of a Viking ship–more like a knarr, a merchant's ship, rather than a warship. The third was from the south, one that would be used around the waters of Miklagard. It confirmed Gun's account of the allegiance that had wiped out her crew and forced her to take refuge with the tribe.

It worried Jarl that he didn't know how many men this would add to the Rus's numbers, and they already outnumbered him. As the sun rose over the trees to his back, the slaves worked the field. Jarl saw that the guide had returned with a man from another band. They were waiting in silence below him. As the sun rose higher, there was a commotion in the Rus camp. Jarl saw scores of men, including at least fifteen black-clad southerners, quickly disappear into the huts at the rear of the encampment, leaving just twenty or so Rus visible. Most notable was the giant Olaf Olafsson, who stood a head taller than the rest of his men. The camp quieted again as Jarl's longboat became visible, moving with the current down the river. It was the same as when Jarl had landed five years before. The Rus acted friendly, only four of them approaching the boat with Olaf and helping pull the ship ashore.

Jarl watched while his men were shown huts far removed from where the rest of Olaf's fighters were hidden. Then Jarl climbed down, leaving the native still sitting on a higher branch to see if anything changed. Once on the ground, he called Gun, the guide, and the men she'd collected from the other groups and led them further into the woods. When it was safe to talk, he began to revise his plan but was stopped by the arrival of the village chief. He'd left the children with the woman. He spoke with Gun in his native tongue. At first Gun seemed concerned, and then she was calm.

"A man who was away from our village when you arrived returned and followed our trail. He is staying with the children," said Gun.

Jarl could see that the chief was determined to stay. At his belt was a beautiful blue blade with a jewel on the pommel and the axe he had been given as a gift.

Jarl explained to the group what he had seen and the difficulty the expanded field presented. He told them of the two guards and the need to silence them. Gun translated as Jarl spoke. The guide followed, talking to the chief with flourishes of his hands. The chief stood still for a moment, then spoke in halting Norse.

"We," he said, pointing at the four natives in the group. "We kill Rus guards."

"It must be done quietly. We need them killed as the shield wall is forming. If it is done too long before, or if they raise an alarm, the Rus will not have gathered in strength. We need all the attention on our boat crew to get our bowmen across the field to use their bows."

Gun again translated. The chief stood firm. "We kill them on your signal."

Jarl knew that none of his men would be able to get near the guards. They could shoot them with arrows, but even in death they might cry out and warn the Rus. The chief stood still as the four tribesmen moved to his back.

"They say they can do it. I believe them," said Gun, turning and listening to what the chief was saying to his men. She explained to Jarl what their plan was. He nodded, then gave the group instructions that they were to take back to those who waited at the edge of the forest. It would be a long night.

"I would have you stay behind with the bowmen," said Jarl as the others left and he and Gun were alone. "If something happens, you must take care of the children."

"I go with you after I shoot," said Gun. Her voice was flat, showing no emotion, only resolve. "I've not lost you for four years only to lose you again."

Jarl could not dissuade her, and after a while he stopped trying, taking her deep into the woods where they would not be disturbed as they rediscovered each other after years of thinking the other was dead.

The chief and their guide, under the cover of darkness, crept into the field of crops. They didn't return, but
when the sun again rose above the trees and the slaves
were summoned into the field, Jarl saw that the chief
and the guide, their cloaks discarded, their shirts dirty
and ripped, were tethered together among the workers.
The two Rus, as they had the day before, took up their
positions.

Above Jarl, the sentry in the tree dropped a rock. It
was a sign that the crew had left the boat but had not yet
formed a shield wall. Jarl gave a low whistle, and immediately his archers readied their bows.

There was a commotion in the village. The native in
the tree dropped two stones, the signal that the men from
the longboat were forming their shield wall. Jarl and his
men watched as the chief and the four he'd chosen rose
from the ground with the blades they had buried the night
before, slashing the guards' throats. There was no cry, no
sound other than the slaves digging in the soil, recovering the weapons that had been left for them. Jarl's men
and the native bowmen rushed from the woods across
the field from both the north and the south, arrows in
their bows notched at the ready, as the sound of shields
being hammered filled the air.

The Rus compound came alive like a bee's nest disturbed. Men rushed out of the dwellings, directed by Olaf
Olafsson, forming a semi-circle around the twenty-five
Vikings, who were pounding their swords against their
shields. The line of Rus reached the shore on either side
of the Viking shield wall.

Jarl took his group of Vikings and native bowmen
through the huts that had housed the slaves. Behind his

men's shield wall, he saw several bodies hanging over the sides of the Rus boat and the southern vessel. Assured that all the Rus were in place, Jarl waved for his bowmen to set loose their arrows. Fifty arrows rose like a cloud of insects. Another fifty were in the air before the first hit. The effect was devastating. Half the Rus and black-clad southerners fell to the ground as yet another flurry of arrows struck home. Behind him, Jarl saw the slaves, some with knives, some with digging tools, standing in front of the archers, directed by the chief.

The Rus, who had numbered well over a hundred warriors and had been aided by fifteen black-coated men of the vizier's palace guard, were now equal to the number of Vikings. Arrows still flying, Jarl led his Vikings with a war cry toward the back of the Rus line. The Rus were in total confusion. With a shield wall in front of them, Vikings attacking from the rear, and arrows still claiming lives with each volley, many started to flee. As the two bands came together, the arrows started picking off the Rus who tried to escape the trap. None made it to the woods. Women among the slaves who had been working the field ran to where the first Rus were hit and began pulling out the arrows. They took knives and axes from the fallen men and cut their throats, making sure they were dead.

Jarl stole a look to the rear to see what was causing the screams of the fallen Rus. He suspected that the women had been used for more than field work. This had not been planned. His admiration of the old chief increased with each death wail. He turned back to the battle in front of him and saw, as he'd hoped, that the Rus had not had time to put on mail, only grabbing their shields. Olafsson had thought to quickly overwhelm the small shield line with sheer numbers. Jarl looked for the giant and found him to his left, wielding a great axe. There was an arrow sticking from his thigh, but he seemed not to notice it.

As he moved toward the giant, two Rus moved in front of him. Jarl would be at a disadvantage if both attacked together. Before Olafsson could join them, there was a flash of brown that passed Jarl's shield. Loki, Gun's dog, hit the man's shield, clambering over it and closing his jaws on the man's throat. The Rus went down, leaving only a single warrior between Jarl and Olafsson. Jarl swung his axe and splintered the shield of the man facing him, sending him to the ground and lowering the sharpened butt of the handle with tremendous force onto the man's chest.

Turning, Jarl saw the giant making his way toward him with a look of recognition on his face.

"You! You are mine," he shouted at Jarl.

CHAPTER 56
DRY DRAYTON, ENGLAND–THE PRESENT

Inspector Small accepted the congratulations of his staff as they all raised their coffee cups in a toast. The small conference room was crowded with patrolmen and staff. Small had just arrested the gang of criminals who had been stealing golf clubs from tourists' cars and had branched out to computers. He had suspected an export company, and when a destination in the Middle East was listed, a city they had never exported to before, he'd obtained permission for the harbor master to search the consignment. It consisted almost entirely of stolen computers covered with an inch of English woolens. It was easy to break the three owners of the shipping company to get the names of the gang members who were committing the actual robberies. The arrest was clean, and Small's group was given a commendation for the second time in two weeks.

No sooner were the cups put down than Small's cell phone rang. He looked at the screen and moved to his office. It was Gerald Bawkin, who had called when the Whistling Pig case had started. He knew from his earlier conversation that Bawkin was highly placed in the government, but the man had never disclosed his position or branch. Small couldn't resist taking his chance. "I was wondering if I could ask you about some inconsistencies in the assassination attempt on the Labor leader."

"Interesting," said Bawkin. "I've been watching you work for the last month. The arrest of the gang preying on visiting golfers was particularly well done. I think you would better serve the country working for me. The pay is appreciably more, and you've shown intelligence and an inquisitive mind that would do nicely in the new position."

"Yes, but ..."

"No buts," said Bawkin before Small could finish his sentence. "Someone will be contacting you. I hope, if you pass scrutiny, you will consider the position. As to the other matter, it's been looked into at a higher level than mine. I would strongly suggest that you cease all inquiries into the incident."

Small knew when to heed advice. In the future, he might be interested in events connected to the two families, but he would certainly not investigate them.

"I look forward to the opportunity to serve, and I fully understand your concern. Thank you for your confidence in my ability. May I ask what your branch is?"

"MV," was the short reply before the line disconnected.

DNIEPER RIVER, 945

There was one Rus between Jarl and Olaf Olafsson. The giant Rus pushed him toward Jarl. The unfortunate man stumbled and was dispatched with a single blow from

Jarl's axe. Olafsson moved toward Jarl, but the fallen man was in his way. Jarl realized that both the length of the Rus's arm and that of his two-bladed axe put him at a disadvantage. He spent the time Olafsson took to climb over the body putting his axe in his belt and drawing his sword. He would use his knowledge of how the smaller southerners had fought the Varangians. The slope of the land toward the river was also an advantage, but not a great one.

The Rus swung his axe parallel to the ground, aiming at Jarl's head. Jarl moved backward and saw the blade pass not more than a foot in front of his eyes. Only Olafsson's great strength prevented the momentum from spinning him around, exposing his side. Jarl thrust low at the man's legs, but Olafsson's shield came down, deflecting the blade, which cut a finger-length slash on his calf.

Olaf bellowed in pain but still managed to raise his battle axe above his head and strike downward. Jarl raised his shield, angling it so the blade would be deflected rather than take the force full on. The axe hit the shield, but the power behind it turned it at an acute angle. The great blade slid off into Jarl's right foot, causing him to fall, his shield on the ground to his left, pinned there by Olafsson's foot. Olafsson again raised his axe, but Jarl thrust his sword up under the Rus's tunic and into his groin.

There was a low growl as Loki, having torn the throat of one Rus, crashed heavily into Olafsson from behind, biting deeply into Olafsson's leg and causing him to topple. The giant's axe fell in front of him with only its own weight behind it. The axe's blade was initially stopped by Jarl's chest mail, but so great was Olafsson's weight that it forced the rear edge of his two-sided great axe to cut deep into the giant's heart. At the same time, the axe separated the links of Jarl's mail, pushing the blade into the muscle and bone of Jarl's shoulder.

Just then Gun came up from behind. She reached down and slid her hand under the giant's head, slitting his throat. She called for help to pull the Rus off her husband. As they rolled Olafsson's great bulk off Jarl, Gun saw the gaping wound and screamed. She wrenched the axe away and saw a gush of blood. She had lived with Jarl's death for three years, finally coming to grips with her grief. Now it came flooding back as she lifted him and hugged him against her chest. His eyes looked at her. He mouthed, "Love," but no words escaped his lips. With a shudder, he passed out. Her wail of grief sounded above the diminishing sounds of battle as she tried to stem the flow of blood.

There were few Rus left fighting, and the sound of metal clashing had been replaced by the smell of blood. All the Rus who tried to flee were downed by arrows long before they reached the trees. Those who were left were given no quarter, not allowed to surrender. Gun called for the healer and saw, to her surprise, that their two boys were with the woman, moving among the fallen Rus.

The healer rushed to Gun's side, gently pulling her away from Jarl's form. As the sounds of battle diminished, she took a cloth that was damp with a foul-smelling liquid and packed it into the wound at his shoulder. She gave a quick glance at the wound on his foot, shook her head, and looked back at his shoulder. The flow of blood had slowed. She gently removed the rag and saw where the blood was flowing from with regular pulses. She used a ligature from the bag at her waist to tie the vessel off. Blood still filled the wound, but it no longer flowed freely. She placed the foul-smelling cloth back in and called two of the tribesmen to her side, giving them instructions on how to construct a litter. Gun asked a question, but the healer didn't answer. Her attention was now focused on the gash in Jarl's foot.

For the next four days, Gun hardly moved from Jarl's side. They moved Jarl to one of the huts, but after seeing the condition of the dwelling, they made a tent of sail cloth outside while they burnt a flameless fire inside to rid the hut of its insects and vermin. The healer used the rest of the morning to close Jarl's wounds, wiping them with the strong drink they'd found in the huts of the black-clad southerners.

"Will he live?" asked Gun as the healer rose to look to the rest of the wounded.

"It is in God's hands. He's lost much blood, but his pulse remains steady, if not strong. He will never use his right arm again if he does. It is his foot that is the worry, for the flesh is wasting. There was dirt in the wound from his boot, as well as from the ground. The blood does not flow as strongly there. If he does live, he might lose his leg if the foul smell comes."

"What can I do?"

"Wash the wounds often with a clean cloth and the strong drink. Give him water and food if he wakes," said the healer.

Of Jarl's men they had lost five, and four more were injured, but three were expected to survive. Two of the tribesmen had suffered injuries to their legs when some of the Rus who had been downed by arrows proved to be not quite dead–a condition that was soon remedied.

Jarl was alive. Gun worried that even with the skill of the tribe's healer, he might not last another day. But each morning he grew more alert, though speaking with great effort.

Aksel Johansson took charge of the men. Both he and the chief came regularly to Gun to receive instructions. It took the day of the battle and most of the next to bury the dead. The tribesmen, the freed slaves, and the Vikings worked side by side to dig a ditch deep enough to cover the bodies. The seven Vikings who had passed on to Valhalla were shrouded and placed in one of the Rus boats with their weapons and some of the livestock the Rus had kept in a pen. The boat was pushed into the current and fired. It was a fitting burial for those who had been so brave.

"Go to Olaf's lodge and dig the floor," said Gun to Aksel Johansson after the fire-ship had sunk. "Four years ago, it was where he hid the band's treasure. I do not think he had the imagination to change his habit."

Johansson returned in less than an hour. "You were right. It is a great treasure. It will fill our ship."

After calling for the healer, Gun left Jarl's side and went with Johansson to Olafsson's dwelling. Much of the loot was already piled outside. Aksel had overestimated the amount. It was a rich finding, but not as much as they had taken four years before. It would fill two-thirds of the ship.

"Store it on our ship and cover it. I would rather it not be seen by passing vessels," Gun said as she started back to Jarl's side. "And ask the chief to come to me."

The chief asked about Jarl, who must have heard him, as he raised his head and said, "Thank you for your bowmen. Gun tells me all the Rus and southerners are dead."

"It is true," said the old man, with Gun translating for both of them.

"The men are uncomfortable being this near the river and so far from home," said Gun.

Jarl gave a weak nod, and the chief left, thanking Jarl for ridding the tribe of the Rus. He had more to say but would speak to Gun later, as he could see that Jarl was spent.

Alone, Gun said to Jarl, "The chief is worried about other Rus taking revenge. I have a plan for that. It can wait. You rest."

The afternoon of the third day, Gun gathered the tribesmen as they were readying to leave. She placed a leather pouch containing some of the coin and another containing a handful of jewels from Olaf's treasure into the chief's hand. His men had already greatly profited by looting the fallen Rus of their weapons.

Gun faced the assembled group, speaking loudly. She told them to spread the story of a one-handed warrior woman leading a band of Vikings that had come from the north and attacked the Rus, killing all in an act of revenge. There was to be no mention of any help from the villagers, only the fear that the Vikings would turn east and attack them as well. Gun told them that if they repeated the story enough, and acted truly afraid, their help in killing the Rus would never be known.

Following the burial and the Viking funeral, Gun and her remaining Vikings stood at the bank of the river, threatening a number of boats as they sailed south. The tribesmen hid in the trees. If the tribesmen were ready to leave, so were the men of Gun's crew. The longer they stayed, the more chance of some group from either the north or the south coming to seek revenge or the treasure. With every passing vessel, the threat grew. Only Jarl's weakened condition stopped them from sailing. Gun sensed the mood of the crew and spoke to Aksel.

"I have one more task. I will do it today, and we will leave tomorrow at first light," said Gun on the morning of the fifth day.

"The men accept you as their leader," said Aksel. "As do I. It is good that we leave this place, though."

All the Rus vessels had been burned or destroyed. Only their Viking longboat remained on the shore. Jarl was stronger, but the healer warned that he was still not out of danger. With the healer at Jarl's side, Gun took four Vikings and her two boys and rowed the ship to the western bank. She took them to the cliff above the hidden cave and removed a portion of the hidden treasure, enough to fully load their ship. She was the last to leave the cave, which had been her solitary dwelling before she had found the tribe that had taken her in and helped her birth her two children.

She sealed it with stones, protecting it from the bats which, if allowed, would surely again find its cool darkness welcoming. The men carried the treasure back to their longship, along with the two boys, who each carried a burden of a small sack. At the river, they secured the cargo, again covering it, and rowed back across the river.

The next morning, on the sixth day after the battle, the tribe having left, they moved Jarl to the longboat, placing him on furs directly under the stern steering platform. Their last act was to burn all the Rus dwellings to the ground.

Gun stood on the steering platform, holding the oar against her side, the wind blowing her now almost completely blond hair. She had the men pull against the current as they rowed north toward Kiev and home. In front of her were her two children, with the great hound, Loki, sleeping contentedly between them. Below the steering platform was the village's healer, who still watched over Jarl.

EPILOGUE

Gun returned home with her two children at the start of winter. Jarl had survived but would forever be without use of his right arm and would walk with a limp, missing half his foot. Eric Red Hand, Gun's father, greeted them warmly, taking great pride in his two grandchildren and bestowing on them all that his own sons would have had if they had survived. Gun sought out the families of the men who had died in the vizier's attack on her camp beneath the rapids and gave them part of the treasure their men would have carried home had they lived.

Jarl was resigned to never again go a-Viking. He was rich beyond need. He sent word to Bjorn that the land in the Angles was his as long as he supported Hamerton and his daughter. He was to tell Hamerton that he was dead, in part because of the embarrassment he felt over being so badly injured, and in part because his love for Gun would not allow him to love another. He was ignorant of the twin boys who had been born in Ajaccio and the single boy he had fathered on the Isle of the Angles. He was unaware of the bloodlines that would be passed down through the centuries, just as Gun's sons would.

Jarl stayed at Red Hand's side. He would never again wield a sword or axe in battle, but his wisdom and battle luck were still prized by both his men and Red Hand.

Red Hand lived for twelve years after their return, long enough to see his two grandsons turn into young men. Jarl suspected that they had a secret way of communicating with each other, like he and his brothers had, but neither he nor Gun said anything. Red Hand died during his sixty-eighth winter, a contented man, leaving his vast holdings to Jarl and Gun who passed them to their sons.

THE END

www.ingramcontent.com/pod-product-compliance
Lightning Source LLC
Chambersburg PA
CBHW051229260626

47162CB00002B/331